THE LAST STRAW

SHARON SALA

THE LAST STRAW

mira

ISBN-13: 978-0-7783-3199-5

The Last Straw

This edition published by arrangement with Harlequin Books S.A.

For questions and comments about the quality of this book, please contact us at CustomerService@Harlequin.com.

Mira
22 Adelaide St. West, 40th Floor
Toronto, Ontario M5H 4E3, Canada
BookClubbish.com

Printed in U.S.A.

Love is the only emotion we have that can grow exponentially,
spread faster than the speed of light and never die.

I dedicate this book to the people who love and aren't afraid to show it.

To the love I lost, and to the bright spirit he is now,
who still waits for me to follow.

This book is for Bobby.

THE LAST STRAW

CHAPTER ONE

After ten days of nonstop work at Addison-Tunnell Ad Agency, twenty-nine-year-old executive Rachel Dean was finally on her way home. The presentation was finished and ready to present tomorrow.

It was just after 7 p.m., and thanks to traffic on the Dallas Beltway, it took almost forty-five minutes to reach the historic district where she lived. The apartment she rented was in an old mansion called the Detter House. It had been renovated into apartments by the present owner about twenty years ago, and rare openings in the residence were a hot leasing commodity.

The two-story wings on either side of the midsection were now all apartments. The midsection had been turned into a communal lobby on the first floor with big-screen televisions, and the second floor was the central elevator system that led to both north and south wings.

There was a full basement beneath the central part, and the grounds surrounding it provided covered parking for the residents, a pool and an area for outdoor entertaining.

Rachel loved living here, and breathed a sigh of relief when the grand edifice appeared in her view. She took the turn up the drive and then drove around back to her covered parking space. Living alone for as long as she had, Rachel had a tendency to talk to herself, which was evident when she grabbed her purse and briefcase to exit the car.

"Oh, my Lord…my feet are killing me. I have never been so glad to get home."

She waved to some of the residents who were outside grilling by the heated pool as she passed.

"Come join us!" one man called.

"Another time," Rachel said. "I'm bushed!"

He gave her a thumbs-up, then turned back to the grill.

The grilling meat smelled good, but all she wanted was a shower, a bowl of soup and to kick back and put up her feet.

She took the elevator to the second floor, then down the hall to her apartment in the north wing. It was habit to lock the door behind her as she went in, and habit that she left her purse on the hall table and her briefcase on the floor beside it, before heading to the bedroom to change.

The floors were shining, and the woodwork dusted. Today had been the day the cleaning service came, and the scent of lemon oil and lilac followed her from room to room. Lilac was her latest choice of air freshener, and a subtle hint that they were also her favorite flower.

She stripped off her clothes, changing into old blue jeans and a long-sleeved Dallas Cowboys sweatshirt. She traded her high heels for socks and tennis shoes, then picked up the clothes she'd just removed, along with what was in her hamper, and took them to the laundry and started the load to wash.

The washer was filling with water as she went to the pantry to get a can of chicken noodle soup. She thought about making herself a sandwich, as she poured the soup into a bowl to heat, but opted for cheese and crackers to go with it instead.

She was waiting for the microwave to stop when she began hearing faint strains of music. It sounded like the cookout at the pool was turning into a party. She knew she'd be welcome if she joined them, but the thought of getting back into party clothes was too much, and despite the heated pool, the evenings were getting too cool now for her to enjoy a swim.

The microwave dinged as she was taking her plate of cheese and crackers to the table. She turned on the iPad she'd left there this morning, and then made herself something to drink. As she stepped back to the microwave to get her soup, she caught a glimpse of her own reflection.

Her features were a bit muddled, but the basic outline of her short dark curls and pug nose was obvious. She wasn't drop-dead gorgeous, but she liked who she was, and that was enough. When she lifted the hot soup from the microwave, the scent made her stomach growl as she carried it to the table.

She reached for the iPad, pulled up the book she'd been reading, then tested the heat of the soup before she took her first bite. The warmth of the soup, and the homey taste of the noodles, were reminders of her childhood. She ate with relish, wishing her older sister, Millie, who still lived in their hometown of Tulsa, Oklahoma, were with her, and then got lost in the story as she ate.

She was about halfway through her meal when she heard the sound of laughter coming from the back of her apartment. It sounded like it was in her bedroom, which made no sense, because she lived alone.

Frowning, she put down her spoon and got up to investigate. There was no hesitation or fear as she walked into her bedroom. But she was surprised that her television was on.

"What in the world?" she muttered, and began looking around for the remote to turn it off.

When she finally spied it on the shelf below the television, instead of the bedside table where she always kept it, she assumed the cleaning crew had moved it, but it still didn't explain why it had suddenly turned on.

Focused solely on getting to the remote, she didn't hear the soft sound of a footfall behind her. Then the stabbing pain at the nape of her neck was shocking, and caught her unawares. She screamed, thinking something had just stung her, and was reaching for the back of her neck when the room began to spin, and then everything went black.

It was five minutes to 4 a.m. when Charlie Dodge's cell phone signaled a text. He rolled over in bed, saw the time and groaned. Who would be texting him at this time of the morning?

Then he saw it was from Wyrick.

"What the hell?" he muttered, then threw back the covers and sat up on the side of the bed as he pulled up the message.

Stay off the beltway this morning. There's going to be a massive pileup.

"What the hell, again?" he muttered.

Frustrated and sleepy, he forgot he was only wearing gym shorts as he got up and strode across the hall to her bedroom, then pounded on the door.

There was a long moment of silence, and then he pounded again, and got a very cranky response.

"Are you bleeding?"

He rolled his eyes. "No."

The tone of her voice had not softened. "Then what the hell? It's 4 a.m."

"Why, yes, it is. So why are you sending me random texts at this hour?" he shouted.

There was another, even longer moment of silence, and then

the door swung inward, and Wyrick was standing in the shadows wearing pink flannel pajamas with little white lambs on them—a complete dichotomy to the red–and–black dragon tattoo beneath.

He'd seen her in those pajamas before, and was always surprised by how vulnerable she looked without the war paint she wore in public.

As for Wyrick, she'd seen Charlie's bare chest, hard abs and long bare legs before, and was still struggling to pull out of the nightmare she'd been having when he knocked.

"I didn't send you a text!" she snapped.

Charlie shoved the phone in her face.

She turned on the light and then looked at the phone, and as she did, the color faded from her face. That was when he realized she was as startled by the text as he'd been.

"What's wrong?" he asked.

She turned around and went to get her phone off the charger, then brought it back to the door, pulled up his number with their message history and handed it to him.

"Look for yourself. The last text I sent to you was yesterday… from the office…telling you what I wanted for lunch."

Charlie frowned. "But this is plainly from you. So unless someone has hacked you, this doesn't make sense."

"It's impossible to hack me. I need to sit down," she said, and dropped onto the side of her bed.

Charlie followed, and sat down beside her, waiting in silence.

Finally, she took a deep breath and started talking.

"I can't believe this happened. I was dreaming this. It was a thought in my dream. Not an awake thought. A dream thought. I am going to have to think about this a bit, but the bottom line is, I think I just bypassed the need to use a phone to send you messages."

In that moment Charlie felt the world shift beneath his feet.

He didn't know what to say, but he'd long since given up being shocked by her growing abilities.

"Leave it to you to find a way to beat a monthly phone bill," he muttered. "So is this text true? About the imminent crash?"

She nodded.

"Is there any way we could notify someone to prevent it?"

A muscle jerked in the side of her jaw.

"No. It is what it is," she said.

"Then we take backstreets to work. Thanks for the heads-up. I'm going to shower."

"It's too early to go to work," Wyrick said.

"Agreed. But sleep is impossible now, so I'm still gonna shower," Charlie said, and left her sitting.

When he got back to his room, he shut the door between them and headed for the bathroom. Later, as he was rinsing the shampoo from his hair, he kept thinking of her—and of him—and how their lives had changed in the past few months.

Universal Theorem was responsible for all she was. But they'd become so threatened by her existence, that they'd tried to kill her. And after losing his wife, Annie, there was nothing to tie him to his previous lifestyle, which was why he was in residence at the estate where she now lived.

He owed his life to Wyrick. She was a warrior. She backed down from no one. But it appeared she'd just shocked herself. She was still evolving, and this time she'd projected the energy to create a text message and send it, while she was asleep. Freaky weird, but cool as hell. If this was the way this day was going to begin, he could only imagine what the rest of it would be like.

Unfortunately, Wyrick wasn't as unaffected by this as Charlie seemed to be. She was still sitting on her bed, trying to come to terms with the shock of what she'd just done.

She had stunned herself. The ramifications of being able to

send a text message with her mind wasn't something she would have ever believed possible, and yet, she'd done it.

She scrubbed her face with her hands, as if trying to wipe away the reality of who she was, then got up and walked into her bathroom and stared at herself in the mirror.

I am such a freak. If I had hair, I'd be pulling it. The upside of that is, if I start growing horns, they'll be easy to see.

Then she turned away from her own reflection and followed Charlie's lead, stripped, tossed her pajamas in the laundry and got into the shower.

The heat of the pounding water eased the tension in her shoulders, and slowly, she began to relax. What had happened was a little startling, but considering everything else that was evolving within her, it was just one more thing to accept.

The upside of the latest revelation was Charlie. He was unflappable. As soon as she got out, she dressed in sweats and headed downstairs.

Wyrick was, in no way, a domestic goddess, but she was thinking along the lines of "feed a cold, starve a fever," as she went. She felt weird, like she hadn't eaten in days, and guessed food would be the first step in taking that away.

She could toast a mean waffle when the need arose, and this morning, in light of the fact that she'd just bypassed text messaging as the world knew and understood it, eating seemed like the thing to do.

By the time Charlie came down, she had coffee made, and a platter of toasted waffles on the table, with butter and syrup in containers beside them.

"Seriously, Martha Stewart?" Charlie said as he walked into the room and smelled the waffles.

She turned toward him, the fork in her hand in a gesture of defense.

"If you ever want another bear claw in your office again, you might want to shut it," she snapped.

He grinned, but had the good sense not to respond. Instead, he poured himself a cup of coffee, waited for her to sit down and then joined her.

A brief wash of regret moved through Charlie as he thought of all the times he and Annie had sat down to breakfast like this, but because of the early-onset Alzheimer's she had suffered, he'd lost that life with her a long time before he lost the woman.

They ate in relative silence for a few minutes, until he got up to refill his coffee and carried the carafe to the table and topped off her cup, as well.

"Did we tie up all the loose ends on the missing twins' case?" Charlie asked.

Wyrick nodded. "The police were given all of the information you got on the guy connected to the human trafficking ring. Last I heard, they'd picked him up, but I have no idea if he turned on his people. All I know is, those girls are lucky you found them when you did. They were bound for Dubai."

"*We* found them. Never belittle the online tracking you do," Charlie said.

Wyrick said nothing, but the praise went deep. She was dedicated to never letting this man down. Even when he made her crazy, his place in her life was ingrained.

Charlie pointed to the last waffle on the plate.

"You gonna eat that?" he asked.

"I can't," Wyrick said.

He frowned. "Why?"

"It has your name on it," Wyrick said.

It took him a second to realize she'd actually made a joke, and then laughed out loud as he forked it onto his plate.

"That's a good one," he said, then buttered it up and drowned it in syrup, just the way he liked it.

Wyrick got up and carried her dishes to the sink. No need to sit there and get all comfy-cozy with the boss—even if he was living under her roof for the sole purpose of keeping her alive.

"I'm going to check my email," she said. "I'll be ready to leave for work around 7:30."

Charlie had a mouthful of waffle, and nodded as she left the kitchen.

Wyrick thought about going out to the greenhouse to pick some of Merlin's tomatoes first, then decided against it. She'd get them tonight when they came home. She'd been putting off checking online messages and email, but this morning it felt like the thing to do.

The office in the old mansion was grand—all cherrywood, overstuffed leather furniture and floor-to-ceiling bookcases, and every time she walked in, she half expected to see her old friend, Merlin, sitting behind the desk, sporting his long white hair and beard. He hadn't needed a pointed hat and magic. He'd been wizard-smart without the trimmings.

It was sad to know someone that brilliant and vital was gone, and she was still struggling with the fact that he'd named her his heir. She didn't need the money. She had too much of it already, and it still couldn't buy her what she needed most—the anonymity of a personal life.

But the gift of that which he loved most, this estate in the heart of old Dallas, was a treasure she didn't take lightly. She missed him. She missed his wit.

Except for Charlie, Merlin was the only other person she'd ever trusted, and cancer took him, just like Alzheimer's had taken Charlie's Annie. But that was life, and she obviously wasn't through living hers, so she sat down in Merlin's chair, booted up one of her personal computers and went to work.

She had messages from her stockbroker.

Messages regarding the stats on her gaming company. Messages about her newest patents.

Messages from every company she owned.

And alerts from websites connected to religious communities who were posting about her. A few referred to her as an angel from God. A larger number of them considered her a benign cancer upon humanity, who should never have been born.

But there were a couple with large followings who posted dire warnings about the wisdom of leaving her alive in the world, and having prayer meetings in secret places to pray for her death.

Those were the ones she kept an eye on. Getting Universal Theorem out of her life had come at a huge cost. It had unleashed the madness of people who used religion to pursue their own personal, and often selfish, agendas.

One group stood out among the rest as one of the most dangerous. The congregation was small, but the online presence was larger. They called themselves the Church of The Righteous, and had a website that was a hotbed of disinformation and religious rants, and currently, a lot of that had to do with her.

So far she'd had no personal contact with them, but she suspected she would. She wasn't exactly afraid, but she was leery of bad men with personal power agendas. UT had taught her that.

She responded to her stockbroker's questions, sent information and orders as needed to her holdings and then went to get ready for work.

The weather was changing along with the days as they moved into fall. And on days when the weather was overcast, it was also cold. She opted for black leather and long sleeves on her blouse, silver knee-high boots and red-and-silver eye shadow, with a slash of red on her lips. After dropping her phone into her purse, she slung the strap over her shoulder and headed downstairs to get the rest of her things.

Charlie was kicked back in the living room, flipping channels on the morning news shows, when she walked in. He looked up, then turned off the TV and stood.

Wyrick's eyes narrowed as she quickly looked away.

Damn man. He made everything he wore look sexy, including the black Levi's, the white shirt and the Western-cut black blazer he had on today. Even his boots were shining. She refused to watch when he settled that black Stetson on his head, and left the house ahead of him, knowing he would follow.

"I'm stopping to get bear claws on the way. Don't forget. Stay off the beltway," she said.

"I'm not likely to forget that, and I have to get gas. See you at the office," Charlie said.

They both got in their cars. Wyrick used her remote to open the iron gates at the front of the estate, and Charlie used his to close them as they drove through. As always, Wyrick kept an eye out for people who didn't belong, and Charlie kept an eye out for her, by following the tracker she'd put on her phone so he'd always know where she was.

They took backstreets toward Charlie's office building, and parted ways when Wyrick pulled in to a strip mall and parked in front of a little bakery.

Even though Charlie had eaten waffles for breakfast, he was already thinking about coffee and crunching on sugar-glazed bear claws at the office. By the time he got to the station to refuel, Wyrick was back in her car and on her way to the office.

She beat him there because she needed to be first. She liked going into the quiet rooms, turning on lights and booting up computers. She liked making coffee and putting the pastries under the glass dome on the coffee bar. And she liked, most of all, sitting at her desk and hearing the stride of Charlie's footsteps as he came up the hall toward the office, then waiting for his key in the door.

Before, he used to come striding in, bringing life and energy into the space. But that was before people started trying to kill her. Now they had bulletproof frosted glass in the door, a security camera in the hall outside and people had to wait to be buzzed in. Wyrick resented the loss of her freedom, but she'd done what it took to feel safe, so there was that.

By the time Charlie finally arrived, Wyrick had gone through the messages, had notes on his desk and was entering direct deposit payments into their office accounts.

"Morning," he said as he passed her desk.

"Bear claws at the coffee bar. Messages on your desk," she said without looking up.

Charlie nodded. Here, their relationship was back on a boss-to-employee basis. At home, they stood on equal ground, free to argue. Free to admit shit to each other that they never spoke aloud outside those walls.

He stopped at the coffee bar and poured himself a cup of coffee, snagged a bear claw on a napkin and went into his office. He left his hat on the rack, and the jacket below it, and went to work.

Rachel Dean woke up with a bad taste in her mouth and a pain in her neck. But when she rolled over and opened her eyes, she saw a single bulb burning from a fixture beside an air vent in a cement ceiling, the bare mattress she was lying on and the four walls of a concrete, windowless cell. She screamed. The horror of no echo told her how solid the walls had to be to deaden the sound.

She didn't know where she was, or how she'd gotten here. The last thing she remembered was going into her bedroom to turn off the television, and then… Oh, my God! The pain in her neck! That hadn't been an insect sting. She'd been drugged. In her own home!

The room spun around her as she sat up and ran her fingers

through her hair, then rubbed at the back of her neck. At that moment she panicked all over again.

Her presentation was this morning, and she wasn't going to be there! What would her boss think? Hopefully, her secretary knew how to retrieve it. Someone else would give it. Someone else would get the client.

And then reality set in.

Missing a presentation was the least of her troubles. There was every possibility she would die here. Except for the mattress on which she was sitting, the only other things in the room were an old sink hanging precariously from one wall, and an ancient commode. Then she finally focused on the door—the huge metal door! Maybe, just maybe, it wasn't locked.

But when she got to her feet and staggered toward it, her hopes were dashed. It wouldn't budge. She doubled up her fists and began pounding on it, screaming over and over for help. The sound of her voice was diluted within the small space, but it didn't silence her. She pounded until her hands were throbbing, and her throat was sore from screaming before she finally dropped to her knees, sobbing hysterically.

She cried until her eyes were swollen, her throat now downright raw, before she crawled back to the mattress. But she was afraid to close her eyes for fear of what would come through the door, so she curled up in a ball against the wall, her knees beneath her chin, and waited.

CHAPTER TWO

Sonny Burch was a forty-something-year-old man with blond thinning hair and pale green eyes. He claimed being six feet tall, but he wasn't. Without the lifts in his shoes, he was barely five-nine. To make up for his lack of height, he worked out—keeping his arms and shoulders muscular, and his belly flat. At work people called him Boss, but he always thought of himself as Sonny, because that was what his mother had called him.

Sonny arrived at his office and went straight into a meeting. There was cake in the conference room in honor of a colleague's birthday. He liked cake, but his personal celebrations always had to do with playing the game, and winning the prize.

Sonny was a man who led two lives—a man who wore two faces. His public face and his private face. But he excused that as a given because he was a Gemini—the sign of the twins. He was good, and he was evil. He liked to make people laugh, and he liked to make people cry.

And when he went home after work today, he would get to play the game. It had been four years since he'd given in to this need, and knowing who was waiting for him made it hard to concentrate on work. He equated his obsession to being on a diet, and then finally giving himself a long-awaited treat, and he was starving for this high—the high of watching her bleed, and hearing her scream.

Rachel woke up again with the hangover from hell. The remnants of the drugs were still in her system, and the first thing she saw when she opened her eyes was that single lightbulb high above her head, burning away the dark.

This time, without the initial shock masking everything else, she caught an underlying stench of urine, and a steady drip coming from somewhere behind her. This wasn't a bad dream. This was real, and she had no idea how long she'd been here. Without clocks or windows, or anything to mark time, all she felt was extreme thirst. She rolled over to get up, and again, the room began to spin. So she tried again, this time stopping when she was sitting in an upright position, and when the spinning stopped, she managed to stand and headed straight for the door, praying with every step that this time the knob would turn, and the door would open. But it would not.

She doubled up her fists and began pounding on the door.

"Help! Help me!" she screamed, until her hands were throbbing, and her voice was raw.

She turned her back to the door, her hands clutched beneath her breasts, in complete disbelief. The truth was staring her in the face and she still couldn't grasp it.

Why had this happened? Was she the victim of human trafficking, or was the person who took her some kind of serial rapist? Would he kill her, or just torture her until she wished she *were* dead?

She staggered to the sink hanging near the ancient toilet, then turned on the tap. Both water and air came out in a sputtering whoosh, along with some bits of rust. She let it run until it was clear, then leaned over the sink and sluiced her face until the last of the drugged feeling was gone, then cupped her hands beneath the flow, and drank without thought of contamination.

She flushed the toilet just to see if it worked, and then stood, staring at the disappearing water circling the rust-stained bowl before she finally allowed herself to use it, then flushed it again.

Looking back at the old mattress, she suddenly focused on the faded stains within the fabric and realized they looked like bloodstains. Faint and faded, but bloodstains, nevertheless. She shuddered in renewed horror. She didn't want to die, but she wouldn't go down without a fight.

Unwilling to lie back down, she stood in the middle of the floor until the muscles in her legs were trembling from the strain, and the room was beginning to spin.

Staggering back to the mattress, she sat down, still facing the door, and again, the remnants of the drugs still in her system pulled her under.

Rachel Dean's absence had not gone unnoticed at Addison-Tunnell. Her secretary, Lucy Arnold, was in a panic. Their boss, Russ Addison, was in a bigger panic. The clients were in the conference room waiting.

"Call her apartment!" he ordered.

"I already called five times!" Lucy cried. "This isn't like Rachel. Something is wrong!"

Russ shoved a hand through his hair in frustration.

"Who else is familiar with this project?"

"Uh…maybe Ralph? He did some initial research for her. I can get the file to him."

"Then do it!" Addison said. "I'll let him know what's happening and talk to the clients myself until he gets in there."

"Yes, sir!" Lucy said.

"And then check on Rachel again," Addison said.

Lucy pulled up the files on Rachel's computer, did a quick search for the right one, then sent it to Ralph. She didn't know what had gone wrong, but she was just sick for Rachel. She'd worked so hard on it.

As soon as it went through, she pulled up Rachel's personnel file and began looking for contact information, then made a frantic call to Wayne Dyer, the manager of the building where Rachel lived.

Wayne lived in a ground-floor apartment on the premises and was at his desk in the manager's office, working on accounts, when the phone rang.

"Detter House. This is Wayne."

"Mr. Dyer, this is Lucy Arnold, from Addison-Tunnell Advertising Agency. I'm Rachel Dean's secretary. Rachel lives in apartment 210 on the second floor of your residence, and she didn't come in to work this morning. She didn't call, and she's not answering her phone. We're extremely concerned. She had a very important presentation this morning and would never have missed this. We're asking if you could do a wellness check?"

Wayne frowned.

"I'm sorry to hear this. Yes, of course, I'll be happy to check on her."

"Oh, thank you," Lucy said. "Please call me back as soon as you do."

"Yes, I will. I have your number on caller ID. Give me a few minutes to get to that wing of the building."

"Thank you. Thank you so much," Lucy said. "I'll be waiting for your call."

She hung up the phone and then sat, staring off into space, trying not to imagine the worst, while Wayne picked up a passkey and headed for the elevator.

He wasn't overly concerned with what he'd find. He didn't know Rachel Dean's personal habits, but it wouldn't be the first time a resident had overslept. He was just hoping she hadn't taken a fall, or was passed out from being drugged up or drunk. That would be completely embarrassing.

He took the elevator up, exited on the second floor and headed down the north hall to apartment 210, then knocked and waited, but no one answered. He knocked again, and then called out her name.

"Rachel! Rachel Dean! It's Wayne Dyer."

Still no response.

He unlocked the door, and then the dead bolt before pushing it open. Even then, he still didn't cross the threshold.

"Rachel! It's me, Wayne Dyer! Your boss has requested a wellness check. I'm coming in!" he yelled, and then walked into the foyer, leaving the door open behind him as he started his search.

He could hear voices in the back of the apartment and hoped she wasn't in bed with someone, then recognized the voices of two talk show hosts on the program he'd been watching. The sound he was hearing was the television.

"Rachel! Hello? Hello? Are you there?"

Again, he got no response.

By now his heart was beginning to race. *Oh, God, just please don't let her be dead*, he thought as he poked his head into her bedroom.

The television was on. The bathroom door was open, but it was empty. The walk-in closet door was open, but she wasn't in there. As he left the bedroom and headed toward the kitchen, he was starting to grow concerned. But it wasn't until he saw a partially filled bowl of congealed soup and the dried cheese on a half-eaten cracker that it began to dawn on him that she was gone.

Her iPad was beside the food, as if she'd just gotten up and walked away from a meal. But that food had been there for hours, and it wasn't breakfast food. He went back to the living room, taking note of her briefcase on the floor, and her purse on the table beside the door.

"This isn't looking good," Wayne muttered, then left, locking the door behind him, and headed back downstairs on a run.

He knew what she drove, and wanted to see if her car was gone. But when he stepped out the back of the building and saw the little red Fiat still parked in her assigned parking spot, his heart skipped a beat.

He turned around and ran back to his office. His hands were shaking as he punched in the numbers, and waited for it to ring, and then her secretary answered immediately.

"This is Lucy."

"Lucy, this is Wayne Dyer. Rachel isn't in her apartment. The television is on in her bedroom. There is a partially eaten meal from last night still on her dining table. Her car is still here. Her purse and briefcase are still in her apartment. Have you called her sister? She might know something. Do you have her contact information?"

"Yes, yes, I do. I'll call her right now, and thank you," Lucy said.

"Of course, and please keep me updated when you know something more."

Lucy heard the line go dead when he disconnected, but she was already looking for the contact info for Rachel's sister. She'd heard her talk about her often, and knew they were close. If there had been a family emergency, Millie Chriss would know.

She finally found the info and made the call, and as she was waiting for Millie to answer, Lucy kept thinking of Rachel's purse and car still on the premises. Even if it had been a family emergency, she would not have left the purse behind.

Millie had just dropped her husband, Ray, off at the airport, and was on her way home when her phone rang. When she saw the call was from Addison-Tunnell, she smiled. It was Rachel. She hit Bluetooth to answer for hands-free driving, and took the exit off the freeway to head home.

"Hello?"

"Mrs. Chriss, this is Lucy Arnold, Rachel's secretary. Do you have a minute?"

Millie frowned. *God, please don't let Rachel have been in a wreck.*

"What's wrong?" Millie asked, and then heard Lucy hesitate. It was enough to intensify her concern.

"Well, we're not sure. Rachel had a big presentation this morning and didn't make it into work. She didn't call in, which isn't like her. And she didn't answer any of our calls. Was there, by chance, a family emergency?"

Millie's heart sank.

"No. Nothing like that! Oh, my God. Have you checked her apartment? Maybe she fell!"

"I already had the manager do a wellness check. The apartment was locked, but she wasn't inside. He said there was food leftover on the table from last night. Her purse and briefcase are still there, and so is her car. But she's gone."

Millie moaned. "Oh, my God. Oh, my God! Have you called the police?"

"Not yet. We wanted to check with you first."

"Call them!" Millie cried. "Call them now. I'm on my way home. Keep me updated. If you haven't heard anything by tonight, I'll be heading that way tomorrow morning."

"Yes, I will. I'm so sorry to be the bearer of bad news."

"I'll be in touch with the Dallas Police myself today. You're reporting her as a missing person, right?"

"Yes, ma'am," Lucy said.

Millie braked for a red light, her voice shaking.

"You report it, and I'll follow up and deal with them."

"I will," Lucy said, disconnected and then called Russ Addison. Reporting a missing employee carried more weight when it was the boss doing the reporting.

Once she filled him in on what she'd found out, Russ Addison became concerned, as well.

"Yes, I'll make the call to Missing Persons myself, and fill them in on what we know," Russ said.

Back in Tulsa, Millie Chriss was in a panic, and too far away to help. She was in shock. She was nauseated, but too scared to cry. She wanted to call Ray, but he was on a plane bound for Seattle. She and Rachel were all the family each other had. She couldn't lose her.

"Please, baby. Wherever you are, please be safe. If you're in trouble, I'll find you… I swear."

Detective Darren Floyd was at his desk finishing up a report when his phone rang. He hit Save, then turned around to answer.

"Missing Persons. Detective Floyd speaking."

"Darren, this is Russell Addison."

"Russ! My old roomie. What's going on?"

Russ Addison smiled, remembering their college days together, then got down to business.

"This is actually a serious call. I have an employee who didn't show up for work this morning, and the circumstances are worrying. She'd been working on this presentation for two weeks, and was primed to deliver. We've called without getting an answer, and then had the building manager do a wellness check."

"Talk to me," Darren said, and reached for a pen and paper.

Russ began explaining the situation, from Rachel Dean's work ethic, to the building manager's findings in her apartment.

"So her name is Rachel Dean? What's her home address?" Darren asked.

Russ read it from her personnel file. "She lives at the Det-

ter House. You know, that big mansion they turned into apartments in the historic district?"

Darren frowned.

"Yes, I know it. It's pricey."

"She's well paid, and worth every penny. She's one of my best
ad execs. This is an official missing person report. Can you look
into it personally?"

"Yes. My partner and I will head out there now. Does the
building manager live on the premises?"

"Yes. At least, that's my understanding," Russ said. "Also,
Rachel Dean has only one living family member. Her name is
Millie Chriss. She lives in Tulsa, but they're very close, so be
prepared for her to contact you. And while I do want to know
what you find out, from now on please refer all of your discovery and questions to her sister, because she has been notified
her sister is missing."

"Do you have a contact number for her?" Darren asked.

"Yes," Russ said, and read it to him.

"Okay... I've got all I need for now. I'll be in touch."

"Thanks," Russ said. "I owe you."

"Nah...just doing my job, buddy. Take care," Darren said.
He grabbed his notes, slipped them into his pocket and stood.

"Hey, Waylon! We've got a new one. Let's go."

Waylon Mills grabbed his jacket and slipped it on over his
gun and shoulder holster as he followed his partner out of the
precinct.

Wayne Dyer was getting ready to run some errands when he
received a call from a Dallas police detective, telling him they
were on the way to the Detter House to investigate a report of
a missing person from the residence, and asked him to be on
site to let them into her apartment.

He readily agreed, and then spent the next twenty minutes

nervously waiting for them to arrive. When they walked into the manager's office flashing their badges, his stomach knotted. He'd never had business with the police before, and he was starting to realize that if something really had happened to Rachel Dean, they might consider him a suspect.

"Mr. Dyer?"

"Yes, but call me Wayne."

Floyd nodded. "I'm Detective Floyd. This is my partner, Detective Mills. We need access to Rachel Dean's apartment."

"Yes, sir. I have the passkey. Follow me," Wayne said, and led them to the elevator, then up to the second floor of the north wing.

Both detectives were checking out security cameras as they headed up the hall.

"Are there security cameras in every hallway in the building?" Mills asked.

"Yes, sir. At both ends of each hallway," Wayne said.

"What about inside the apartments?" Floyd asked.

"That's strictly up to the residents. I don't believe Rachel did, but you can check it out."

"We'll need a copy of the security footage on the premises from the last twenty-four hours," Floyd said.

"I'll get it for you. You can pick it up on your way out," Wayne said. "Okay…here we are," he said, and stopped at the door to apartment 210, unlocked it, then led the way in. The moment they entered the apartment, they heard voices.

"Someone's talking back there," Mills said, pointing down a hall off the foyer.

"It's the television in the bedroom," Wayne said. "It was on when I came in to do the wellness check. I didn't mess with anything or touch anything. Her purse and briefcase are here at the entry, just as I saw them when I walked in. There's partially eaten food on the table in the kitchen, but it's not breakfast food, and it looks like it's been there for hours. I also checked to see if her car was still on the premises, and it is. It's the little red Fiat in the parking garage out back. After that I called the secretary at Addison-Tunnell, who'd asked for the wellness check, to report what I'd found, and then you guys called. That's the extent of my knowledge about this."

"Does Rachel Dean have a boyfriend?" Detective Floyd asked.

Wayne shrugged. "I couldn't say, but I've never seen her with anyone in particular. She's really nice and cute, but she seems focused on her career."

"We're going to do a walk-through," Floyd said. "If we need anything else, we'll call."

"What about locking up?" Wayne asked.

"Can we lock it from the inside and just pull the door shut?" Mills asked.

"No, sir," Wayne said. "How about I leave the passkey with you, and when you've finished up, just drop it off when you pick up the security footage."

"Will do," Mills said, and took the key, then closed the door behind Dyer after he left.

Floyd glanced around the foyer, then into the living room to their right. Nothing was disturbed, or appeared to be out of place.

"Let's start in the kitchen," Floyd said. "You know what to look for."

Mills saw the utility room and checked it first.

"Hey, there's a load of laundry in the washer that wasn't ever put in the dryer," he said as he came back out.

Floyd pointed to the table. "We've got a half-eaten bowl of noodle soup, a dead iPad and the cheese on this plate is hard and curling at the edges. This is not breakfast food. This is from last night, for sure."

Mills nodded. "Looks like she was reading something on her iPad while she ate, and was interrupted."

"Maybe she got sick and headed to the bathroom?"

"Dyer didn't mention any signs of that, but we're about to find out," Mills said, and followed the sounds of the television all the way down the hall and into her bedroom.

"The bed is made. Doesn't look like she slept in it last night," Floyd said.

Mills stood for a moment, eyeing the setup of the room.

"Why would the TV be on, if she was eating her meal in the kitchen? She obviously wasn't watching TV in bed, because the bed hasn't been disturbed since it was made, and the remote is all the way across the room by the television. Nobody watches TV like that."

Floyd's eyes narrowed. There was no simple explanation for any of this. He stepped into the bathroom, eyeing the perfectly folded towel and washcloth hanging on the towel rack, then felt the soap inside the shower. It was dry. Everything in the room was pristine.

"She didn't shower in here last night," he said, and then eyed footsteps in the carpeting that went in and out of the walk-in closet, but there was nothing obvious to be seen in there, either.

"There's no blood. No sign of a fight. Nothing has been disturbed. But she's damn sure gone," Floyd said.

"Maybe that security footage will show something different," Mills said.

"I want to look at it now," Floyd said. "Call Dyer and tell him we're coming down."

Mills made the call, and was talking to Dyer as they left, locking the door and heading back to the elevator.

Viewing the footage only compounded the puzzle. It showed Wayne letting in a cleaning crew around 10 a.m. yesterday, and then coming back just after 1 p.m. to lock up when they left.

"Do you do this for all of the residents?" Detective Mills asked.

"You mean, letting in cleaning crews and repairmen? Yes. It's part of my job. Slick Floors is the cleaning service. They have a contract with Detter House, but they never have free access to the rooms. I always let them in and lock up after they're gone."

Then they fast-forwarded the footage to the next person to enter her apartment.

"Who's that?" Floyd asked.

"That's Rachel. She often works late at her office."

It was the first time they were seeing the face of the woman who'd gone missing. Pretty, dark curly hair. A little over five feet tall. The time stamp was just before 8 p.m. when she went into her apartment. She never came out again. After that the next person to show up at her door on the footage was Dyer going in for the wellness check this morning.

"This is very disturbing," Floyd said. "There's not another way out of her apartment. There's no back door, and the fire exit is down the hall, so she would have had to come out of her apartment to get out of this building, no matter where she made an exit. I'm calling in our team from the crime lab. They'll do a sweep of the apartment. If there are answers to be had there, they'll find them. So for now I'm keeping the passkey until they're finished."

Wayne nodded. "If there's anything I can do to help, don't hesitate to ask."

"We'll be in touch," Floyd said.

CHAPTER THREE

The day at Dodge Investigations was slow, but productive. Charlie was gone most of the afternoon, testifying in a court case, and Wyrick was in the office at her desk, shopping online at Whole Foods, contemplating which box of cereal to order, when the phone rang. She paused, then swiveled around and reached for the phone.

"Dodge Investigations."

"I need to hire Charlie Dodge. I'm being blackmailed and—"

Wyrick frowned. "Then call the police. Charlie Dodge is in the business of finding people who've gone missing."

"I can't! If I call the police, my wife will—"

"Your mistakes and your pissed-off wife are your business, but nothing my boss will ever get mixed up in. You have two choices. Pay your blackmailer, or call the cops."

She hung up, then turned back to her pending grocery order, moved the cursor to sugarcoated rice crisps and clicked. Charlie liked those.

A short while later she got a text from Charlie.

Lock up the office and go home when you want. I'm still waiting to testify. The judge gave the opposing council a thirty-minute recess. Just be careful.

She sent him a thumbs-up emoji, and went about shutting things down. There were two cherry Danish left at the coffee bar from the assortment she'd brought this morning, so she boxed them up to take home, then grabbed her things and headed for the door.

She had her bag over her shoulder, and the key in her hand as she opened the door to go out. She had just enough time to see a tall, skinny man in jeans and a black plaid shirt coming at her, pushing her back inside. She kicked at him, sending him stumbling backward, but before she could get the Taser out of her bag, he swung at her. She ducked. His fist hit her on the shoulder instead of her face, knocking her backward.

She knew when he kicked the door shut that he'd come to kill her, so she grabbed her bag, yanked out the Taser and fired as he was pulling a gun from the waistband of his jeans.

The prongs hit him in the face.

He flew backward as if she'd punched him, slamming against the door, and then falling onto the floor, seizing and jerking from the electric shocks rolling through his body.

Wyrick rolled over, dug her phone from her pocket and called 911. As soon as help was dispatched, she hung up, then ran into Charlie's office for a pair of handcuffs, went back to where he lay jerking and moaning, kicked the bottom of his shoe, then leaned over him long enough to meet his enraged gaze.

"You are a true piece of shit," she said calmly, then rolled him facedown and yanked his arms behind his back and cuffed him, before she pulled the prongs from his face, then dragged him away from the door and opened it wide, so the police could get in.

Spittle was running from the corner of his mouth, and he was moaning between every other breath, and yet he managed to mumble.

"Devil woman."

The skin crawled on the back of her neck. She should have known! He was one of them. She leaned over and dug the wallet from his hip pocket.

"Thief," he hissed.

She could see the side of his face was turning splotchy and red where the Taser prongs had penetrated the flesh, and blood was oozing from the wounds, dripping down his cheek onto the floor beneath him. But she had no empathy for his pain.

"The pot calling the kettle black. You're the one who came in here to kill me, and it's all on video," she muttered, and then the moment she touched the wallet, she knew he was part of The Righteous.

She pulled out his driver's license, took a picture of it, put it back in the wallet, then shoved it in his pocket. She had a new enemy and he had a name.

Barrett Taylor.

Taylor heard the click when she took the picture, and guessed what she'd just done. And when she'd returned the wallet to his pocket, he began to panic. His people wouldn't be happy this had happened.

"Others comin'…know what you are," he mumbled.

A chill went up Wyrick's back, and then she got mad. More coming? No, by God! Not again!

She kicked the bottom of his boot again.

"And now I know who *you* are, too…and where you live. And, I know what you are, and what you came to do. The Righteous are not going to be happy with you. You know what they'll do. They don't like failure, do they?"

He shuddered. "How you—?"

"If you really knew who I was, you wouldn't have had to ask that question. Looks to me like they set you up to be the sacrificial goat to get rid of me. Did you know that ahead of time? Is this your little cult's version of dying for the cause, or are you just that stupid?"

He moaned. "Jus' doin' Lord's work."

"God didn't tell you to do this. The leader of your little swamp-rat cult told you."

If he could, Taylor would have spit in her face, but his drool was already running on the floor because he still couldn't feel his lips.

Wyrick was beginning to hear sirens, and so did Taylor.

He closed his eyes, still moaning from the pain, and wished he could begin this day all over again.

"Feels like you got hold of a hot wire and can't let go, doesn't it?" Wyrick said. "Be glad it was me who caught you and not Charlie. He would have shot you where you stood for what you did to me, before he ever bothered to call the cops."

After that Barrett Taylor went mum. He heard the police cars pulling to a screeching halt in the parking lot outside the building, and made his peace with what was.

Two officers took the stairwell up, as two others took the elevator, thereby blocking off all avenues of exit. They merged in the hallway, and headed up the hall toward the office of Dodge Investigations, coming in with their guns drawn.

Once they realized Wyrick was standing upright, and the intruder was handcuffed facedown on the floor, they holstered their weapons.

The first officer introduced himself. "Ma'am... Wyrick, I'm Officer Bullard. Are you okay?"

"Obviously," she said.

"Is he the only one?" Bullard asked.

She nodded.

"Exactly what happened here?"

So Wyrick proceeded to explain.

"It's all going to be on the security cams. They are at both ends of the hall outside, as well as one over the door to our office, and then there are ones in here, as well. He was waiting for me. When I opened the door to leave, he kicked it in, hit me with his fist, then was reaching for his gun when I Tasered him. I pulled his wallet and took a picture of his driver's license, then put it back in his pocket. Knowing the identities of my enemies is what keeps me alive, even though his cult isn't known for brilliance…just hate. He was going for the gun when I fired the Taser."

Officer Bullard frowned. "Cult? You know him?"

"I know who he belongs to. They call themselves the Church of The Righteous. They're based in Louisiana, and have been throwing out all kinds of warnings on their website about my existence, saying I'm an abomination, ranting about how I need to be 'taken care of.' Taylor just bragged there are others coming after me, too. Needless to say, I'm pressing charges against him for assault and attempted murder."

Officers Oliver and Jackson pulled Barrett Taylor to his feet. Oliver then began searching him for the gun, while Jackson got an evidence bag. When Jackson began to pat him down, he grimaced.

"Dang it, Oliver. He pissed his pants. It's your turn to transport a wet one."

"I couldn't help it," Taylor said, glaring at Wyrick.

Wyrick glared back. "A rather embarrassing side effect of getting Tasered. Be glad I didn't shoot you in the balls, because that was my first target."

Taylor blanched, and then looked away as the officer bagged his gun.

"Get him out of here," Bullard said, then glanced back at

Wyrick as they led him away in handcuffs. "Ma'am, does Charlie know about this?"

"He's in court. I'll tell him later," Wyrick said.

"I'll just walk you to your car," Bullard said, and then grinned. "Just in case there's another one out there, you can protect the both of us."

She ignored his attempt at humor, because she was anything but amused.

"I'll get video footage from the security cameras to you tomorrow morning. Thank you for your prompt response."

"Yes, ma'am," Bullard said.

They rode the elevator down in silence, then she exited the building and headed for her Ferrari, got in and sped off, heading straight to Whole Foods to pick up her grocery order. But even after she was on her way home, she kept thinking, *Charlie is going to be pissed*.

And Charlie was pissed. He'd spent the whole afternoon waiting to testify, only to be told late in the afternoon that the defendant pled out on the assault charges, and got off with time served, which amounted to two months and a fine.

He still couldn't believe it. He'd witnessed the man assault a waitress, who wound up with a broken nose and jaw, her front teeth getting knocked out in the process, and this was her justice? He found out later the man was her ex-husband, and that she'd had a protective order against him. If Charlie hadn't taken him down, he might have killed her.

The longer he stayed in this business, the more disenchanted he was becoming with the justice system. Sometimes it wasn't about the crime, as much as how much power and money you had to buy your way out of trouble. All he wanted now was just to get home.

Living with Wyrick was often aggravating as hell, but she

was also the anchor to his world. Knowing she needed him had changed his focus from the overwhelming grief of losing Annie. Wyrick was the weight that kept everything level in his life, and gave him purpose for still being in this world.

When he finally reached the drive leading up to the mansion, he hit the remote and drove through the iron gates as they opened, then hit the remote again, closing them behind him as he passed.

The weather looked iffy today, so he parked in the covered garage behind the mansion, just in case there was any threat of hail later on tonight, and headed toward the house. The wind was sharp and getting chilly as he glanced up at the sky. Fall was upon them and winter wouldn't be far behind. Time was moving too fast. He was passing the greenhouse when he saw movement inside and smiled.

Wyrick was in there, and likely picking some of her old landlord's tomatoes. Technically, they were her tomatoes now, since she'd inherited his property, but she still called them Merlin's tomatoes.

He opened the door to the greenhouse and looked in. She was all the way at the back, and as he'd guessed, was filling a small bowl with patio tomatoes.

"Hey!" he called out. "I'm home. Need any help?"

She turned, a rare smile on her face. "No. I've got it. I'll be in soon."

He gave her a thumbs-up, shut the door and then jogged up the steps to the veranda, and into the house through the kitchen.

The room was warm and welcoming, and there was something heating in the oven, because he could smell it. Wyrick wasn't much for cooking, but neither was he. She could heat food up without burning it, and microwave like a beast.

It was enough skill to sustain them, and when the occasion

demanded, they went out to eat, or ordered in. Their routine was far smoother than their relationship, but it was what it was.

Anxious now to get out of the clothes he'd worn to court, he headed upstairs on a run.

By the time he came back down in old jeans and a long-sleeved T-shirt, Wyrick was back in the kitchen washing tomatoes.

A timer went off just as Charlie walked in.

"Is that timer for what's in the oven?" he asked.

She nodded.

He waited for further instructions, but when she stayed silent, he sighed.

"Want me to take it out?"

"You'll have to if you want to eat it," she said.

He rolled his eyes, grabbed a couple of pot holders and opened the oven door, pulled out some kind of casserole in a foil container and set it on a burner to cool.

"Smells good. You outdid yourself tonight," he drawled.

"It's supposed to be beef Stroganoff...or something like that, but it's basically beef tips and noodles in sauce. There's stuff for salad in the refrigerator—if you can handle a pair of scissors to open the bag of salad greens, then follow the directions."

He frowned. "You're exceptionally pissy tonight. What's wrong?"

He heard her sigh, then watched her shoulders slump.

"You're going to be mad, so I thought I'd just be mad first and save you the trouble."

His frown deepened.

"What happened?"

"I'll tell you while we eat. You do better with food in your belly."

"I am not a savage beast to be tamed with a thick piece of steak," he muttered.

"It's beef tips and noodles, and yes, you are."

"Fine. I'll make the salad," he said.

She added a handful of the little tomatoes to the bowl of greens, then carried the casserole to the table while he stirred the dressing into the salad.

They sat, then looked up at each other over empty plates.

"What happened?" Charlie asked.

"You haven't take a bite of—"

"Dammit, Wyrick. I am not your priest. I'm your friend, and when you remember to acknowledge it… I am also your boss. Talk to me."

And so she did, from beginning to end.

"Shit," Charlie muttered when she stopped talking. "Were you scared?"

"No. But by the time I got through with him, he was," she said.

Relief washed through him.

"You said you got a picture of his driver's license?"

She nodded.

"After dinner you will send it to me, please. You do your research. I'll do mine. Understood?"

"Yes."

"Okay, then," Charlie said and scooped out a big serving of the Stroganoff onto his plate, added salad next to it and took his first bite, chewed and then swallowed. "It's good. You outdid yourself," he said.

"Stifle the sarcasm. Next time, you cook," she muttered, then served herself and started eating.

They ate in silence now, but the tension was gone.

Charlie felt the prickly energy of the wall she kept between them, and Wyrick knew he wasn't going to let this go, which was fine with her, because neither was she.

★ ★ ★

Barrett Taylor had taken a risk after being booked into jail by using his one phone call on Jeremiah Raver, the leader of the church.

To say Raver was angry was putting it mildly.

"I trusted you to do a simple job, and your incompetence is only going to bring negative attention to us," Raver shouted.

But Barrett was pissed at Raver for not telling him the whole story about that woman.

"That's just it. It wasn't a simple job. You said she was an unnatural abomination. You said she had powers that belonged only to God, but you neglected to mention she was psychic. You didn't tell me she was six fucking feet tall. She knew everything about my presence without touching me. What was I supposed to be? The fatted calf? The lure? Did you just decide to sacrifice me for her?"

Raver blinked. Rebellion within The Righteous was unheard of. And the fact that Barrett had figured this out made him uncomfortable.

"It wasn't like that," Raver said.

"Then get me a lawyer and get me the fuck out of here," Barrett said. "I'm not sacrificing myself for anyone."

Raver didn't like what he was hearing.

"Are you threatening me?"

Barrett lowered his voice. "You hung me out to dry, Raver. You figure it out." He hung up. But once the link was broken between him and Raver, his defiance faded. This was going to be a learning experience, for sure.

The game was on with Rachel Dean, and it was all Sonny could think about on the way home. He stopped off at a fast-food drive-through, ordered chicken nuggets and fries and a bottle of water and then drove away.

Rachel was exactly what he'd been needing—a little after-work entertainment was always good for releasing unspent energy and relieving stress.

The weatherman was predicting a light frost tonight. Maybe he'd take her a blanket along with her food. He didn't want her to get sick before he was done with her. That had happened to him once before. When that one had died in her sleep, he was disappointed to have been cheated out of being the one to deliver the death blow. It was always the delicious denouement to the game.

Rachel had paced and screamed for help, and pounded on the door off and on for hours. She finally fell asleep from exhaustion, only to be awakened sometime later by a hard slap across her face.

She woke up with a scream. There was a man on his hands and knees above her, tearing at her clothing—and she knew him!

"You!" she cried, and tried to push him off, kicking and slapping at him in desperation.

Even as she was hammering at his shoulders, and trying to claw his face, he was laughing. Then he drew back his fist and hit her on the jaw, knocking her unconscious.

When she came to again, she was naked, and he was on top of her and in her, holding a knife against her throat.

"Move, and you'll cut your own throat," Sonny said, and then leaned down and whispered against her ear. "I don't mind fucking a dead woman. I've done it before."

She saw the expression on his face, and then her own reflection in his eyes, and froze.

The next few minutes were an eternity of pain and despair, and when he finally collapsed on top of her, the knife slid lightly across her throat, bringing blood.

He leaned down, licked it slowly, then kissed her viciously, biting her mouth before he got up.

"Dinner is served," he said, pointing to a sack on the floor by the sink, and then he was gone.

Rachel staggered to her feet, picked up the clothing he'd ripped off her and went to the sink. Using her underwear for a rag, she began washing. At first, the rag was red with blood, but the cut on her throat finally stopped bleeding, and then she washed every inch of her body, desperate to get the feel of him off her skin.

She noticed he'd left her a blanket with the food, but she was without soap. Without clean clothes. Without hope. And yet, she knew if she ever got a chance to escape, she needed to be strong enough to do it. After she dressed she picked up the sack of food he'd brought, carried it to the far corner of the room, away from the mattress, and dug out cold chicken nuggets and fries. She gagged on the first couple of bites, but then took a small sip from the bottle of water he'd included, and waited until the nausea passed. After that she ate with solemn determination, tasting nothing but revenge.

It took Millie forever to get home. She got stuck in traffic due to a wreck up ahead, and then as traffic finally started moving, they were all detoured into an older part of the city, and then just when she thought she was in the clear, her car began losing speed. She pulled over to the first access road, and called her car service.

After being towed to a repair shop, they told her the alternator had gone out, and so she sat for two hours, waiting for them to run down the part on the other side of Tulsa.

While she was waiting, she'd called Addison-Tunnell, and asked if they'd made the missing person report to Dallas PD.

"Yes, we did. Mr. Addison reported it himself. If you'll hold a couple of minutes, I'll get contact info for you and text it to your phone."

"Thank you," Millie said, and disconnected. Her gut was in knots and she was so scared it was hard to breathe.

A few minutes later she got the text, pulled up the name and number and quickly made the call. It rang twice, and then a man's voice was in her ear.

"Detective Floyd, Missing Persons."

"Detective Floyd, this is Millie Chriss. I'm Rachel Dean's sister, and I was told you are the officer looking into my sister's disappearance."

"Yes, ma'am."

"Do you know anything? What can you tell me?" Millie asked.

"We know she's missing, and under suspicious circumstances. I'm with the crime scene team right now. We're in her apartment gathering evidence, but with no signs of a struggle, or any evidence of foul play, we're at a bit of a loss. We're hoping something will pop from what we're gathering."

"I'm coming to Dallas tomorrow. Even if I can't help, I need to be there. Rachel and I are all that's left of our family. I can't lose her. I just can't," Millie said, her voice breaking from emotion.

"We'll do everything we can," Floyd said. "I have your phone number. If we find out anything, you'll be the first to know."

"Thank you," Millie said.

She disconnected, then began sending Ray a text, explaining what had happened, and that she was leaving for Dallas in the morning. He wouldn't get the message until he landed, but he'd call her once he did, and she needed to hear his voice.

Another two hours passed before her car was fixed, and she was on her way home. Once she got there, she got a suitcase from the closet and began packing. She didn't know how long she was going to be gone, but she wasn't coming back until Rachel was found.

She'd missed lunch, and was too upset to be hungry, but she knew she needed to eat. She was in the kitchen getting out a loaf of bread when her phone rang. She grabbed it, praying it would be the Dallas Police telling her they'd found Rachel, but it was Ray.

"Hello?"

"Millie, honey! What the hell?" Ray said. "Rachel's missing?"

"Yes!" she wailed, then sat down at the kitchen table and began giving him details. "I'm already packed. I'm heading to Dallas early tomorrow morning. I know I can't really do anything to help, but I feel like I have to be there...to be close."

"Of course. Where are you going to stay?"

"At the same place we always stay when we visit, the Warwick Melrose on Oak Lawn," Millie said.

"Do you need me to join you? I will. I hate to think of you waiting all on your own," Ray said.

Millie wanted to be selfish and say yes. But this conference was important for him.

"No, I'll be fine. You go to your meetings. Do your thing and I'll keep you updated if there's any news."

Ray groaned. "I hate this. I'm sick about Rachel. And I'm so sad for you. We have to have faith they'll find her."

Tears finally rolled as her voice began to shake.

"They have to. They just have to."

"I know, baby. I know. Listen… I've got to go. I love you. I'll check in with you after I get to Seattle, okay?"

Millie sighed. "Yes, yes, I love you, too. Be safe, sweetheart."

"And you drive safe tomorrow. Don't get distracted by worrying and get yourself hurt," Ray said.

"I won't. I promise. I'll feel better just knowing I'm heading her way. Talk to you later. I love you."

"I love you, too," Ray said and disconnected.

Millie laid the phone down, then looked up at the cuckoo clock on the kitchen wall, ticking away precious time. She tried not to think of what horrors Rachel might be enduring, willing herself not to even think that Rachel might already be dead.

Unaware of the ensuing drama regarding Rachel Dean's disappearance, Charlie worked late into the night, running background checks on Barrett Taylor, and on all of the people he could find names for who were connected to The Righteous organization. From what he could tell, a preacher named Jeremiah Raver was at the head of it.

Taylor was just the hit man—an ex-con who'd done time in Florida, and in Alabama, although his current place of residence was listed in Baton Rouge, Louisiana. He'd been arrested for armed robbery, breaking and entering, possession of stolen property, car theft and drug possession. This murder attempt was new, or at least something he'd never been caught doing before.

Charlie guessed Wyrick probably had all of this and more, and had dirt on the entire organization, but she had a tendency to keep her troubles to herself, and he wanted to know what she was facing now—not after it all fell in on top of her again.

He finally went to bed, satisfied with what he'd learned, and wisely did not bring it up again at breakfast the next morning.

By the time he and Wyrick left for work, he was better informed about the whole organization and how they worked, but Taylor mentioned there were others coming for her, too, and he didn't know what they looked like. He couldn't do anything about that, but he wanted to make sure Barrett Taylor didn't bond out of jail. So he called in a favor from a friend in the Dallas PD. The phone rang twice, and then the call picked up on the third ring.

"Lieutenant Wagner."

"Tony, this is Charlie Dodge."

"Hey, Charlie. Good to hear from you… I think. What's going on? Everything okay with Wyrick? I was told there was an attempted break-in at your office yesterday evening, and she was involved."

"That's why I'm calling, and yes, she's okay. No thanks to me because I was in court waiting to testify," Charlie said. "The man who attacked Wyrick is a convicted felon named Barrett Taylor. He has an ugly little rap sheet, and broke a couple of laws for himself just driving across state lines to come after her. When she opened the door to go home for the evening, he was in the hall waiting for her. He kicked it in, punched her and knocked her down, and was reaching for his gun when she Tasered him. Even after she had him cuffed he kept threatening her, telling her there were others coming after her, too, and I need to make sure he is charged with everything you can make stick to him. He belongs to a cult called the Church of The Righteous, and it appears they're out to get her. I'm not letting that happen again."

"I appreciate your concern. I'll make sure no balls are dropped when he's formally charged."

"Thanks, Tony. I really appreciate it," Charlie said and disconnected.

He glanced up in the rearview mirror, but Wyrick was nowhere in sight. He'd lost track of her while he was talking, but they were headed to the same place, and he would bet money she'd beat him there.

By the time he got to the office, Wyrick was already in work mode.

"No bear claws. You have apple fritters, and a butt load of messages," she said as he walked in.

He grinned. "I like apple fritters."

"I know that," she said.

"Are there any pressing issues?" Charlie asked.

"Not unless you decide to take the bullshit case, which is the message on top."

Charlie frowned. "Well, hell. If the day is starting with bullshit, then I'm gonna need two apple fritters to even begin," he said and kept walking.

Wyrick hid a grin. She loved it when Charlie got all pissy, as long as it wasn't with her.

Rachel Dean woke with a gasp, and then moaned.

"This has to be a bad dream. This can't really be happening to me. Why can't I wake up?"

Just the sound of her own voice settled the moment of panic, and then she slowly unwrapped herself from the blanket.

But when she tried to stand, she was so sore she could barely move. She finally got to her feet, but it hurt to walk. When she began checking her body, and saw the bruising and the cuts, the pain began to make sense.

She went straight to the toilet, then washed her hands at the sink before refilling her water bottle from the tap. Her throat was burning where he'd cut her, and she feared it would get infected, but without a mirror to see, all she could do was wash it again.

As always, she went straight to the door and tried to open it, but it was still locked. She went through the same routine, beating on the door, screaming for help until hearing the panic in her own voice made it worse, so she crawled back onto the mattress and rolled herself up in the blanket.

She was cold, hungry and at the same time sick to her stomach with fear. She thought of Millie, afraid she'd never see her again—and thought of her job, and how hard she'd worked to get to where she was, only to know she was losing it all. The sadness she felt was undercoated with a growing rage.

Why was God letting this happen?

Then tears rolled.

The reality of her situation was that no one deserved this. Ever. But for whatever reason, it had happened to her, and she wasn't ready to die.

CHAPTER FOUR

Millie Chriss was already in Oklahoma City by 9 a.m., and heading for the I35-I40 interchange. It was going to take more than three hours to get to Dallas, plus the time it took to get to her hotel. As she was approaching the interchange, she deftly moved into the far left lane of I35 to take the southbound turn-off that would take her into Texas.

The highway straightened out after she headed south, and with the sun on her left shoulder, and her attention on the crazy amount of traffic, she kept driving, every mile taking her that much closer to Rachel.

Detectives Floyd and Mills were frustrated. Even though the Rachel Dean case was new, they had nothing that would even lead them in the general direction of finding out where she'd gone, or if someone had taken her.

Between them, they'd worked hundreds of crime scenes in their careers, but this one was a puzzle. Unless the crime scene team came up with some DNA, they were at a loss.

They'd interviewed every resident at the Detter House yesterday, and talked to at least eight people who'd been outside grilling, who'd seen her come home alone the evening before. They knew from the security footage that she also entered her apartment alone, and then basically disappeared into thin air.

They'd confiscated security footage from the exterior and interior of the property, checked her car and confiscated her personal laptop. One of the techs had it at the lab now, going through it, looking for clues—like a relationship no one knew about—or looking for threats she might have received, looking for a hidden lifestyle.

It wouldn't be the first time a seemingly "good girl" was also walking on the wild side. It didn't appear likely, but detectives didn't operate on odds. They worked with facts, and now and then, gut instinct. Unfortunately, right now they were short on both.

Sonny woke up with a hard-on for Rachel. He had options. He could call in sick and play with her all day. Or he could go to work, and spend the day in anticipation.

The thing about playing with her all day was the less than appealing location, and lack of ambience. The mattress was filthy. The room was cold. He wanted in her, but since he did not want to spend the day there, work won out.

He crawled out of bed and headed for the shower.

Charlie was in his office going through morning messages and personal email when Wyrick walked in.

"Turn on the television to KTVT."

Charlie reached for the remote and aimed it at the television.

"Why am I doing this?" he asked, seeing film footage of police at a location, and then the picture of a young woman flashing across the screen.

"That woman went missing from the Detter House. We're going to get that case."

Charlie frowned. "I'd ask how do you know that, but that would be redundant. Have we been contacted by family yet?"

"No, but we will. Tomorrow morning."

"Who is she?" Charlie asked.

"Her name is Rachel Dean. I'm going to start a background check on her now."

Charlie nodded. "They just said on the report that she's an ad executive with Addison-Tunnell."

Wyrick nodded. "Her sister isn't going to be able to afford us, but she's going to put her house up for collateral to get the money. I'm going to tell her we have a fund set aside for situations like this, and I'll be good for whatever costs we incur."

"I'm down with that," Charlie said. "But why pro bono her… why now?"

"Because it feels like Rachel Dean is still alive, but not for long. And Merlin gave me all that money…which I already didn't need. Might as well put some of it to good use."

"I won't tell," Charlie said.

Wyrick frowned. "Tell what?"

"That you aren't as fierce as you look, and that there really is a heart beneath that dragon."

She glared, her eyes narrowing. "As you were," she muttered and walked out of his office, slamming the door behind her.

Charlie grinned. It was rare to be able to get under her skin, but when he did, it was something to celebrate. He glanced at the clock.

Noon. On the dot.

Lunch was happening somewhere.

He got up and opened the door between them.

"Hey…lunch is on me if you'll order."

Wyrick paused, then looked up from her computer.

"What do you want to eat?" she asked.

"Two Arby's roast beef sandwiches with horseradish sauce and fries."

"How high-class of you," she drawled, then pulled up an open window, clicked on a link and began scanning the menu for the Arby's nearest their location.

He ignored the dig. It was payback because of what he'd said earlier, but he didn't care. He poked the dragon, but he was a grown-ass man and big enough to take it. He went back to get his phone and Stetson, then stopped at her desk on the way out.

"Just so I know they got the right order, what are you having?" he asked.

"I wanted crow, but it wasn't on the menu, so I'm having one of what you're having."

He grinned again, and by the time he got out into the hall he was laughing.

Damn, but it feels good to laugh. I need to do it more often.

Goose bumps rose on Wyrick's arms when she heard his laughter fading away as he disappeared down the hall.

She frowned. *Damn man is too sexy for his own good. He should have to wear a warning sign that says Too Hot To Handle.*

Millie Chriss reached her hotel just after 1 p.m. and checked in. Now that she was here, she needed to know wheels were turning and things were happening. Maybe they had news. Maybe they had a lead. And she wanted to let Detective Floyd know she was in Dallas. So she pulled up his number and called. Just when she thought it was going to go to voice mail, he answered.

"Detective Floyd. Missing Persons."

"Good afternoon, Detective Floyd. This is Millie Chriss, Rachel Dean's sister. I wanted you to know that I am now in Dallas, and staying at the Warwick Melrose. Do you have any news?"

Floyd hated to be the bearer of bad news.

"No, ma'am, but it's early. Evidence was gathered from the scene only yesterday and it will take time to—"

Millie's heart sank. The disappointment was huge, and she interrupted, her voice trembling with barely suppressed emotion. "It's not early for Rachel. What *I* know is that tonight will be the third night my sister has not slept in her own bed. God only knows what's happened to her, but I have to believe she's still alive. Time is not on her side. Am I right?"

"I can't argue with any of that," Floyd said. "Just know that we're not taking this lightly. When we have something valid to go on, I will let you know."

"Yes, all right," Millie said, then disconnected and burst into tears.

She was still crying when her cell phone rang, and when she saw it was from Ray, she groaned. She'd promised to let him know when she got into Dallas.

"Hey, honey," she said.

"I'm just checking on you. Are you still traveling?" Ray asked.

"No, but I haven't been here long. I'm in my room at the hotel and just got off the phone with Detective Floyd."

"Any news?" Ray asked.

Millie burst into tears all over again. "Not yet. They haven't found anything in her apartment that even gives them a clue as to what happened to her."

She heard Ray sigh.

"I'm sorry. I'm worried sick for Rachel, and I know you are, too. But I'm also worried about you. I still think I should—"

Millie grabbed a handful of tissues and wiped her face.

"No, no, I'm fine. It was just a momentary letdown when the detective said they still didn't know anything. But I'm scared, Ray. She was missing a whole night before we even knew about it. Tonight will be the third night. I'm afraid the police won't find her in time to save her."

"Listen, I've been thinking. Remember that private investigator and his partner who made the news a while back? I think his name was Dodge? His partner was the woman who took down that international consortium for medical malpractice, and a whole bunch of other stuff?"

"Oh. Yes, I remember. But what's that—"

"I looked it up. Dodge Security and Investigations is based in Dallas, and their recovery rate on missing persons is huge. He's made the headlines over and over for finding lost kids and other people who've gone missing. And his partner, that woman they call Wyrick…they say she's brilliant on a genius level…and psychic. If you want, see if you can hire him."

Millie's heart skipped. "Oh, Ray…honey…we probably can't afford him."

"Rachel is family. If we have to, we can take a second mortgage out on our house."

"Really?" Millie asked.

"Yes, really," he said.

"Okay…yes… I'll give the police until tomorrow morning, and if they don't get anything positive from the tests at the crime scene lab, then I'll call them. And thank you… I love you for this."

"I love you, too," Ray said. "Call me anytime. There's no meeting more important than us finding Rachel."

"I will," Millie said. "And just so you know…you are my hero, Ray Chriss. I'll call you tonight."

"I'll be waiting," Ray said. "Now wash away your tears and go get yourself something to eat. Making yourself sick with worry won't help anyone. Love you."

"Love you, too," Millie said, and then the call ended.

She sat for a few moments, thinking about what Ray had

said. It was the first hopeful thing she'd heard since all of this happened. Then she got up, washed her face and repaired her makeup. Maybe by the time she found a place to eat, she'd have an appetite to go with it.

Barrett Taylor's meeting with Marsh Fielding, the Dallas lawyer Raver hired to represent him, did not go well.

"So what am I facing?" Taylor asked.

Fielding pulled up his notes and started going down the list.

"According to the arrest report, you have been charged with stalking, breaking and entering, assault, attempted murder and carrying a firearm across state lines with intent to do harm."

Taylor's heart sank. "What kind of deal can I get?"

"There's no way to whitewash an attempted murder caught on video. Unless you have something to give them in return for a lighter sentence, you don't have anything to bargain with to get a deal."

"There are other men coming after her," Taylor said.

"Do you know who they are?" Fielding asked.

Taylor slumped. "No, only that he was sending three. I left first."

Fielding shrugged. "Then you have no bargaining power."

"Figures," Taylor muttered. "When is my arraignment?"

Fielding looked up from his notes. "Tomorrow. You will enter a plea of guilty or not guilty. It's your decision."

Barrett Taylor frowned. "What are my chances if I go to trial?"

"You mean of getting off free?"

Taylor nodded.

"Absolutely none. You don't know the woman you attacked. You had no prior history with her. You crossed state lines with a weapon, and with one purpose…to kill her, and they have that on video, am I right?"

Taylor glared.

"Am I right?" Fielding asked again.

Barrett Taylor leaned forward, his voice shaking with anger.

"Yes, you're right. But she is an abomination in the eyes of God. The Righteous have a duty to the world to rid it of alien life forms."

Marsh Fielding blinked.

"As your lawyer, I would advise you to keep that opinion to yourself. And just between us, how many alien life forms have you previously dispensed with?"

"Me personally? She would have been my first," Taylor said.

Marsh shuddered, reminding himself that everyone deserved representation in a court of law.

"Okay. Just making sure I know what we're dealing with. So how are you going to plead?"

"Not guilty," Taylor said. "I know how the system works. The judge will hear my plea. Then there'll be a hearing to set bail, and—"

Fielding interrupted, "You know as well as I do that a judge can refuse that. The DA can use your track record and the cold manner in which you stalked her as a reason to deny bail. Also, they may consider you a flight risk. If that's the case, you won't get out before your trial, which could be months, sometimes more than a year. Just so you know."

"That's not fair!" Taylor shouted, then looked around the small conference room and lowered his voice. "That's not right."

"Well, neither is murder. What you did is frowned upon in this country. You aren't allowed to decide who lives or dies. You made an attempt on someone's life, and it was caught on video. I don't know if you're aware of it, but your attempt on Jade Wyrick's life pissed off some important people. You tried to kill a woman who is, at this moment in time, the single, most famous woman on the planet. And you got caught doing it. By her. I'll see what I can do tomorrow, but don't expect miracles."

Taylor slumped where he sat. So much for trying out religion. It didn't feel so good anymore.

Wyrick was still running background checks on Rachel Dean when Charlie left. She'd reminded him that they could have the food delivered, but Charlie wanted to get it because he said it was quicker. The truth was that Charlie didn't like sitting behind a desk, and when they weren't out on a case, he was doomed to desk work. As for reading the background she was getting on Rachel, it was like reading a bio of a woman's fast track to success.

Rachel graduated from Memorial High School in Tulsa, Oklahoma, and was at Tulsa University when her parents were killed in an accident. After her parents' deaths, her sister, Millie, and her husband, Ray Chriss, moved Rachel in with them and helped her finish college. Her degree was a Bachelor of Arts, majoring in business, and minoring in marketing and advertising, and she was hired straight out of college by Addison-Tunnell, an advertising company in Dallas. She had worked her way up to ad executive, with a growing list of clients.

As far as Wyrick could tell, Rachel's only serious romance was in college, and it ended when her parents were killed. From what she'd learned so far, Rachel's focus was on her career, and not a relationship.

But none of this information ruled out unknown stalkers, or being the victim of a random act of violence. She was still running searches when Charlie came back with lunch.

She heard the key in the lock and knew it had to be him, but she was still jumpy enough from the attempt on her life to reach for her Taser.

Then the door swung inward and he walked in with their lunch in a bag.

"Don't shoot. I bring offerings of roast beef and horseradish," he said and kicked the door shut behind him.

"Let's eat at the conference table in my office. It's nice outside today. At least we can look at it from there."

She nodded, then washed up in her private bathroom before following him into the office. He was at the wet bar.

"I'm assuming you want a Pepsi," he said.

"Please," she said and sat down, letting Charlie dispense the food from the sack after he came back. She pulled a curly fry from the container and popped it into her mouth, savoring the salty taste as she chewed. "Thanks for lunch," she added.

"Tax deduction," he said.

She glared.

He grinned and opened two packets of horseradish sauce and squeezed them all over his first sandwich before taking a bite.

Wyrick squeezed a packet of the same sauce on hers, and then they settled into eating.

The office phone rang while they were eating. But when she started to get up to answer, Charlie stopped her.

"It's lunchtime. Let it go to voice mail."

So she did, reaching instead for another curly fry. She tilted her head back, and dangled it over her mouth before dropping it in.

Charlie glanced at the soft curve of her lower lip, and as he did, saw a single grain of salt glistening beneath the lights from the chandelier hanging over the conference table. At that point his thoughts flooded with interesting ways to remove it, none of which needed to be voiced. Then she picked up a napkin to wipe her lips and solved the problem for him.

He looked down at his sandwich and took another bite and gave himself a talking-to.

Just fucking chew it, Charlie, and don't go there.

So he did, then sauced up his second sandwich and finished it, too.

Wyrick went back to work while Charlie gathered up their refuse and tossed it into the trash.

Jeremiah Raver was the fourth generation of a family who'd lived out their lives in the Louisiana swamps, subsisting on whatever they could hunt or grow. But from birth, Jeremiah had been scared spitless of the swamp and its critters—from snakes to gators, and everything in between.

He had been the butt of jokes in the Raver family his entire life, until he announced, at the age of seventeen, that God had called him to preach. At first, the news was shocking to the family. But his mama grabbed on to that with both hands. He wasn't a coward, after all. He was a warrior for the Lord, and that was that.

Now his mama and daddy were long gone, and he was nearing his fiftieth birthday, and still preaching The Word every Sunday. He founded the church over thirty years ago, but after witnessing Jade Wyrick's live press conference some months back, he'd been horrified by her appearance. And after a dream he'd had about her, he'd awakened with the belief that it was his mission to cleanse the world of her presence.

He began the online posts about her without thinking of the possible consequences, and took their war with the devil to the virtual world. As the months passed by, his fervor grew.

Finally, he chose three men from his congregation that he felt would be willing warriors for God. He chose each of them separately, speaking to them in confidence, and then gave each a picture of her, the location of her place of work and where she lived.

Barrett Taylor was the first man he sent, because he knew

Taylor was a convicted felon. He'd been so certain Taylor would succeed. Then Taylor got himself caught and jailed, and now Raver was worried.

He called in Jessup Wallis, and gave him the same orders, and then as insurance, called in his last man, Farrell Kitt, and gave him the same instructions. They did not know about each other, or that Barrett Taylor had already failed and was in jail. All they knew was that they were on a mission for the Lord.

Now that Jeremiah had reset his plan, he felt it was time to make himself scarce. The cops knew he was the pastor of the church attached to Taylor's charges, and Taylor had already threatened Raver, if he didn't get out of jail.

Jeremiah knew there was only one place he could go and disappear. Back where he'd grown up. He grabbed a suitcase full of clothes and some canned goods, and headed to his brother's place in the bayou.

Wyrick had everything she could find on Rachel Dean in a file. Now they were just waiting for the sister to show up and hire them. And while Charlie was in his office on the phone, she pulled up The Righteous website to see if there was any chatter about Barrett Taylor's arrest.

To her dismay, no one knew he had failed, so there was no deterrent for the others. No fear of also being caught. But there was more than chatter. It was an outright call to war to destroy her. She needed to get to her own computers and stop this before it got out of hand. The underlying tone of the comments, no matter how vague they tried to word it, was plain for her to see. She was world-weary and heartsick as she stared at the monitor, trying to figure out how to protect herself now.

And that was how Charlie found her. He knew by her body language something had happened.

"What's wrong?" he asked.

Wyrick jumped. She hadn't heard him come out of his office.

"I need to go home and get to my computers. If I don't stop The Righteous now, it's going to be Universal Theorem all over again."

"Are there others coming now?"

Wyrick looked up, a little surprised that he'd already figured that out.

"Taylor said there were," Wyrick said.

"Then go. Do whatever you have to do. I'll close up and be right behind you."

She wouldn't look at him for fear he'd see the tears in her eyes. She was so sick of this. The war was never going to be over, but she was going to make them sorry that they'd fired the first shot. She turned off her computer and picked up her things, but when she started out the door, Charlie was right behind her.

"I thought you were going to—"

"I'm walking you to your car," he said. "Taylor was armed. So am I."

She blinked, then saw the gun he was holding and didn't argue. They said nothing to each other in the elevator. Charlie made her wait at the door as he stepped out into the parking lot, looking around for unfamiliar vehicles, and then motioned her out.

He didn't have to tell her not to dawdle as they headed for the Ferrari. He waited until she was inside before he spoke.

"Straight home," he said. "I won't be far behind."

She nodded.

"And whatever you're about to do, make them sorry," he added.

"Their walls are already crumbling. They just don't know it yet," she said, then started the car and drove away.

Charlie watched until she was out of sight before he hurried back inside to close up shop. He was less than fifteen minutes behind her when he left the parking lot, heading home.

CHAPTER FIVE

Wyrick didn't breathe easy until she was safely inside the mansion, then she dropped her things and made a run for the office. By the time she had her research files pulled up on the church and its leader, she was in strike mode.

This was like taking down Universal Theorem, only on a smaller level, but it was going to cause just as much damage within The Righteous organization as it had done to UT. And since this involved money laundering for a man named Preston Davis, who was selling stolen weapons, she had enough to make them sweat.

She and Charlie had worked with Special Agent Hank Raines of the FBI twice now, and while they'd had their differences, she also knew she could trust him.

So she sent him an email, explaining what was happening. She sent a link to the Church of The Righteous website, and copies of posts from the website that highlighted their intent toward her. She sent a copy of the security footage from their office depicting the attack and threats Barrett Taylor made against her, and the file she'd been collecting on their illegal activities.

She needed The Righteous discredited, the illegal activities exposed and the other hit men scrambling to save their own asses in the hopes they'd abandon their quest to end her life. And to do that, she had another public statement to make to the media that would strengthen her intent.

She was offering up a quarter of a million dollar bounty per man for their name and picture. That was all. Just their identities.

To protect herself from criminal charges, the bounty would immediately be nullified if the men were harmed in any way. Once they were identified, they were going to get a crash course in what it felt like to be targeted by society and the media, and it should send Jeremiah Raver into a panic of his own. Now all she had to do was make her announcement before anyone could stop her.

She had the video already prepared, and had attached it to the email she sent to Raines. The only thing left to do now was upload it to the public media sites. Then Charlie arrived.

She heard him calling her name, got up and walked out into the hall.

"I'm in the office."

A few moments later he appeared in the doorway with a Pepsi in one hand, and a Hershey bar in the other.

"I thought you might need this," he said.

Wyrick took them, gladly.

"Thanks. You're just in time," she said and went back into the office.

"In time for what?" Charlie said as he watched her plop back down in the chair, unscrew the lid off her Pepsi, then peel back the wrapping on the Hershey bar and pop a little square into her mouth.

She let the chocolate melt on her tongue, then swallowed it before she answered.

"I just sent a file to Hank Raines that's going to put a big kink in The Righteous organization."

He frowned. "Why? What did you discover?"

"They're laundering money from the sale of stolen weapons."

"Are you serious?" Charlie said.

She nodded, then took a drink of her Pepsi. "But that's not all. Give me a second. I need to send this video to the media."

"Video? Wait. Who's on it?" Charlie asked.

"Me. Offering a quarter of a million dollars per hit man, for their names and pictures. We both know they can't be arrested unless they make an attempt on my life, and I'm not willing to take the chance that they will oblige me and screw up as badly as Barrett Taylor did. But this bounty will sure slow their asses down. As soon as I verify their identities, I'm making them and their connection to The Righteous public. I've also put these safeguards in place. The bounty can't go to anyone connected to the cult, because I'll be damned if I let them profit off me when they're trying to kill me, and it will be nullified if either of the men are harmed. Also, if anyone makes a false claim, then I'll file charges against them for bearing false witness, and attempting to obtain money under fraudulent pretenses."

"I'm not sure all of that is legal," Charlie said.

Wyrick looked up at him. "I don't really care. You're the only reason I'm still alive, and the law can't do anything to the other two men unless they make a move toward me. So I'm changing up their choices."

She turned to the computer monitor, pulled up the media list, attached her video and hit Send.

"Ta-da!" she said, and then popped another square of chocolate into her mouth.

Charlie was speechless. It was the gutsiest move he'd ever known anyone to make, but Jade Wyrick was a law unto herself. He also understood her desperation, and the need for haste.

There was no way to predict when the next attempt to take her out might happen. And a quarter of a million dollars was a hell of a lot of money. She hadn't threatened anyone's life. She was just paying for names and pictures.

"*Ta-da* is an understatement," Charlie muttered.

"Don't worry," Wyrick said. "The faster this hits the media, the safer I become."

"I get the concept, but the certainty of a positive outcome is iffy."

Wyrick leaned back in her chair and stared Charlie down without speaking. Finally, he was the one to give.

"What?"

"You still don't understand," she said.

"Understand what?" Charlie said.

"My entire existence began based on uncertainty. How many different DNA donors should Universal Theorem use on the embryo that became me? How many others failed before I became viable? What did they hope to achieve, other than the curiosity of seeing if they could do it? Did Universal Theorem ever once consider the humanity of my existence? Why was I born a genius? Did they intend to weaponize me for my brain? Why do I know things before they happen? How is it that I have patents for things that will not be useful for another fifty years? Why is loss and suffering more familiar to me than laughter? Will I ever burn out? Will I wake up some morning with the realization that the expiration date on the vast knowledge that is second nature to me has suddenly arrived? Am I going to go out in a pop and a flash of fire, like a diode in an old television set, or will I be curled up in a ball in some institution, drooling and picking at sores I've made on my body? Every fucking thing about me is uncertain, and to exist in this world, I can't let myself care."

Charlie felt sick. He wanted to put his arms around her, but she would have decked him for the show of sympathy. Instead, he shrugged and put his hands in his pockets.

"I am so accustomed to you being you, I forget what you already went through before we even met. Sorry for the momentary loss of focus. We deal with what we have to as it comes. Just don't forget... I'm on your side. Always."

Wyrick shrugged. She needed to change the subject before she started crying.

"Want to make a bet that Agent Raines calls you instead of me?" she asked.

Charlie frowned.

"Why would he be calling me when you're the one who sent the file?"

"Because he's scared of me, and we both know it," Wyrick said.

"If I agree with you, why would I bet against you?" he asked.

Her eyes narrowed. "For the hell of it?"

He grinned. "Okay...so what do I win if you're wrong, and he calls you first?"

"I'll be responsible for dinner for a whole week," Wyrick said.

"And if he calls me first...which we both know is likely going to happen...then I have to furnish a week of dinners?" Charlie said.

"That's the bet," Wyrick said.

"That's not a bet. That's whitewashing the fact that you don't want to do dinner for a week. So why don't I save us both some time, and just offer to do that anyway?"

"Sure, okay...since you offered," Wyrick said.

"I suppose that starts tonight?" Charlie asked.

"I'm good with that," Wyrick said.

He laughed. "Do you have a preference?"

"No. I'm fine with whatever floats your boat," she said.

"Well, that would be water...if I had a boat to float," he muttered. "I'm going to see what we have in the freezer."

"I bought groceries yesterday. There are lots of choices."

He sighed. "Yeah, right. Anyway...since you've already launched another war, why don't you go get into something comfy and put your feet up. I'm going to change, then I'll just be in the galley of that boat, making your dinner."

"Whining does not become you," Wyrick said, then picked up what was left of her pop and candy and left the office, heading down the hall to take the elevator up to her room, while Charlie chose the other way and jogged up the stairs.

Wyrick exited the elevator just as Charlie appeared at the head of the landing. They paused, staring at each other from separate ends of the hall, and then Wyrick suddenly crammed the last bite of chocolate into her mouth, chewing and swallowing it as she screwed down the lid on her Pepsi.

Charlie saw the look on her face, and knew almost instantly what she was about to do.

"You haven't got a chance in hell," he shouted and started running, just as she bolted toward him.

Their bedrooms were in the middle of the hall and directly across from each other. Now the race was on to see who could get inside first.

Wyrick knew it was going to be close. She was fast, but so was Charlie, and his legs were long. Really long. She had the Pepsi in one hand, swinging it as she ran, and Charlie was laughing at her as they came closer and closer. Then all of a sudden he was in his room, slamming the door behind him.

"Dammit!" Wyrick shouted.

She was paused in the hall, gasping for breath and thinking she was severely out of shape, when the Pepsi she'd been running with suddenly blew. She screamed, both in shock and dismay as the lid hit the ceiling, then came down at her feet as carbonated cola spewed everywhere.

Charlie heard what sounded like a shot, and then the scream, and panicked. He turned and yanked the door open, ready to do battle, then saw her standing in the hall, the empty Pepsi bottle still in her hand, and what had been left of it now dripping from her face, and her clothes and the wall.

Awash with relief, he grinned.

"Shut your damn door," Wyrick said.

He did, but by then he was laughing.

She looked down at herself. What a freaking mess.

But she'd made Charlie laugh again. Her good deed for the day.

She went into her room, changed into old clothes, then headed downstairs to get cleaning supplies. She had walls to wash down, and a floor to mop.

Charlie was changing out of what he'd worn to work when his cell phone rang. He glanced at caller ID and then sighed.

Special Agent Raines.

And this is why he hadn't made that bet.

He sat down on the side of his bed, guessing that Raines was losing his mind over what Wyrick had just done.

"Hello."

"What the fucking hell is Wyrick thinking?"

"Hello, Agent Raines. Out of curiosity, why didn't you call her and ask her yourself?"

"Because," Raines muttered.

Charlie sighed. "So I take it you have not read everything she sent you, or you wouldn't be asking me this."

"I saw that video, and I already know the havoc this is going to cause," Raines said.

"You should have read it all before you called, because then you'd know a religious cult called the Church of The Righteous has dispatched three hit men to kill her. One already tried. He's sitting in a Dallas jail in deep shit. She sent you a video of the incident, along with all of the info that ties him to The Righteous, and I wasn't even there. It happened at the office, and I was in court, waiting to testify on a case."

"Jesus," Raines muttered. "But she's put a bounty on these men's heads."

"No, she did not, and you know it. All she asked for were their identities. If any of them are harmed in any way, or interfered with, the cash reward is nullified, and if anyone gives her a fake name trying to get the money, she'll file charges against them for fraud."

"What's she going to do with the info?" Raines asked.

"Reveal them to the world for who they are...and what they were willing to do to her, for no other reason than that she was born. I back her fully, so there's that," Charlie added.

"Fine. So what's with the Church of The Righteous...other than a religious cult?"

"Dammit, Raines. Read what she sent. The preacher is money laundering for a man named Preston Davis, who's buying and selling stolen weapons. Go do your job and give them something more to worry about than what they can do to her," Charlie said and hung up.

Hank Raines groaned. His wife was planning to grill T-bones tonight, and now he was going to be late going home for dinner. He turned back to his computer, pulled up the rest of the files that Wyrick'd sent and started reading. By the time he had finished, his toes were curling in his shoes. He didn't know how much of the information Wyrick sent was clean enough to use. They'd have to verify it from their end before they could act, but she was a wonder.

He reached for the phone to call his boss. His guess was they'd pass it off to the ATF, and if they did, they were going to have a field day with this.

The video Wyrick sent to the media had set its own fire. Another message from the famous Jade Wyrick was solid gold, and when they began airing it, it blew up across social media, and the comment threads for every station that had aired it.

Preston Davis had gone to a family funeral in Baton Rouge, and was sitting at his aunt's house having pie and coffee, when someone pointed at the television.

"Would you look at that!" someone said.

He turned around just as Jeremiah Raver's face flashed on the screen. He set his food aside and walked closer, but by then the story was over. It was bothering him that someone he did business with had made national news. He needed to know what it was about without showing the concern he was feeling.

"Hey, Shirley, what was that all about?" he asked.

His cousin looked up at him from where she was sitting.

"That's the preacher who heads up the Church of The Righteous over near Paulette."

"So what's going on?" Preston asked.

"Oh…they say he's been preaching against a woman named Jade Wyrick, calling her an alien, and an abomination in the eyes of the Lord because of how she was born. A man in Dallas, Texas, was just arrested for trying to kill the Wyrick woman, and he claims his preacher sent him to do the deed. And it appears he's not the only one. The Wyrick woman claims the preacher sent three men after her, so two more are still out there. She just put a quarter of a million dollar bounty on each of the other two men. She don't want them dead or nothin'. She just wants their names and a picture. She's about to blast their little secret society out of the water. What a mess. What a mess."

"Indeed," Preston said, but his mind was racing.

If the law got after Raver, and began digging deeper into his business dealings, that could mean trouble for him. It appeared he needed to do a little housecleaning himself, before things got out of hand.

Within hours of the video's airing, every member of Raver's church was in a panic. Was this going to fall back on them? Were they going to be arrested for abetting an attempted murder, when it was something they knew nothing about?

One by one, they began calling Jeremiah Raver, demanding answers, demanding their names be taken off the church register, but he wasn't answering. They wanted the whole thing to go away, and their connections to him and the church off the World Wide Web.

And all the while this was going on, Jessup Wallis and Farrell Kitt were en route to Dallas, with no idea of what they were driving into.

Jeremiah was at his brother Samuel's house in the bayou, and the cell service was spotty. He was anxious about what was happening, but he couldn't get a call in or out. He needed to know what was going on to protect himself, so he got in the car and started driving until he got a strong cell signal, then pulled over on the old dirt road and started checking messages.

That was when he found all the missed calls from his church members. After listening to the panic and the anger in their voices, he realized the depth of trouble he was in. He had severely underestimated Jade Wyrick. If she had found out all this, then there was a chance she knew about his other activities, too. The men he did business with weren't fond of publicity, and if they wanted the link between them destroyed, erasing their names in his contacts wouldn't do it. They'd want him dead.

He needed to go home long enough to get to his computer and take down the website and delete the files in his email. He drove back to Samuel's to let his sister-in-law, Maisie, know where he was going, and found his brother sitting on the porch.

And from the look on Samuel's face, he wasn't happy. The more Jeremiah thought about it, the more he came to believe Samuel was there waiting for him. But he had more important things to deal with than whatever was up his brother's butt.

"Hey, Samuel… I'm gonna be gone for a while. There's some stuff I need to do at home."

Samuel already knew his brother had come here to hide. He didn't hold with any of Jeremiah's preaching or his shady dealings.

"Do what you gotta do," Samuel said. "But watch your back. Your business partners ain't the kind to take kindly to publicity."

Jeremiah stared. "What are you talking about? You don't know my business. And what do you mean about publicity?"

"We might live in the bayou, but we ain't stupid, brother. I know what you been doin'. Ain't no one here got the money to donate what you take in at church."

"How do you know what—"

"Maisie works at the bank in Paulette, remember? And while you were out, we saw the video that Wyrick woman you been preaching against aired on TV, so we also know you sent men to kill her. It says in the Bible, *Thou shall not kill*, and you're a preacher who sent hit men to kill someone! That don't set right with us. I think you need to just go on and take your stuff back with you when you leave. We don't want you bringing your bad juju here."

Jeremiah frowned. All of a sudden, the frantic messages from his church members were starting to make sense.

"Video? What video?" Jeremiah asked.

"It seems that Wyrick woman caught the first man you sent. He's in jail. But he told her there were two more coming after her. I guess she didn't take kindly to that, because she has offered a quarter of a million dollar bounty on each one. She don't want them. Just their identities. And she said can't nobody hurt 'em, or they don't get the dough. She's gonna plaster their pictures all over that social media you're so fond of, so everyone will know you're the one behind it."

Jeremiah groaned. Barrett Taylor had blabbed about the other men.

"But, Samuel, I don't have anywhere else to go."

Samuel shrugged. "I am not my brother's keeper. You lit the fuse to this. We'll say a prayer for your mortal soul, and that's the best I can offer. Just don't tell me where you're goin', because I won't lie to the law if they come looking for you. But if I don't know where you are, then my conscience will be clear."

"Some brother you are," Jeremiah muttered.

"That's kinda what I was thinking about you," Samuel said and stood up, looming a good five inches above his brother's head. "Y'all go on now. Get your stuff and go about your business, preacher man."

Jeremiah ducked his head and went inside. To his surprise, Maisie had already packed his bag. It was sitting in the middle of the bed, and she was nowhere to be seen. He grabbed it and headed out the door, threw it in the backseat of the car and as he drove away, knew he'd never see them again.

It took him over an hour to get home, and as he approached the road leading up to the house, he slowed down considerably, making sure there weren't any parish police cars parked off in the trees.

Once he got to the house, he ran straight to the office and began taking down the website. He was still at it when he got a call. He recognized Preston Davis's number, but he didn't take time to answer. Preston was the moneyman. The one he did business with, and he didn't have time to talk.

But Preston called again, and again, and kept calling until Jeremiah finally answered.

"Hello."

"What the hell have you done…putting out a hit on some woman and bringing down the law on top of all we have going?"

"It wasn't supposed to happen that way," Raver said. "She's evil. She's the Devil's daughter, and she needs to disappear. I had a vision and—"

"No, *you're* the one who needs to disappear," Preston said.

Jeremiah felt the warning all the way to his toes.

"I'm taking down the website and packing right now. Just calm down. They don't know anything about you."

"You don't know that," Preston said and hung up.

The knot in Jeremiah's belly tightened, but he didn't have time to dwell on Preston's attitude right now. He turned back to the computer and kept dismantling the site, and deleting everything he could find about it online, then deleted all his email until everything was gone.

He leaned back with a big sigh of relief, thinking he'd covered all his tracks, and then got up and went to pack up his clothes.

Jeremiah might be a fool, but Preston Davis was not. He was certain that, if worse came to worse, Raver would give them all up, as part of a plea deal on his own behalf.

So while Jeremiah was erasing the Church of The Righteous from the web, Preston Davis sent a man to Raver's home to erase him.

Two hours later Jeremiah came out of the house with the last of his things—two suitcases full of clothes. He had a bag in each hand and was heading for his car when he saw movement in the trees beyond the house.

He paused, his heart racing, staring intently, trying to discern if it was animal or man. But he never got a chance to figure it out, because Preston's hit man put a bullet between Jeremiah's eyes.

Between one breath and the next, he died. He fell flat on his back, the suitcases beside him, while the blood from his body poured out of the gaping hole in the back of his head. He'd lived his adult life preaching about Jesus, but he was about to meet his Maker on a whole other playing field.

Jessup Wallis was in Texas, driving westbound on I20 and coming up on Longview when he got a call from his girlfriend, Britta.

"Hey, honey, what's up?"

"Jessup, a woman just put out a quarter of a million dollar bounty for the name and picture of each man Jeremiah Raver sent to get her. And since you told me your trip was just an errand for your preacher man, I'm assuming one of them is you."

Jessup felt the blood draining from his face. He swerved to the side of the interstate and stopped the car before he passed out.

"What? What the hell? How did she find out? She can't do that. Why, that's outright murder for hire!" he said, then Britta snorted in his ear, a sign she was not pleased with him.

"She found out because Barrett Taylor gave y'all up. She took him down with a Taser, and then got it all on video, so he's sitting in jail facing a butt load of charges. As for the murder for hire comment, what the fuck do you call what y'all were gonna do to her?" Britta cried.

"We ain't takin' no money," he muttered.

"No, but if your job was to kill her, then that makes you a hit man. The good part is, she don't want none of you dead. She just wants your identities."

Jessup groaned. "What for?"

"She's gonna plaster them all over the media for free, so you'll know what it feels like to be targeted. And just so you know, your preacher's gone missing."

"The bastard," Jessup muttered. "Raver starts a war and then he's the first one to turn tail and run. So whoever turns me in gets the money?"

"Yes. But it can't be anyone connected to the church or to you."

"Shit. What do I do?" Jessup muttered.

"Well, it don't take a genius to figure that out. Turn your ass around and come home. Did you tell anyone else where you were going?"

Jessup groaned. "I might have mentioned it when I was drinking with the boys last night, but I ain't sure. I was pretty lit."

"You'll know soon enough," Britta said.

Jessup groaned again. "Thanks for lettin' me know, sugar. I'm gonna turn around right now and head back. I'll likely get home sometime tomorrow. I can't believe Raver. I didn't sign up to be betrayed by my own preacher. He preaches hellfire and damnation for sinners, and then turns tail and runs when his own hide is in danger? I did not sign up for this. They can't arrest me. I didn't do anything."

"Whatever…but don't think you're coming back to shack up with me. I never wanted anything to do with your church, and I got my own reputation to worry about now. I can't be tied up to you in any way, and have my picture all over the Facebook and the Twitter."

"But, baby…you can't just—"

"I'll put your clothes on the porch," she said.

The line went dead in his ear.

Jessup stared at the phone, and then laid it down in the seat, pulled back onto the highway and began looking for a place to turn around.

CHAPTER SIX

Farrell Kitt was a thirty-something-year-old farmer with a pregnant wife and three kids—the oldest having just turned nine. His devotion to the Church of The Righteous was just one heartbeat less than his devotion to his family.

His one regret was that his wife, Judy, did not share his love of his church, and refused to go herself, or let him take their children there. She didn't know what he was doing when he packed up and left this morning, other than he'd promised to do a favor for Jeremiah. He was a long way from home, but was still on I49 in Louisiana, heading to Shreveport, when his cell phone rang. When he saw it was Judy, he smiled and answered.

"Hello, sugar. How's my favorite girl?"

Judy was crying and screaming, and it scared him to death. All he could think was that something had happened to one of the kids, as he pulled over to the shoulder of the interstate.

"Judy, honey! Take a breath. I can't understand a word you're saying." He heard her inhale and then blow her nose. The kids were all crying in the background, and now his belly was in knots. "What's wrong? What's wrong?"

"It's everywhere—all over the TV and internet. My sister saw it on Facebook and called me, so I looked and seen it with my own eyes. That woman Jeremiah keeps preaching about...the one he calls a devil? She's gone and put out a quarter of a million dollar bounty on two men she claims Raver sent to kill her. Are you one of them? Is that the favor you were doing for him?"

Farrell felt like he was going to puke.

"You don't understand," he said.

"It's true? You're really one of them? Oh, my God! You are a raving idiot. You're the one who doesn't understand!" Judy cried. "If you're one of them, then there is a bounty on your head."

"What? What? She can't do that! That's murder for hire!"

"You're a fool! A damn fool!" Judy cried. "You're the one out to kill, and she don't want you dead." Then she began outlining what she knew, finishing up with the one positive aspect. "If anyone hurts you in any way, the bounty is nullified and they get arrested."

"How did she—"

"Barrett Taylor is in jail. He talked after she took him down, and he told her there was more comin' after her, so this happened."

"Call Preacher Raver! Ask him what I should do!"

Judy started crying all over again.

"He's not answering his phone and no one's seen him. Wherever you are, turn around and come home. Don't no one have to know, if you didn't tell. I sure didn't."

"But our church people could guess...and they'll talk," Farrell said. "Even if they can't collect, they might give me up in an effort to distance themselves from the church."

"Just come home," Judy begged.

"Yes, yes, I will," Farrell said. "I'll hunt me a place to turn around and be there as soon as I can. I'm sorry. I'm sorry. Just calm down. It'll be okay."

The line went dead in his ear. And just like that, his passion to end a life had dwindled to cold sweat and a knot in his belly. Judy was furious, and that Wyrick woman had called them out. He couldn't get over it. A quarter of a million dollars. More money than he'd ever imagined he would be worth.

Sonny was in his apartment, watching the evening news as he changed out of his work clothes. When he heard the journalist mention the name Wyrick, he looked up. The woman fascinated him. He'd seen her live press conference on TV months back and knew all about her. He'd even fantasized about making her his like Rachel was, but knew that opportunity would never arise.

Still, he upped the volume to see what she was talking about, and then sat watching the way her lips moved, and her eyes narrowed. She didn't have breasts. She didn't have hair. And yet, he'd never been more attracted to a woman in his life than he was to her. She looked like a cross between a drag queen and an alien, and she was so damn hot it made him shake just thinking about holding her beneath him.

And then he began to focus on what she was saying in the video and realized Jade Wyrick had just put out a quarter-million-dollar bounty on each of two men some religious group had sent to kill her.

He slapped his leg and whooped with glee.

"Damn woman. You are freaking amazing."

He watched until the video ended, then turned off the television. Wyrick was a dream, but he already had a woman more his type waiting, and he didn't want to disappoint her.

The cell was cold, but Rachel was burning up. She was sick. Maybe the cut in her throat was infected. Maybe he'd broken her ribs when he hit her. All she knew was that it hurt to breathe, and it hurt to walk.

She had no idea what time it was, but she was scared to death that he'd come back, and at the same time, afraid he wouldn't. She'd made up her mind that this time she was not going to submit. It didn't make what he wanted to do to her any easier, because he got off on her pain, and he liked to see her bleed. If she was going to die, she was going to die fighting.

She staggered to her feet and stumbled to the sink again to sluice her burning face with cold water before returning to the mattress, then pulled the blanket up to her chin and stared at the door.

She didn't know if she was hallucinating, or if it was real when the door finally opened, then reality hit when she saw him slip inside, and heard the door lock behind him.

"Hey, my beauty. This is no way to greet your lover. I brought you a burger and fries and some water," he said.

Rachel stayed beneath the blanket, waiting. She was nauseated and shaking, but this time she had no doubts as to what he was bent on doing.

Sonny dropped the bag of food and the water in a corner of the room, and then started taking off his clothes. He was aroused and smiling as he picked up the knife and headed toward her.

"You can take them off, or I'll cut them off," he said.

Rachel didn't move.

Sonny frowned. Her face was flushed and her eyes were glassy. He grabbed the blanket and yanked it from her body, and when he did, he saw the festering wound at her neck.

Shit. She's sick.

But he'd been thinking about her all day and wouldn't be denied. He dropped down on his knees beside her and started yanking off her clothes, expecting resistance. But there was none. This was disappointing, and he was beginning to lose his arousal, so he poked at the bruises as they were revealed, expecting a reaction. Her nostrils flared slightly, but that was all.

"Come on, bitch. You know what I like," Sonny mumbled, and pinched both her breasts.

It took everything Rachel had not to react. Not to fight. She was still biding her time, watching for an opening—for him to look away, even if for a moment.

Sonny wasn't expecting the severity of bruising on her body. She was dark blue and purple everywhere. Maybe he'd been a little rough the first time around. He sure didn't want her disabled. Not yet. They'd just begun their little affair.

"Hey. Snap out of it," he said and slapped her, crushing her mouth against her teeth.

When the blood gushed, he grinned. That was more like it.

"Did you miss me, baby?" he crooned. "I missed you. We're going to have a real good time tonight."

When he rolled Rachel over onto her back, and shoved his knee between her legs, she flopped lifelessly. He frowned, and looked around for his knife. A little pain would sharpen her senses.

It was the moment Rachel had been waiting for. She grabbed his dick with one hand, squeezing and digging in her nails with every ounce of strength she had left, and then twisted it.

Before he could react, she reached toward him with her other hand and stabbed her fingernails into his chest, scratching him all the way down to his belly button.

Sonny was in shock. The pain was excruciating.

He began screaming and cursing, hitting her and grabbing at her hand, begging her to let go. The harder he hit her, the more she twisted.

Finally, in a last ditch effort, he doubled up his fist and hit her hard enough to knock her out. The moment he was free, he rolled over onto his side, sobbing and holding himself…afraid to look for fear his dick would come off in his own hands.

He wanted to kill her. Right then. Right where she lay. But

he was paralyzed by the pain. When he finally got to his feet, he made it as far as the sink when nausea hit. He spun and threw up in the commode until his sides were aching.

He didn't know Rachel had regained consciousness, or that she was crawling toward his knife until he her heard her moving. By the time he looked over his shoulder, she had the knife in her hand and was on her hands and knees.

He couldn't fight her like this. She'd almost unmanned him. All he could think to do was get out of her reach. With every ounce of strength he had left, he grabbed his clothes and made a run for the door, then fumbled with the keypad trying to unlock it. His heart was pounding, his fingers shaking.

She was only feet away and coming at him when he fell through the doorway, slamming it shut, automatically locking the door behind him.

He was bleeding, and swollen and as naked as the day he'd been born. It felt like she'd broken his dick. He needed to get home and get ice on it, ASAP. No way could he go to the ER with all these scratches, and an injury like this. He would be arrested for rape, and they'd start looking for a victim.

It took every ounce of strength he had left to get dressed and get home, sobbing with every step that he took. He'd go back to her again, but this time he'd take a gun and put a hole in her head.

When the door slammed shut in Rachel's face, she collapsed in despair. Her jaw was throbbing, her mouth was swelling and now so was her eye. She'd been close. So close. But she had a weapon now. She had his knife.

It was a good thing, and a bad thing.

He'd come back. But now that she had his knife, he couldn't afford to come back without a gun.

She needed to even the playing field a little, and the only way she could think was to put out the light. If she could break the bulb, then he couldn't see her. He wouldn't be expecting darkness, or for her to be right at the door. If she was lucky, she could stab him as he entered and make a run for it. After what she'd done to him tonight, it would be her only chance.

She got her clothes back on, all except for one shoe, then pulled the mattress to the corner nearest the door. By now her eye was almost shut, and she kept sluicing water over her face, hoping to deter some of the swelling.

Finally, she was as clean as she was going to get, and thought about the food that he'd brought. The mere idea of eating made her sick to her stomach, and it was going to hurt her jaw to chew, but she had to keep up her strength.

With every cold, greasy bite she took, she looked up through her one good eye, staring intently at the single bulb in the center of the ceiling, gauging how high it was as she chewed, and planning how hard she would have to throw her shoe to break it.

She finally finished her food, washed up, then carefully looked around at the new location of her bed, and positioned the blanket and the knife where she could find them in the dark. Then she paced off the number of steps from the foot of the mattress to the sink and the toilet, then counted them again going back. Afterward, she closed her eyes and did it again, and again, until she was confident she could find them in the dark.

Then she picked up her shoe, eyed the bulb and made her first throw. The shoe didn't even hit the ceiling. With only one eye to gauge the distance, she'd underestimated the height. So she kept retrieving the shoe and throwing it again, harder and harder, over and over, until finally, it hit the target.

To her dismay, the bulb didn't break. She was so tired and so frustrated that she just stood there, screaming, sobbing, cursing, berating every man who ever lived, until she couldn't catch her breath, and then she stopped. This wasn't getting her anywhere, and she didn't dare take the time to quit and rest.

She hobbled over to retrieve the shoe, then went back to stand by the edge of the mattress. She looked up again—the shoe clutched against her chest—then reared back and threw it, watching the arc, and then, once again, the contact.

But this time there was a flash as the bulb shattered and everything went black. In a panic, she covered her face, protecting her eyes as the glass from the broken bulb rained down around her.

When she opened them again, it was to total darkness. She couldn't see her hand in front of her face, and the shock became reality. She'd never been in the presence of a complete absence of light. The air suddenly felt thick—too thick to breathe. It took her a few seconds to realize it was her own panic, and not the air that was choking her. She needed to calm down. She needed to rest, so she slowly turned, then eased down to her knees and crawled forward until she felt the mattress. The disgusting object had become a touchstone to safety, because now she knew where she was.

She crawled up on it, rolled herself up in the blanket and then felt around until she found the knife and held it close. She needed to be listening for the lock to release, and be watching for the door to come open and attack him before he realized the room was dark.

Sonny was back in his place. He'd taken a shower and disinfected the scratches on his chest, but he was in too much pain to sleep. So he sat up in his recliner all night, sobbing from the pain, popping over-the-counter pain pills, and alternating the ice packs in his lap.

He was tired. So tired, and he'd taken so many pain pills that it should have made him sick, but they didn't even faze the pain.

He was still awake when the sun came up, and in no shape to

go to work, so he called in sick, claiming he'd taken a bad fall, and was going to take the rest of the week off.

He finally fell asleep around 10 a.m. and dreamed of a woman who turned into a tiger and castrated him with her claws.

He woke up in a sweat, still hurting, popped some more painkillers, then crawled into bed with a fresh ice pack and willed himself back to sleep.

Millie Chriss was awake by daybreak. She quickly showered and dressed, then went down to breakfast, biding her time until it was late enough to call Detective Floyd.

After she ordered, she called Ray to let him know her plans, and that they'd connect later this evening for a longer talk.

"Just be careful," Ray said.

"I will," Millie promised, and then the connection ended.

She laid her phone aside and looked up at all of the other diners going about their mornings, thinking of how much safety and freedom is taken for granted.

Her baby sister was in trouble. She wouldn't have just disappeared for three nights now without letting someone know where she'd gone, but where in God's name was she? What had happened to her? Was she hurt? Was she even still alive? The uncertainty was making Millie crazy.

After her food arrived, she ate for the nourishment, then went back to her room. It was time to start laying out a new plan, and the first order of business was finding out if the evidence taken from Rachel's apartment had yielded any clues.

She made a call to Detective Floyd and said a prayer for good news as she waited for him to answer.

Darren Floyd was in morning traffic on the beltway on his way to the precinct when his phone rang. He answered on Bluetooth so he could keep both hands on the wheel.

"Detective Floyd speaking," he said.

"Good morning, Detective Floyd. This is Millie Chriss. I was wondering if you had any news."

He sighed. "No, ma'am. I'm sorry, but there was nothing new from the crime lab."

Millie's heart sank.

"This is not what I had hoped to hear. What's next?"

"I understand your concern, but we're not quitting on her. This just isn't making it easy."

Millie hesitated a second, unsure of how this would be received, and then decided she didn't care what they thought. This was about Rachel's life. Not their hurt feelings.

"I want you to know that I plan to contact Charlie Dodge. If I can hire him, he will also be looking for her."

Detective Floyd was well aware of Dodge's reputation for finding the lost, and he knew Charlie had a hole card in his assistant, Wyrick.

"That's fine. We can't tell you not to, nor would we. If he takes your case, he'll check in with us, and we'll go from there."

"Thank you for understanding, but please keep me updated," Millie said and disconnected, then pulled up the contact info for Dodge Investigations and gave them a call.

Wyrick had just opened the office and was at the coffee bar setting it up for the day when the phone rang. She licked a smear of sugar off her thumb and ran to answer.

"Dodge Investigations."

Millie Chriss took a deep breath.

"Yes, hello. This is Millie Chriss. My sister has gone missing. The Dallas PD don't have any leads, and I'm desperate for help. I was wondering if it would be—"

"Can you be here by 10 a.m.?" Wyrick asked.

Millie stuttered. "Uh…oh, my God…yes! Thank you."

"Do you have the address?" Wyrick asked.

"No, but I can—"

"Get a pen and paper and I'll give it to you," Wyrick said.

"Yes, yes, just a second," Millie said and grabbed the little pad of paper and pen off the desk. "Okay, go ahead."

Wyrick told her the address, then added, "Parking is in the rear of the building. Drive safe, Mrs. Chriss. We'll see you at ten."

"Yes, yes, thank you so—" Then she realized the woman had disconnected, and wondered if that was the Wyrick woman that Ray said was psychic, then realized it didn't matter. Millie had just set into motion what she needed to happen.

Even though it was a little early, she went to freshen up her makeup. She needed gas, and there was a lot of Dallas territory and traffic between where she was, and where she needed to be. So as soon as she was ready, she left the hotel.

Charlie arrived at the office a short while later, and in a mood.

"Nearly got sideswiped trying to exit the beltway," he said. "I hope there's a bear claw waiting for me at the coffee bar."

"Two," Wyrick said and got up to go to their printer. "And Millie Chriss will be in at 10."

"Who's Millie—"

Wyrick was gathering a handful of pages coming off their printer. "Remember yesterday when I told you we would get the case on that missing woman, Rachel Dean? Millie is Rachel's sister." She pulled the last page off the rack and handed him the stack. "This is all the information I have on Rachel. There are no secrets in her past. I think whatever happened to her is either stalker related, or an act of random violence."

Charlie took the papers.

"Thanks for printing them off. I hate reading notes on an iPad."

"I know. That's why you're holding them in your hand now. You have about forty-five minutes before she's due, so…"

Charlie took the hint and went into his office, dumped the papers and his briefcase on his desk, then divested himself of his Stetson and jacket before going for bear claws and coffee.

By the time he'd eaten his first one, he was in a better mood, and by the time Millie Chriss arrived, he was primed and ready.

Millie arrived at the door, then hesitated as she realized she had to be buzzed in. She pressed the button and looked up at the camera. Moments later she heard a click as the door unlocked. She turned the knob and walked in.

It would have been an understatement for Millie to say the stunning woman at the desk was a surprise. And then all six-feet-plus of her stood up from the desk and came to greet Millie.

"I'm Wyrick. We spoke on the phone," she said and extended her hand.

Millie clasped it, wondering if her touch would be as electrifying as her appearance, but all she got was a warm squeeze, and then she let go. She was admiring Wyrick's guts, as well as the silver pants and black knee-high boots she was wearing, with a long-sleeved white blouse featuring a neckline that plunged all the way to her waist. The dragon tattoo was startling, but at the same time, amazing, and the blouse gave the red-and-black dragon beneath plenty of room to see out. Its teeth were bared. Its yellow eyes were glittering as if warning people not to get too close.

The silver eye shadow above Wyrick's eyelids made her dark eyes look huge, and the single black tear below drew Millie's eyes to the slash of red on Wyrick's lips, and then she realized the woman was speaking.

"Charlie is waiting to see you," Wyrick said. "Follow me."

Then she led Millie in without delay. "Charlie. Millie Chriss is here."

Charlie stood, and Millie blinked. The man made Wyrick look small, and he was seriously good-looking.

"Mrs. Chriss. Please have a seat," Charlie said. "Wyrick and I work together on all of our cases, so she'll be sitting in."

Millie nodded nervously, then sat. "Thank you for seeing me on such short notice, but my sister has gone missing and—"

Charlie held up his hand.

"No explanations necessary. Wyrick told me yesterday you'd be coming. She's already pulled all of the info on your sister that was available online. So if there's anything you know about her that's very private, now's the time to tell us."

Millie looked over at Wyrick. "But…how did you…?"

Wyrick shrugged. "I saw the report of her having gone missing on the news and…well…sometimes I just know stuff."

Millie nodded as if she understood, but she didn't. Not really.

"Before this conversation goes any further, I have to ask what you charge," Millie said.

"Wyrick handles all of the accounting. I'll let her explain," Charlie said.

Wyrick offered no explanation other than the truth.

"I know this seems intrusive, but I also 'knew' you would have to mortgage your home to raise the money, and we don't ever want to put a family in hardship when they're already worried about a loved one. We have a pro bono fund, and it will take care of all the incurred expenses for this case."

Millie's eyes welled, and then she covered her face and started to cry. "Thank you. Oh, my God, thank you. Rachel is my baby sister. We're the only living members of our family. I've gone through every imaginable hell thinking what might have happened to her. If she's alive, I just want her back. If she's not, I need to find her and bring her home."

"We'll take the case," Charlie said. "And we will find her. At this early date, I can't promise more."

"I understand," Millie said. "I'm just so grateful. I don't even know what to say."

"Tell us about Rachel," Charlie said. "Any relationships? Anybody jealous of her at work? Anything she's mentioned to you in the past few months that she seemed concerned about?"

And so Millie started talking. Wyrick was recording the session and taking notes as she listened. Every now and then, Charlie would stop and ask another question that would take Millie off into another avenue of info.

And then finally, they were done.

"That's all I know, and Rachel wasn't the kind of person who kept secrets from me…or anyone else. She was what you saw…a pretty, career-driven woman with a great outlook on life."

Charlie nodded. "Okay, we have your contact information, and we'll stay in touch. And if we have any other questions as the case progresses, we'll call as we go."

Millie nodded. "I'm not leaving Dallas until she's found."

"Understood," Wyrick said. "Follow me. I'll show you out," and then stood and walked Millie into the outer office, and then opened the door for her.

Millie paused and then turned. "I don't know your story. But the woman I see before me is a gift from God. Thank you, and thank you to Charlie for agreeing to take my case."

Wyrick was touched, but only nodded her head as she let Millie out. When she closed the door and turned around, Charlie was in the doorway, watching her.

"I just got off the phone with Detective Floyd in Missing Persons. He knows we're working the case. And he knows we'll share anything we find. He's also calling the manager at the Detter House to let them know we have the okay to go into Rachel Dean's apartment and look around."

"Give me five minutes and I'll be ready," Wyrick said.

Charlie nodded and walked back into the office.

When he came out again, Wyrick was waiting.

CHAPTER SEVEN

Wayne Dyer hung up the phone and reached for his coffee cup. Detective Floyd had just given him a heads-up that a private investigator was also going to be working with them on the Rachel Dean case, and they had his permission to see the apartment.

Wayne sighed and took a quick sip, then made a face. It was stone-cold. He got up and popped it in the microwave to warm up, then went to get the passkey. This missing person thing wasn't looking good for the Detter House. He'd already called Allen Carson, the owner, notifying him of what had happened. Carson urged Wayne to assist the authorities in every way. He wanted the issue cleared up and swept under the rug before the media turned it into bad PR for future rentals.

Wayne felt caught in the middle of the whole mess. He was the man with the passkey, and a resident disappeared from her own apartment without anyone knowing how, or where she'd gone.

He was the one who let cleaning crews in and out. The one who walked the pest control service through the building and through the respective apartments on a quarterly basis.

He'd let the cleaning crew into Rachel's apartment the day she disappeared, and he'd gone into her apartment on his own to do a wellness check at the request of her employer. Wayne felt like he had a target on his chest, and was just waiting for someone to pull the trigger and blame him for all of it.

When the door to his office opened, the couple who walked in rendered him momentarily speechless.

He'd heard of Charlie Dodge, and he'd seen that woman who worked with him on TV a few months back. But he wasn't prepared for the sheer power of their presence, and then Charlie smiled.

"Mr. Dyer, I'm Charlie Dodge, and this is Wyrick, my assistant. You know why we're here."

"Yes, Detective Floyd called, and please call me Wayne. I'll take you up to Rachel Dean's apartment." He exited with the passkey in his hand as he led the way to the elevator. "I can't tell you how disturbed we all are about this. Rachel is very well-liked here, and we're hoping every day for some positive news."

Just as the detectives had done before them, Charlie and Wyrick took careful note of the way the old mansion had been laid out into separate apartments, and when they exited the elevator and followed Wayne down to apartment 210, they also noticed the security cameras.

"Are those security cameras all in working order?" Charlie asked.

Wayne nodded. "Yes. I made a copy of the twenty-four hours before she disappeared for the police, and I can make a copy for you, as well, if you want."

"Yes," Wyrick said.

"Happy to help," Wayne said as he glanced at her. He started to smile, and then saved it. She was a little scary and too serious to chance it. Then he paused at the door to Rachel's apartment.

"Here we are. She doesn't have security inside her apartment, and that's strictly the leaser's choice. Some do. Some don't."

Charlie removed the yellow strip of crime scene tape that had been taped across the doorway, then Wayne unlocked the door.

"I have a question," Wyrick said. "I understand a cleaning crew was here the day she went missing?"

"Yes. I let them in that morning, and they were gone long before she came home from work," Wayne said.

"How many people in the cleaning crew?" Wyrick asked.

"Three. A man and two women. Do you want me to go in with you, or…"

"No, thanks," Charlie said.

Wayne hesitated, then once again handed over the passkey.

"I'm sure I can trust you to lock up when you're finished. If I'm not in the office, just drop it in the mail slot in the door."

"Will do," Charlie said.

Charlie and Wyrick walked in, shutting the door behind them. Then they stood in the foyer, absorbing the vibes.

Charlie was waiting for her to make the first move.

"Anything?" he asked.

"I don't get any images of a struggle, but I get vibes of different people…probably the cleaning crew," Wyrick said.

"Let's check it out," Charlie said and moved from the foyer into the living room on the right. It was neat and spotless. "I don't think she was even in here after she came home from work," he said. "Nobody sat on the sofa or in any of the chairs, because the throw pillows don't look as if they've been moved since they were fluffed."

Wyrick smirked. "Fluffed?"

Charlie frowned. "Well, what the hell do *you* call it?"

"I think the most common phrase is 'plumping up' the pillows," she said and walked back out into the hall.

"I never claimed interior decorating as part of my résumé," he muttered and followed her as she moved up the hall.

Wyrick grinned, but only because he couldn't see her face, and then paused at the junction. They could either go left or forward, so they chose to go forward, and wound up in the kitchen/dining area, with a visible utility area off the kitchen.

The table was bare, but Wyrick saw differently.

"There was food here…and an iPad. She was reading it. The police collected it for evidence, but it wasn't breakfast food. It was from the night before…the night she went missing," Wyrick said.

Wyrick touched the chairs at the table. "Something disturbed her meal. She got up and never came back."

Charlie wandered into the utility room and lifted the lid on the washer, then the dryer, before walking back into the kitchen.

"There are clothes in the washer. They got washed, but never put in the dryer, and I'm also just realizing there's no other exit out of this apartment but the one we came in. There's a window overlooking part of the parking area, but no fire escape. Is this even up to code?"

Wyrick shrugged. "I saw signs over a door down the hall that said Fire Escape, so it's like a hotel. I guess you have to get to the end of the hall to get to a separate stairwell other than the one at the entrance downstairs."

"And according to Rachel's sister, and Detective Floyd, they have her on camera going in and never coming out," Charlie said.

Wyrick led the way out of the kitchen, and then pointed down the other hall.

"This is just a one-bedroom apartment, so let's check that out next. Right now the only vibes I'm picking up on are hers. Like I'm seeing everything through her eyes, and nothing seems amiss," Wyrick said.

"Millie Chriss told us the television was on when Dyer did the wellness check. He claims he didn't touch anything, and it was still on when the police came. It's not on now, so I'm guessing the team from the crime lab turned it off after dusting for prints," Charlie said, and then turned the doorknob and walked in while Wyrick paused on the threshold.

"Bed wasn't slept in," Charlie said and walked into the bathroom. Clean towels were still folded on the rack and the shower door was spotless. "She didn't shower after she got home," he added.

Wyrick hadn't moved, still looking at the setup, the furniture all in place. No signs of a struggle. The only strange thing she noticed was that the remote was lying beside the television, which was all the way across the room from the bed.

"Why would she turn on a television in here if she was eating her meal and reading in the kitchen?" Wyrick said. "And why is the remote all the way across the room, and not beside her bed, where you would expect it to be?"

"Maybe the cleaning crew did it," Charlie said.

"If Rachel had left it on while she was getting dressed for work, she would have still heard it playing before she left and turned it off. Even if the cleaning crew turned it on to listen to while they worked, they would not have left it playing, either, and she would have not wanted it playing if she's in another room, reading," Wyrick said.

"Agreed," Charlie said and then stepped into the big walk-in closet to look around, but everything was neatly hanging, or on shelving. "Are you picking up on anything in this room?" he asked as he exited.

Wyrick frowned. "I can see her in here, and then everything goes black. Whatever happened to her, I don't think she saw it coming."

"Dammit," Charlie muttered.

"I'm getting a really bad headache," Wyrick muttered. "I need air."

"Then we're done in here for now," Charlie said. "You're picking up on shit even you can't see. Let's get back to the office and regroup on where to go from here."

Wyrick didn't argue. They locked up the apartment and headed back to the manager's office and walked in.

Wayne was on the phone with one of the residents.

"Someone just walked in. Can you hold a moment?" he said.

"We brought back your key," Charlie said. "But we may need to come back later."

"No problem," Wayne said. "Have a nice evening." Then he went back to his call as Charlie and Wyrick left. "Sorry, George. The PI Rachel Dean's family hired was taking a look at her apartment. Now, you said your shower has a leak?"

"Rachel Dean…you mean the woman who went missing from here?" George asked on the other end of the line.

"Yes. Her family hired Charlie Dodge. I heard he's the best. Maybe he and Wyrick will find her. Now, what's up with your shower?"

"It drips, and it's driving me nuts at night trying to sleep."

"I'm sorry. I'll get a work order going and get it fixed ASAP."

"Thanks," George said and hung up.

Wayne made a note to himself to call a plumber and dropped the passkey in a drawer.

Charlie and Wyrick drove in silence for several minutes until Wyrick suddenly spoke.

"If there are any blueprints for the original property, I want to see them. I know there would be some from the reconstruction that was done twenty years ago, but I'm not sure about original blueprints from a building that old."

Charlie glanced at her before moving into another lane of traffic.

"Are you thinking there could be secret passages?"

Wyrick wouldn't commit to that. "I'm not thinking anything specific. Right now it's about covering all the bases."

"If you find them, send them to me. That's something I can easily do. What I want you to do is run background checks on all of the residents. Call Wayne Dyer for their names. Rachel Dean might not have any secrets in her past, but that doesn't mean the rest of them are lily-white," Charlie said.

Wyrick nodded and made the call.

Wayne was looking for his car keys when his phone rang. He had an appointment to get a haircut, and was already cutting it close.

"Hello. This is Wayne."

"This is Wyrick. Charlie would like a list of names of all the residents. Could you please send us the list via email?"

"Yes, but I'm leaving for an appointment right now. I'll do it as soon as I return. What's the email address?"

Wyrick gave it to him and disconnected.

"He's going out. He'll send it later," she said, then began rubbing at the space above her nose, trying to rub away the painful throb.

She'd been so sure that just going there would give them some answers, but instead, they'd hit the same wall the police had encountered. So she leaned back and closed her eyes.

"Is your headache getting better?" Charlie asked.

"Yes."

"There are some painkillers in the console if you need them," he said.

"I'm good. I'm just thinking."

After that Charlie stopped talking. He didn't want to interrupt a genius in motion.

Wyrick hadn't given the hit man bounty much thought after making the threat. She was guessing they were in hiding, and if confronted, would all claim innocence. But she also knew a quarter of a million dollars would prompt some greedy people in the know to start pointing fingers. She didn't have any preconceived expectations of what the feedback would be like, but she was curious.

"Have you had any hits on the hit men's identities?" Charlie asked.

"I hadn't this morning, but I'll wait until I get home this evening to check. I'm keeping all of that on my computers, because I know those can't be hacked."

Charlie took the on-ramp to get back on the beltway and get back to their office, thinking what a force of nature she was.

"If you ever want to change occupations, you'd make one hell of a weapon for the government."

"No, I wouldn't. They have too many rules about hacking. I'm absolutely positive they wouldn't like how I get my information. Remember how uptight Hank Raines got when I was running facial recognition, getting the identities of the girls who were in the Fourth Dimension because he needed proof that they were there to get his search warrants?"

Charlie frowned. "I remember plenty from that case. He crossed a couple of lines with us that I did not appreciate, especially trying to confiscate your drone to get the cloaking technology you had on it."

Wyrick shrugged. "You call it confiscate. I call it stealing."

Charlie glanced up in the rearview mirror as he moved into the outside lane and sped up.

"Well, you put an end to that when you threw it in the firepit at the cabin and let them all watch it go up in flames. It was, in my opinion, one of your finer moments," he said. "Want to pick up lunch somewhere, or are you up to a public outing?"

Wyrick glanced at him. "I'm good with either, but I'm thinking you're angling for dining out."

"A Stackhouse burger and fries sure sounds good," Charlie said.

"I'm in," Wyrick said. "You're buying. It'll be a tax write-off."

He laughed. "I can do that."

A few minutes later Charlie pulled off Gaston Avenue into the Stackhouse Burgers parking lot, found a parking place and killed the engine.

Wyrick shoved her laptop back into her bag and pushed it under the seat, pulled down the visor to look in the mirror, which caught Charlie's attention. He'd never seen her do that before.

"What's wrong?" he asked.

"Just checking to make sure my hair is okay," she drawled.

"Don't be a smart-ass," Charlie said. "I'm serious."

Wyrick sighed. "It feels like something is in my eye, but I can't see anything."

"Let me look," Charlie said.

Wyrick hesitated. That would put her closer to him than was comfortable, but her eye was burning.

"Whatever," she muttered and leaned across the seat.

Charlie tilted her head back, then gently pulled up the upper lid, then the lower one down, looking for something that didn't belong.

"See anything?" Wyrick asked.

"I don't… Wait. There's a speck of something just inside the lower edge. Don't move. Let me get a tissue. I think I can get it out," he said, then felt for the box of tissues in the console and pulled one out.

When he aimed the tiny corner of a tissue toward her eye, it took everything within her not to blink, so she focused on the faint wisps of gray hair at his temples and how blue his eyes were instead.

"Got it!" he crowed, and showed her the speck on the tip of the tissue.

Wyrick breathed a sigh of relief, blinking more easily now. "Thanks, Doc."

Charlie grinned. "I'll send you my bill. And your hair's fine, so let's go eat."

Wyrick gave him a look, but he ignored her. To her, that was one of the best parts of Charlie Dodge. He was full of shit and made no apologies for it.

The moment they entered, a number of the diners looked up, and within moments the whispers began.

Charlie glared on her behalf.

Wyrick ignored all of them.

The diners knew who she was.

What Wyrick didn't know was, after revealing herself and her abilities to the world, most of the people in Dallas had come to consider her as "theirs."

They were used to the rich and famous mingling among them. Famous athletes from the Dallas Cowboys football team were always out and about, and movie stars came and went here, as well. It wasn't unusual for a film crew to be in the state somewhere filming.

Wyrick was in the same category—someone who deserved the right to be left the hell alone. But it didn't stop them from looking, and today she was looking fine. She was, in fact, a sight to behold—and always in the company of Charlie Dodge, who had his own reputation going even before she became a part of his world.

Wyrick felt the energy in the room, but it was nothing threatening, so she ignored them as they sat down.

A waiter appeared, took their drink orders and left them

reading the menus. Wyrick glanced at hers briefly, then closed it and set it aside.

Charlie was still looking at choices when he noticed what she'd done.

"That was fast," he said.

Wyrick shrugged. "They have chili-cheese fries."

"No burger to go with them?" Charlie asked.

"An order of chili-cheese fries is all the grease my veins can take in one sitting."

He laughed, and a warmth settled in Wyrick's heart.

They waited without conversation. Charlie answered a text, and Wyrick did a quick check of her email.

When their food finally came, Charlie's double-patty burger was too thick to bite into, so he squished it down with the flat of his hand before he took a bite.

Wyrick fussed with her food, stirring the chili and cheese into the fries with her fork until they were equally coated, then forked up a neat bite.

"Mmm… Oh, my God," she said and closed her eyes.

Charlie looked up just as she said that, saw the ecstasy on her face, and for a few moments forgot what he was doing. She so rarely exhibited any kind of emotion, and seeing that look on her face made him wonder how she'd look making love.

Then the moment he thought it, it shocked him. That had no place in their relationship. It was business or nothing, and he didn't want to lose her. So he reached for the salt shaker, salted his burger, then took another bite.

Wyrick had finished her fries and was still sipping on her drink, waiting for Charlie to finish, when she caught movement from the corner of her eye. She glanced over, then stilled.

There was a little girl coming straight for her with a look of awe on her face, and she knew why. The child was frail, and thin, and as bald as Wyrick, and she was about the same age as Wyrick had been when UT took her away from her mother.

The little girl stopped at the table, looked up at Wyrick's head.

Wyrick leaned over. "It's okay if you want to feel it," Wyrick whispered.

The little girl smiled, then slid her hand across the soft, smooth skin and began rubbing it.

In turn, Wyrick reached for the little girl, laid her hand on her head and closed her eyes.

Immediately, she saw the child's sickness—the cancer cells in her blood and in her bones, the tumor in her brain, and then the beating heart in the frail little body it was trying to keep alive.

She didn't think about consequences. She just focused on what was wrong, and with all of the healing energy she could gather, started working to make it all right.

The parents were dealing with a toddler who'd made a mess, and when they suddenly realized their daughter wasn't at the table, they began to panic. Then the mother saw her across the room, and saw what she was doing, and quietly sat as her eyes filled with tears, letting the moment between Wyrick and her child play out.

Charlie had a lump in his throat, and couldn't have spoken if he'd had to. He'd never seen this tender, gentle side of Wyrick, and it struck him to the core. They didn't know the moment was being filmed by the child's father, along with a roomful of diners.

And then all of a sudden the little girl let go, and when she did, Wyrick drew back.

"What's your name?" the child asked.

Wyrick leaned down again and whispered in her ear.

"My name is Jade."

"I'm Bethie. You're just like me," she said.

"No. I think you're much prettier," Wyrick said.

And then the mother appeared and took her daughter by the hand.

"We're so sorry Bethie bothered you. Our baby made a mess and we didn't realize she'd left the table."

"On the contrary," Wyrick said and winked at Bethie. "This might just be the single best thing that has ever happened to me."

The little girl giggled, and then they were gone.

Wyrick was suddenly aware that she'd let down her guard in public, and now she wouldn't look at Charlie, or anyone else. But when he laid down some money and stood, the silence of the room wrapped around her like a hug as they left.

Even after they were in the car and back on the beltway, she had nothing to say. She was suddenly so tired, and a little sad, so she leaned back and closed her eyes.

Charlie felt her withdrawal and honored it, knowing something beyond the obvious about that child had triggered her in a very deep way.

By the time they reached the office, Wyrick was all business again and went straight to her desk.

"I'm going to see if I can find blueprints for the property."

"If you can, send all of it to me. I'll compare the specs. If there are any secret rooms or passages, they should show up in the blueprints from the renovation."

Wyrick went to work, while Charlie went to his office.

The whole time Barrett Taylor was being arraigned, he had a bad feeling about the outcome. His lawyer, Marsh Fielding, had filled him in earlier about Jade Wyrick's video, and that Jeremiah Raver wasn't answering his phone. All Barrett kept thinking was, if he'd done what he'd come here to do, none of this would be happening. His failure had caused a landslide.

After the charges were read, he pled not guilty. But despite the lawyer's pleas on his behalf, the district attorney's claims that the evidence against Taylor, coupled with his priors and the charges filed, made him a flight risk.

The judge denied bail.

Barrett Taylor was sent back to jail to await a trial date.

It wasn't what he wanted, and it definitely wasn't what Jeremiah Raver had wanted. The Dallas media had already picked up on it, and on the bounty Wyrick had put out on the men coming after her. It only made the story bigger. The Church of The Righteous had finally gotten media attention, but not in a good way.

Sonny was recovering slowly from his near emasculation, but at least he could walk now. His dick was still purple and sore, and it hurt to pee. He just hoped he'd be back in working order when he healed. And the scratches Rachel had put on his chest were scabbing over.

He wasn't messing with her again. She'd turned out to be a big disappointment, and it was time to move on. She was feverish before. Maybe by the time he went back she'd be dead, which would save him the trouble of killing her.

But he wasn't quite up to speed strength-wise, and so he decided to wait at least another day or so, until he knew he was strong enough to move the body. He also knew she'd be hungry, but so what. She could die on an empty stomach as easily as on a full one, and it served her right.

Rachel had no idea how long she'd been in the dark. She'd stayed awake until fever took her under, and now she was in and out of consciousness. The cut on her throat was swollen and too sore to touch, and her body throbbed with every heartbeat.

She dreamed her mother was with her, whispering in her ear to stay strong. Sometimes she thought she could hear Millie talking just outside the door, but no matter how hard she screamed, Millie never heard her.

Other times she dreamed the doorway was open, and imagined Sonny coming at her in the dark, but she didn't have any legs, so she couldn't get away.

In her more cognizant moments, she had enough sense to get up and feel her way to the sink to drink. She could live a long time without food, but not without water, so staying hydrated became her conscious focus.

She lost the knife, and spent frantic moments trying to find it, before she passed out. When she woke up again and couldn't see, she thought she'd gone blind, and screamed. It took a few moments before she remembered, and then she started crying.

"Please, God, please let this be over. Either let me die, or send someone to find me."

CHAPTER EIGHT

Wyrick spent a good half hour looking for blueprints and then realized time was not on their side. There were records of blueprints, but none of the really old ones were online, and even if she found the location of the ones for Detter House, requesting the copies would take days.

She was frustrated with the red tape and lack of online availability when it dawned on her that the current owner might be able to help, so she sent a text to Wayne Dyer requesting the owner's name and phone number.

Within minutes Wayne responded with the name, Allen Carson, as well as his cell number, and a message that he was emailing the list of residents to her.

Wyrick then did a quick search of Allen Carson before she called him, just so she'd know who she was talking to.

A picture popped up of a fifty-something man who looked a little bit like Robert De Niro. According to the info, he was a self-made multimillionaire, twice divorced, three grown kids and no black marks against his credit or his business practices. It was enough to start with, so she made the call.

★ ★ ★

Allen Carson was winding up a business lunch at the Dallas Country Club when his cell phone rang. He saw Dodge Security and Investigations come up on caller ID and frowned. He'd never met Charlie Dodge, but the man's reputation preceded him, and so he stood.

"Excuse me, gentlemen. I need to take this," he said and stepped out of the dining area. "Hello. Allen Carson speaking."

"Mr. Carson, my name is Wyrick. I'm calling on behalf of Dodge Investigations in the hopes that you might be able to assist us on a case that happened on one of your properties."

Allen took a deep breath. He couldn't believe he was actually speaking to *the* Jade Wyrick, and had to make himself focus.

"Um… I don't understand," he said.

"Oh, of course. I just assumed… Let me start over. A woman named Rachel Dean has gone missing, and she lives in one of the apartments in Detter House."

"Oh…that, yes, I'm sorry. My manager did notify me of that happening. But what—"

"She went missing *from* her apartment. There's video of her going in, and then she just disappears. The police have no leads. There are no witnesses to anything, and she has no history of trouble with anyone. Her sister hired us to assist the police in finding her. Charlie and I did a walk-through of the apartment this morning without discovering anything."

Now Allen was beginning to sense the problems he'd feared were arising. The family had called in help beyond the Dallas PD.

"That's terrible. Her family must be terrified. How can I help?" he asked.

"We know the structure is old. And then you bought it a little over twenty years ago and renovated it into apartments. By any chance, did you change any of the structural aspects of it during renovations?"

"Well, of course I took down walls and added other walls to create separate dwellings, but only to the interior aspects of the house. The original structure of the building was never altered. Is that what you mean?"

"Yes, and no. What I need to know is if, during renovation, there would have been spaces left between the new walls and the old. Spaces large enough for people to pass through?"

Allen gasped. "No! I would never have okayed anything like that…and in fact, there would not have been a need to make the floor space smaller. The draw for rental property is always where to get the most space for the money."

"Understood," Wyrick said. "Now, I have one more question. By any chance when you purchased the mansion…did you ever have an occasion to see the original blueprints for Detter House?"

The skin crawled on the back of Allen's neck. All of a sudden, he knew where this was going. They were talking about secret passages here. Oh, God. That would end the trust factor of ever renting property there again.

"Actually, we found the original blueprints in the main library during renovation," Allen said. "Before I became a builder, I was an architect. I've drawn hundreds of blueprints for clients, and collecting blueprints of historic buildings is a hobby of mine. So I have them, as well as the blueprints for the renovation."

Wyrick's heart skipped a beat. What a score!

"Would it be possible for us to borrow them for a time? It's crucial that we rule out even the most random possibilities that might explain how Rachel disappeared."

"Yes, of course," Allen said and glanced at his watch. "It's probably too late for me to messenger them to you today, and I'm not at home. By the time I could get there—"

Wyrick interrupted, "If you'd be agreeable, Charlie or I would gladly come get them this evening. As I said, time is not on our side."

"Yes, of course," Allen said. "I'll be home by six. I live in University Park. I'll text you my address. Just ring the doorbell. My housekeeper will have them for you."

"Thank you for your cooperation," Wyrick said. "We'll take good care of them and get them back to you as soon as we're through."

"Just let me know, and I'll send someone to your office to pick them up, and save you the trip," he said.

"Will do. Thank you again," Wyrick said and hung up, then went to tell Charlie, pausing at the coffee bar on the way to get a sweet roll.

Charlie glanced up as she walked in carrying a cherry Danish.

"Is that for me?" he asked.

"No," she said and took a bite, chewing as she talked. "I found blueprints for the original structure and prints for the renovation. But we have to pick them up."

Charlie glanced at the time. "That was fast, and good job! Where are they, and how much time do I have to go get them?" he asked.

She swallowed her bite, licked the sugar off her thumb and then answered.

"They're at Allen Carson's home. He's an architect, and the owner of the Detter House, and he's really rich."

"As rich as you?" Charlie asked.

She shrugged. "No, but they found the original blueprints in the library when they began reconstruction. He said he collects historic blueprints. And he has the newer ones, too. He said we could pick them both up at his house around six o'clock this evening."

"That's awesome!" Charlie said. "Good call. I'll do it. Just tell me where he lives."

"In University Park. I'll text you the address. I need to see if Dyer has sent the list of residents' names. If he has, I'm going to start running background checks."

"Send me half the names. I can run backgrounds, too, and we'll compile the info at home tonight."

She nodded, then took another bite of Danish and walked out.

Charlie sat back, watching the easy sway of her shoulders in rhythm with her hips, and the stride of such long, perfect legs. Six feet of poetry in motion; he couldn't help but wonder whose DNA was responsible for that.

Unaware she was the subject of her boss's thoughts, Wyrick slid back into her chair, sent Allen Carson's address to Charlie's phone, then pulled up the email. Wayne Dyer had come through. She printed off the list of names and addresses, and took two sheets to Charlie.

"Here you go, and just know that you'll need to leave here no later than five to get all the way to University Park during rush hour traffic."

"Remind me," Charlie said.

"I just did," Wyrick said and strode out of his office at full sail.

He blinked. *Damn woman.* Then he set the alarm on his phone and picked up the list, but he was grinning as he typed the first name in a search bar.

Wyrick started on her list, hoping something popped for them soon.

Hours later Wyrick was forwarding files on the background searches to a computer she had at home when Charlie came out of his office.

"It's five o'clock. I'm off to Allen Carson's home to pick up those blueprints. I'll deal with dinner when I get home," he said.

She glanced up. "I'm leaving, too."

He hesitated.

"I'll be fine. I promise to check outside for vipers and snipers, so go. I can't live in constant fear, okay?"

"Fine," Charlie said and left the office.

But the moment he was gone, Wyrick realized how vulnerable she felt. So she packed up her bag, turned out all the lights and hurried to the elevator.

The ride down was brief. She came out of the car with her keys in hand, turned the corner in the hall and saw Charlie leaning against the wall beside the exit, waiting.

"Don't go having yourself a fit," he said. "I'm just walking you to the car."

"I don't have fits," she said and lifted her chin and waited for him to open the door.

"You had some part of one the other night when you spewed Pepsi all over yourself," he said, then pulled his gun as he exited the building.

She couldn't argue with the truth, and waited as he looked until he was satisfied, before he motioned her out. She went straight to her car with Charlie beside her, then got in.

"Drive safe. I'll call if I'm delayed," he said and then stood back and waited as she drove away.

When she looked in the rearview mirror, he was still in the parking lot, watching her leave. She couldn't think about him right now. There was too much at stake for Rachel Dean to think about how Charlie made her feel.

By the time she got home, all she wanted was to get out of her clothes and makeup and into something comfortable. She parked in the detached garage, then shouldered her bag and headed for the house, passing the greenhouse and the rose garden on the way.

The landscaping crew had obviously come and gone today, because the grass was newly mown and the hedges were clipped.

It was getting late enough in the year that those services would no longer be needed until spring, but the scent of freshly cut grass was pleasant and homey, and today was also the day the twelve-person cleaning service came. She trusted them only because Merlin had trusted them, and they were well aware of the cameras everywhere inside and outside the property, so she had only to check the footage to assure herself they did nothing but clean. Plus, they'd known of her ever since she'd been living downstairs, so her presence upstairs had not changed the status quo of their job.

She was enjoying the scents in the garden, and anticipating the scents of lemon oil that came with the clean house as she hastened her steps, anxious to get inside and get back to the business of finding Rachel.

Charlie was in University Park with his GPS set on Allen Carson's address. He couldn't help but admire the size and the architecture of the homes he was passing, although they were never anything he had aspired to own. He'd learned the hard way that you can't buy the things that matter most in life.

When he finally reached the Carson residence, he pulled up into the circular drive, got out and hurried up the walk to the front door.

The chimes were still echoing as a middle-aged woman in a gray dress opened the door.

He handed her his card. "I'm Charlie Dodge. I'm here to pick up some blueprints."

"Oh, yes, sir. One moment, please," she said and retraced her steps to a hall table a few feet away, picked up two large cardboard tubes and brought them back to him. "Here you are, Mr. Dodge. Have a good evening."

"Tell Mr. Carson I said thank you. We'll return them in a timely fashion," Charlie said and headed back to his Jeep.

He laid them in the backseat and then got in. It was going to take a good forty-five minutes to get home to Wyrick, so he sent her a text to let her know he was on his way, and then left the residence.

The FBI had wasted no time sharing Wyrick's info with the Louisiana division of the ATF, who already had Preston Davis in their sights for other crimes.

After going through the info, the FBI got an arrest warrant for Jeremiah Raver for money laundering, along with a search warrant for his home and for the church. And because the crime had crossed state lines, the FBI had also filed charges against him for ordering the hit on Jade Wyrick.

Special Agent Raines was nervous about the timing. The last time Wyrick gave them info, it was about the Fourth Dimension, and it had been destroyed before they could get to the main man. She had to destroy herself to take them down, and he regretted it.

But he knew there was an FBI team in Louisiana already en route to Jeremiah's residence to serve the warrants, and he had a friend on the team who promised to let him know when Raver was in custody.

Four shiny black SUVs drove up into the yard at the residence of Jeremiah Lee Raver. The first thing they saw was a car with the trunk up, and the backseat full of items.

Agent Vance of the Louisiana FBI was in charge, and he was antsy.

All he wanted was to make a clean arrest and get in and out without a problem. They got out in haste, with weapons drawn as they headed for the house, and then stopped short as they saw the body, crawling with bugs, and the black pool of blood that had soaked into the earth beneath it, and the suitcases, one on either side of him.

"Son of a bitch. That looks like our man," Vance said and immediately realized they could be targets, as well, and turned to his team. "You three, check the perimeter. You two, check the back of the house." Then he glanced at the agent standing beside him. "Call it in. The rest of you follow me."

The agents who'd gone into the tree line had already found where the shooter had been standing. There was a wrapper from a candy bar, and the crushed stub of a cigarette that they marked as evidence, then left it for the crime scene team to bag and tag. They trailed the shooter's tracks back to the road, but there were too many tire tracks to discern what he might have been driving, so they headed back toward the house.

Once Vance and his team were satisfied that the house was empty, they moved through the rooms, careful not to disturb what might become evidence.

One of the first things they found were the computers in the office.

"We already know the website is down, and he likely deleted incriminating files, but the techs might get something from the hard drive."

"I found an address book," one of the agents said. "There are several people with the same last name."

"Get the info," Vance said. "We'll have to call next of kin."

The agent took pictures of the pages, and then left the address book where he'd found it. After that, they went back outside and stood around their vehicles, waiting for the medical examiner and their team from the crime lab to arrive.

Vance was walking around the exterior of the house when he glanced up at the underside of the eaves in front of the house, then stopped.

"Langdon! You and Evers go back into the house and see if

you can find access to the attic. I think I see a security camera up here. It's aimed straight toward the area where the shooter would have been standing. Maybe we'll get lucky."

Glad to have something to do, both agents headed back into the house, and minutes later Evers came running out.

"Security camera in the attic," he said.

Vance hurried inside.

"Access is a pull-down ladder in the hall," Evers said.

Vance hated spiders, and this was Louisiana, but he wanted answers.

"Is there a light?"

"Yes, sir," Evers said. "Langdon is still up there. Watch your head. It has a floor, but it's too low to stand up in."

Vance grabbed on to the handrails and started climbing, emerging into the shallow rafters. He leaned over as he walked to where Langdon was kneeling.

"What've we got?" Vance asked.

Langdon looked up and grinned.

"We got ourselves a shooter. The image is a little blurry, but the lab techs should be able to clean it up some."

"I want enough to run through facial recognition," Vance said.

"Is this the only security camera up here?" Vance asked.

"Yes, sir," Langdon said.

"Then we got lucky," Vance said. "Leave everything as is. The lab will go through the footage."

They were climbing down from the attic when they heard a shout from outside.

"I think the ME is here," Evers said.

Within an hour the team from the crime lab arrived. A couple of them went into the woods to where the shooter stood, photographed the scene and the footprints, then collected the evidence, while other members were inside, collecting the camera from the attic and carrying out the computer. The car was towed for processing.

The ME had put the time of death sometime yesterday, but the security footage would likely verify that. They bagged Raver's body, loaded it into a van and headed for their morgue.

"Shut up the house and tape up the doors," Vance said.

"You can't see the house from the road, so do you want crime scene tape at the road, as well?" Evers asked.

"Yes. And let's get the team and head up the road to the church."

"Shit. I forgot all about that," Langdon said.

Vance shrugged. "It's doubtful he'd put incriminating evidence there, but we have the search warrant. We need to get into his office, and if necessary, confiscate computers there, too. Langdon, you drive. I need to make a phone call as we go."

As Agent Langdon slid behind the wheel, Vance took the passenger seat and made a call to Hank Raines.

Hank was in jeans and a sweatshirt, grilling burgers on his patio. He could hear his wife arguing with one of the kids, and then sudden silence. He grinned. She could shut down an argument as fast as any woman he'd ever known. She was little, but mighty. She was also the love of his life, and the hub of their family.

He raised the grill lid to turn the burgers, and as he did a brief gust of wind blew smoke in his eyes. He turned to the side, blinking to clear his vision, and as he did his phone rang.

When he saw it was Billy Vance, he answered quickly.

"Hey, Billy. How did it go?" Hank asked.

"Well, Raver is dead. Someone took him out yesterday, before we ever got there. We may have some footage from a security camera to point us to the shooter, but it was a hit, for sure.

One shot right between the eyes from fifty yards. I'm guessing his business partners got nervous."

"Dammit," Hank said and began flipping burgers as he talked. "So do you have enough for an arrest warrant on Raver's moneyman?"

"Preston Davis? Yes. That went to the ATF. Wyrick gave us more than enough. I only know the woman by reputation, but she's freaking amazing. Tell her if she ever wants a job, she's got one with us," Vance said.

Hank sighed. "She's not agent material."

"Why the hell not?" Vance asked.

"Because she doesn't give a rat's ass about rules."

Vance laughed. "Copy that. Anyway, we're still on the job, so I've got to go. Thanks again for the info. We owe you."

"We both owe Wyrick," Hank said. "I hate being beholden to that woman. She's brilliant, but she's scary as hell. I don't ever want to make her mad again."

"That sounds like a story," Vance said.

"Someday…over barbecue and beers," Hank said. "Thanks for calling."

Then he took up the burgers and headed inside, and none too soon. The sky had clouded up out of nowhere, and he could already smell rain.

The raid wasn't a total bust. Raver was dead, and his followers were already trying to deny their connections to him and the church. Hopefully, this would keep Wyrick safe—at least for now. As soon as they had their dinner, Hank called Charlie to let him know.

Charlie was in the formal dining room with the blueprints spread out all over the long cherrywood table, checking original measurements of the Detter House against the newer ones, looking for things that didn't add up.

Wyrick was in the office, still running background checks on the current residents. He'd set the timer on his phone to keep track of the time on the frozen lasagna he had baking, but he was hungry, and left the blueprints to check on the food.

He opened the oven to bubbly, lightly browned, cheesy goodness, just as the timer went off on his phone. He took the lasagna out of the oven, set it aside to cool, then turned off the oven.

Since dinner was his job for the rest of the week, he pulled a bag of salad mix out of the refrigerator, dumped it in a bowl, dressed it and put it on the table, then sent Wyrick a text.

Dinner is served, m'lady.

Wyrick heard the ding signaling a text and glanced at her phone, saw it was from Charlie, read it, then saved what she was doing and went to wash up.

Charlie was digging flatware out of a drawer when Wyrick walked in.

"Smells good. I'm starving," she said.

Charlie eyed her fresh face, devoid of makeup, the old Dallas Cowboys shirt she was wearing, and the black leggings beneath it, and carried forks back to the table.

"You've got some long legs to fill up," he said and handed her a fork. "Dig in."

"You, who has a forty-inch inseam, feels the need to discuss long legs," she drawled, then picked off a piece of crusty cheese from the side of the pan and popped it into her mouth.

Charlie wondered how she knew the length of his inseam, then shrugged it off.

Another timer went off. He pulled a sheet pan of toasted garlic bread from the broiler and carried it to the table.

They were in the midst of filling their plates when Charlie's phone rang. He started to let it go to voice mail, and then saw who was calling.

"It's Hank. I better take this," he said.

"Give him my love," Wyrick drawled.

Charlie was laughing when he answered.

"This is Charlie."

"Hey, Charlie… Hank here. I have news. Is Wyrick anywhere around?"

"Why, yes, she's right here. We're just about to have dinner."

"Put the phone on speaker, okay?"

"Sure. Just a sec," Charlie said, punched a button and then set the phone on the table between them. "Okay…we're here," Charlie said.

"Good evening, Wyrick. Sorry to interrupt dinner, but this is information that will interest you."

"I'm listening," she said and took a bite of lasagna.

"The Louisiana FBI went to serve arrest and search warrants on Jeremiah Raver and found his body in the front yard. I won't go into details, but we suspect Preston Davis took offense at the sudden onslaught of publicity, and thought by taking Raver out, no one would find out about the connection between them. Of course, thanks to you, the ATF already has it. I don't know anything about the two other men he sent after you, but once they find out what happened to their leader, I'm thinking they're all going to find the biggest rock to crawl under."

"I believe that's what you call, 'reaping what you sow,'" Wyrick said and reached for a slice of garlic bread.

"Yes, ma'am. Well, that's all I have to share. I hope this is a relief to you, and hasn't upset the dinner you and Charlie are having," Hank said.

"I'm not upset," she said. "Charlie, are you upset?"

"I'm not upset," Charlie said.

"Shit happens and then you die," Wyrick said. "Thanks for calling."

"Are we done?" Charlie asked.

Hank sighed. "Yes. Enjoy your meal," and he disconnected.

Charlie pushed his phone aside and began filling his plate.

"You okay?" he asked.

Wyrick looked up. "Yes. Why wouldn't I be? Raver was the one playing God."

Charlie relaxed. It was what he wanted to hear.

"I haven't found anything on the blueprints yet, but I just got started. What about you? Anything interesting popping on the residents?"

"Nothing yet. I have a couple of searches yet to run."

Charlie winced as a rumble of thunder rolled over the old mansion. "That sounds like we're in for some rain tonight."

"Into each life, some rain must fall," Wyrick said and then rolled her eyes. "I'm just full of parables tonight."

"How about filling up on salad instead?" he said and pushed the bowl toward her.

She looked up. "That was a good one. If I had an eyebrow, I'd arch it. There's hope for you yet."

Charlie didn't like it when she made fun of how she looked.

"Eyebrows are overrated," he said.

Wyrick appreciated the comment and served herself some salad.

Except for the occasional clink of fork to plate, or the clink of ice in a glass, quiet ensued.

CHAPTER NINE

Sonny rubbed his hand across the front of his sweatpants, testing the tenderness in his crotch. He was done with the game and Rachel Dean. He wanted to clean out his little playroom and forget this ever happened.

It wasn't an issue to finish her off tonight, but it would be an issue getting her body out of that room and into his car without hurting himself all over again. He was still considering his options when he heard a big rumble of thunder.

Shit. If it rained, he couldn't get to the burying grounds. Maybe he should just wait another night. He'd be that much stronger, and if it rained enough it would make digging easier.

Thunder rumbled again, and this time bringing with it the wind and the rain. That did it. He gave up the notion and headed to the kitchen to make himself some dinner. He wasn't much of a cook, but he loved chicken potpies, so he took one out of the freezer and popped it into the oven.

Potpie for him.

One more night on earth for her.

★ ★ ★

Rachel didn't know it was night. She didn't know it was rain-ing. But her situation was real. Sometime in the past few hours she'd awakened from a nightmare of fever-driven hallucina-tions, desperate for a drink of water. But instead of following the wall at the foot of the mattress, she forgot where she was, went the wrong way and, with one shoe on and one shoe off, walked across the floor of broken glass.

The shock and then pain of the shards going through the sock and into her foot made her fall. Instinctively, she reached out to catch herself and wound up on her hands and knees in even more of the glass. There was nowhere to walk, nowhere to crawl. She was trapped in the dark that she'd created. Sad to the bone, she rocked back on her heels, threw back her head and screamed.

She was past the prayers. Past making promises about what she'd do with her life if God would just save her. All she wanted now was for it to be over. She didn't know if they'd ever find her body, which made her sad for Millie. But more than any-thing else, she wanted to be dead before Sonny came back. She didn't want to give him the satisfaction of doing it. If she hadn't lost the damn knife, she'd take herself out.

"Don't I matter to anyone? Isn't there one fucking person even looking for me?" Rachel sobbed, then cried until she couldn't breathe.

After a while a resigned calm came to her. The total dark-ness in which she sat was the only safety net between her and Sonny. If he never came back, she would die, but he'd never touch her alive again. And if he did come back, he would be at a disadvantage, because he would not be expecting the darkness.

She also accepted she couldn't stay here forever, so she began brushing away the bits of glass around her. Once she had a space free of glass big enough to sit in, she eased herself down and began picking glass out of her hands, and then her knees, then she felt along the bottom of her sock, pulling out the shards as she went.

Once she was satisfied that she'd done all she could do, she rolled back over onto her hands and knees and felt her way around the room until she found the mattress, then finally found the door.

Reoriented to the direction she was facing, she then made her way to the sink and let the water run free between her fingers until she was satisfied the glass debris had washed away.

Then she leaned over, resting her forearms on the sides of the sink; she cupped her hands, caught enough water to sluice across her face and on the festering sore at her neck, before drinking from the flow.

But when she pulled down her pants at the toilet and felt more glass in her knees, she stayed seated and by feel alone, began picking it out. She could feel blood on her fingers and on her knees, and got back up and washed herself off again, shaking from exhaustion.

Once she got back to her mattress, she crawled back into the corner, then sat with her knees pulled up beneath her chin, and her back against the wall. Her belly growled. From the rumble in her stomach, she guessed it had been more than twenty-four hours since Sonny's last visit.

She knew she'd hurt him.

She hoped it was permanent.

And then she closed her eyes.

In time, her fever turned to chills, waking her again. She needed to find the blanket and began crawling around the mattress, trembling and shaking, and found the knife instead.

The feel of it in her hands gave her courage and strength of purpose, and so she tightened her grip and kept crawling and patting the mattress top until she felt the fuzzy warmth.

Clutching it to her as if she'd just found the Holy Grail, she wrapped the blanket around her, then curled up, making herself as small as she could, with the knife clutched tightly in both hands.

The leftover lasagna from Wyrick and Charlie's dinner had long since been put away, and the dishes were done.

He was back examining the blueprints, and she was in the office. Except for the wind and rain blowing against the windows, the old mansion was quiet.

All of a sudden, Charlie heard Wyrick's footsteps running up the hall toward him. Before he could react, she was standing in the doorway.

"You will not fucking believe what I just found!"

Charlie blinked. "I cannot believe you just said *fucking*."

She shrugged. "I know more curse words. Do you want to hear them, or would you rather find Rachel Dean?"

"Sorry. It was just a surprise. Talk to me," Charlie said.

"Rachel Dean is not the first woman to go missing from Detter House. She's the fourth. Over a period of eleven years."

"Holy shit! Why didn't the police—?"

"I don't think anyone's connected the dots yet," Wyrick said. "The first one who disappeared had no family. Same story, more or less with two more, and neither one of them had family who would have been concerned. But here's the kicker. There hasn't been any activity on their social security numbers since. Not job-wise or otherwise. Rachel Dean is the only one with a living family member who is raising a fuss."

"Were they reported as missing persons?" Charlie asked.

Wyrick nodded. "Initially, yes, and then the cases were closed later after the women were supposedly accounted for."

"We call Detective Floyd first thing tomorrow," Charlie said.

"We also need to go back to Detter House tomorrow. Have you found anything on the old blueprints?" Wyrick asked.

"No, but that only means that if passages were built into the structure, they just didn't want it known," he said.

"Okay, then. We'll deal with that tomorrow. I'm going to wash my hair and go to bed now," Wyrick said and strode out of the room as abruptly as she'd arrived.

Wash her hair. Charlie sighed. She was the most aggravating, most intriguing, most brilliant woman he'd ever known. And she made him crazy, so there was that.

Preston Davis was resting easy now. The man he'd sent to Raver's house had completed the task without issue. But Raver's death also presented another problem. Now he was going to have to find another avenue to funnel his excess cash besides through his own bank. Compared to a lot of others in the business, Preston was small-time. He didn't deal in military weapons, or anything in large quantities. Just weapons taken in robberies that needed to be fenced. He knew people. He'd figure it out. But for now he was backing off.

As it was nearing sunset, he poured himself a double shot of whiskey, picked up his handgun and carried them out onto the veranda. He liked rural Louisiana, just not the swampy parts, and he'd lived out here on his grandpa's land for almost ten years now, ever since the old man's passing, but there was always a snake somewhere waiting to be dispatched, and he hated snakes.

The old antebellum house was smaller than a mansion, but far grander than the simple houses in the surrounding area, and he'd spent most of his youth working for a stockbroker in Charleston before retiring here. He often missed the conveniences of the West Virginia capital, but not enough to want to live there.

He slipped into a wooden rocker, shifted until he was facing west. Then he laid the handgun on the table beside him, took a sip of his whiskey and settled in to watch the end of this day.

A big blue heron flew across his line of vision, and he could already hear the night birds starting to call. He took another sip, wondering what he was going to make for his dinner, when he heard the sounds of vehicles approaching.

He frowned. He wasn't in the mood for company, even though it wasn't unusual for the friends he had to drop in without notice. He took another sip, then set his whiskey on a table and stood up. Out of habit, he slipped his handgun in the back of his waistband and headed for the front yard.

The wraparound porch afforded him the luxury of moving from back to front without going through the house, and he was all the way around the corner and moving toward the front door when he saw the first black SUV.

The windows were tinted, so he couldn't see the driver, but when a second vehicle appeared, and then a third, his heart skipped a beat.

He'd bet his life these were Feds.

Damn Jeremiah Raver to the hellfire and brimstone he preached.

Even before they got out, he was weighing his options.

Did he run?

Did he want to shoot it out and die on the land of his ancestors?

Or did he want to take his chances in court?

Because he knew in his gut he was going to jail.

And then the agents spilled out and headed toward the house with their weapons in their hands.

"ATF! ATF! Put your hands in the air! Put your hands in the air!"

And just like that, Preston's decision was made. He reached behind his back, and when they saw the gun in his hands, they opened fire.

Preston died on the front porch from a gunshot wound to the chest, just as his great-great-great-grandfather had died during the War of Northern Aggression.

Tradition mattered here.

It was, after all, the South.

Early the next morning Special Agent Vance arrived at his office, set down his Starbucks coffee, the one daily indulgence he allowed himself, then eased into his chair and combed his fingers through his hair.

Preston Davis was dead. He'd gotten the message last night on his way home from the office, and immediately sent Hank Raines a text with the info of what had happened.

Billy Vance knew that the ATF team had spent hours collecting evidence at Preston's home. Enough to bring down a whole ring of thieves he'd been doing business with. But notifying Davis's family of the death was not his job. That went to the team who'd gone to serve the warrant. Billy had the Raver family to notify and he was dreading it.

He hated death notifications, but they were part of the job, and after going through the address book they'd found at Raver's house, it hadn't taken much research to find out that Samuel Raver, who was the first name listed under R, was Jeremiah's older brother. So he took a quick sip of his coffee, then punched in the numbers and waited as it began to ring.

Maisie Raver was in the kitchen frying bacon.

The scent was one of Samuel's favorite things in the world, and he was anticipating the breakfast she was making as he finished his shave. When he heard his phone begin to ring, he turned off the water, wiped his hands and ran back into the bedroom. He grabbed the phone from the nightstand, glanced at caller ID and then sat down on the side of the bed before his knees went out from under him.

"Hello?"

"Hello, this is Special Agent Vance, of the Federal Bureau of Investigation. May I speak to Samuel Raver?"

"I'm Samuel."

"Mr. Raver, I'm sorry to disturb you this early in the morning, but it is my duty to inform you that your brother, Jeremiah, is deceased."

Samuel's heart sank, but guilt swirled with the shock, because he also felt a measure of relief that worrying for him was over. He cleared his throat a couple of times before he got himself together enough to speak.

"I'm sad, but I can't say I didn't see this coming," Samuel said.

"When was the last time you spoke to him?" Vance asked.

"He was here for a few hours two days ago, I think. He wanted to stay, but we told him we didn't want his troubles. I told him we'd pray for him. He left. Why is the FBI involved, and how did he die? Did y'all kill him?"

"No, we didn't kill him, but we did go to his house to serve arrest and search warrants, and found him deceased in his yard. He'd been shot."

Samuel groaned. "Lord, Lord, Lord, I feared something like this, but hearing the words just breaks my heart. Do you know who did it? Do you think it has anything to do with that woman he threatened?"

"Inadvertently, maybe. She had nothing to do with his death. But his public desire to see her dead likely called too much attention to himself. It appeared he was packing up to leave. The trunk was up. The car was about half-full of stuff, and there were two packed suitcases beside his body."

Samuel's eyes were full of tears, but he kept thinking, if he hadn't told Jeremiah to leave, whoever killed him might have come to their house looking for him and killed Samuel and Maisie, too.

"What were y'all going to arrest him for?"

Vance hesitated, but the facts would soon be public knowledge. "Money laundering and threatening bodily harm."

Samuel groaned. It was just as he and Maisie had feared.

"Do you know who killed him?" Samuel asked.

"Sorry, this is an ongoing case. I can't say more."

"When do we claim the body?" Samuel asked.

"Someone will call you when the ME releases it. I'm very sorry for your loss," Vance said and disconnected.

Samuel was in shock. He didn't know what the hell Jeremiah had been mixed up in, but he had to call the rest of the family and give them the news.

He got up from the bed, finished shaving and then went to find Maisie. She was his rock, and the calm in every storm life had ever brought to him.

When he walked into the kitchen, she turned around, smiling. Then she saw the look on his face, remembered hearing the phone ring and took the bacon off the stove.

"What's wrong?" she asked.

And so he told her.

The people in the community where Jeremiah lived had seen the black SUVs with the government tags. They'd also seen a van with the medical examiner emblem on the door. They put two and two together and got nine, and while Samuel, who lived way out in the bayou, was just receiving the official word of his brother's death, most of his parishioners already had it figured out before they'd gone to bed the night before.

They didn't know exactly what had happened, but they were ready to blame the government—until the morning news. It appeared their guesstimates were wrong.

The Feds had found him dead when they came to serve an arrest warrant—to a preacher—for money laundering.

Holy shit became the phrase of the day.

★ ★ ★

Since the Church of The Righteous was beginning to crumble, it affirmed a decision that Jordy Gooch, Jessup Wallis's drinking buddy, had been wrestling with ever since he'd heard about the quarter of a million dollar bounty.

Granted, Jessup was drunk when he told Jordy that the preacher was sending him on a holy quest to kill a demon, but in Jordy's mind, that just made him mean *and* stupid.

Then he'd seen the video and put two and two together, and he'd still stayed mum. But with Raver dead, Jordy wanted that money. He'd always wanted to live where it snowed. He'd seen it once when he was a kid, and never forgot. He could get good and lost with a quarter of a million dollars, and never be judged for where he got it.

That video was still all over social media, with the contact info and everything. So he pulled it up on his phone and wrote it all down. Now all he needed was a picture of Jessup, and he had plenty. He just needed to find one where he wasn't drunk and laughing, then send it with the name.

Farrell Kitt was almost home. His panic to see his wife and his kids, and talk to Jeremiah, was uppermost. He was coming up on the church when he saw yellow crime scene tape across the driveway.

"Oh shit, oh shit, oh shit," he groaned.

He didn't know what had happened, but he stomped the accelerator to put as much distance between him and the church as possible. But to get home, he also had to pass where the preacher lived, and when he saw more crime scene tape at the road leading up to Jeremiah's house, his stomach rolled. It was all he could do not to throw up. Something bad had happened. Something worse than the bounty on his head. He was afraid to go home for fear the cops would be waiting for him, and pulled off the side of the road to call Judy. He needed to hear her voice.

It only rang once before Judy answered.

"Where are you?"

"About ten minutes from home. I just drove by the church and Jeremiah's house, and there's crime scene tape everywhere. What the hell happened?"

Judy started crying. "It's just awful. The FBI came to serve warrants on Jeremiah for money laundering, and found him shot dead in the front yard."

Farrell gasped. "What? Money laundering? But—"

"That's not all. Jessup Wallis's girlfriend, Britta, already put Jessup out of her house. His things were all over her porch. I don't know if he's come back to get them, but everyone is pointing fingers at him being one of Raver's chosen."

"What are they sayin' about me?" Farrell asked.

"Nothing that I know of," Judy said. "Your brother David came over this morning to borrow the tractor. He got himself stuck up in his back pasture. He asked where you were, and I said you'd gone into the city for a doctor's appointment, and that you'd be home later today."

"A doctor's appointment? What's supposed to be wrong with me?" Farrell asked.

"I told him you'd been feeling dizzy a lot, and I pressured you into getting a checkup. You know how high blood pressure runs in your family. It was all I could think of."

"Yeah, yeah, that's good. Oh, God, Judy... I'm so sorry I got mixed up in this."

"Just get your ass home," she said.

Farrell put the car back in gear and accelerated, but there was no way to outrun the mistake that he'd made.

It was just before 8 a.m. when Charlie walked into the kitchen. He made himself a cup of coffee, then sat down at the kitchen table to call Detective Floyd, and then his phone rang. It was Hank Raines.

"Good morning, Hank. You're up early."

"Yes, just one of those days," Hank said. "I have an update for you. The ATF went to serve an arrest warrant on Preston Davis, who likely instigated the hit on Raver, hoping to cut the link between them before anyone found out. He resisted arrest and pulled a gun on six armed ATF agents. Needless to say, he's dead. And it is my understanding that the info they confiscated is leading to the arrests of the people Davis had been doing business with."

"Good," Charlie said.

"No problem. Have a good day," Hank said and hung up.

Charlie reached for the notes Wyrick had given him, and called Detective Floyd. The call rang three times, and then he answered.

"Detective Floyd, Dallas PD."

"Hey, Floyd, this is Charlie Dodge. Got a minute?"

"Yes, of course. I was just getting in the car to head to the precinct. What's up?"

"Wyrick was running searches last night and made quite a discovery. Something you may not be aware of."

"Like what?" Floyd asked.

"Rachel Dean isn't the first woman to go missing from the Detter House. She's the fourth. The first one was eleven years ago."

"No way!" Floyd said. "We would have picked up on this ourselves if—"

"Let me finish," Charlie said and laid out what Wyrick had told him, giving him the names of the women and the dates they went missing. But it was the inactive social security numbers for all three of the women that made the case for Wyrick's theory.

"Oh, man. This isn't good," Floyd said. "I've only been with

Missing Persons three years. I was in Homicide before that, so I had no personal info on any of these other cases. I'll pull them immediately. I need to see why they closed the cases and start verifying the inactive numbers."

"We're going back to Detter House soon. Wyrick strongly believes there has to be some kind of hidden passage built into the old structure, and I learned a long time ago not to doubt her instincts."

"Is she really psychic?" Floyd asked. "Don't get me wrong… I'm not discounting her. But I've also never known anyone like her."

"That's because there *is* no one else like her," Charlie said. "If we find out anything new, I'll call."

He disconnected, then laid the phone aside and was getting up to make himself some breakfast when Wyrick entered the kitchen.

"Going in low-key today, I see," he said. "Want a peanut butter and jelly sandwich? I'm gonna make myself one."

She ignored his dig about the silver cat suit and red knee-high boots she was wearing.

"Do we have grape jelly?" she asked.

He nodded.

"Then, yes, I will have a PBGJ, but just one, thank you."

He grinned as she went to make coffee.

PBGJ. Peanut butter and grape jelly. Perfectly Wyrick being perfectly specific.

"I called Detective Floyd. He was understandably shocked and is going to pull the old case files today. I told him we were going back to Detter House," Charlie said.

She nodded as he spoke, but she was watching him making sandwiches, too.

"Uh… Could I have the grape jelly on one side, and the peanut butter on the other?" she asked.

"Yes," he said and never missed a beat.

"Um, you're using creamy peanut butter," she said.

He paused. "Yes."

"If we have crunchy, I would prefer that," she added.

Charlie took a deep breath. "I'll check."

She nodded, then retrieved her cup of coffee from the Keurig and sat down at the table to watch the final construction, knowing full well she was aggravating Charlie Dodge's last nerve.

Finally, the sandwiches were finished, and Charlie plated them up and carried them to the table.

"You didn't cut mine," Wyrick said.

Charlie turned, grabbed a paring knife from the knife block and stabbed it into the center of her sandwich.

"Knock yourself out," he said.

Wyrick hid a grin, then proceeded to cut her sandwich in four squares.

"Hank Raines called this morning. The ATF was serving an arrest warrant on Preston Davis yesterday when he pulled a gun on them. He's dead."

"Cowards always choose the easy way out," she said and stuffed one whole square into her mouth.

Charlie smirked. "Such a dainty little thing you are," he said.

Wyrick chewed and swallowed, then licked a smear of peanut butter from her thumb. She was reaching for another piece when her phone rang. But it was the "Hallelujah" chorus ringtone that startled Charlie and sent Wyrick bolting from her chair.

"What?" he yelled.

"Someone just named one of the hit men. I have to check my email," she said and ran.

She was gone in a flash of silver, the click of her heels marking her speed as she bolted down the hall. But Charlie wanted to see the man's face, because her enemies were his enemies.

Wyrick had the email open, sitting motionless at the monitor, staring at a face.

"Is that one of them?" Charlie asked.

"Maybe…probably," she said.

"What's his name?"

"Jessup Wallis," she said, then switched screens and pulled up a file listing the members of the Church of The Righteous. "His name is on the list of members."

"How can you prove he's one of the three who were sent?" Charlie asked.

"I hacked into Jeremiah Raver's phone records when I was making the case for money laundering. Most of the calls on his phone were from parishioners, or Preston Davis. But after Barrett Taylor tried to kill me, I checked Raver's phone records again. There were three new numbers he'd never called before, but they were local to Raver's area—and made within the past week. One of them belonged to Barrett Taylor, and I already knew he was hit man number one. Then Raver had a call from the Dallas County Jail right after Barrett Taylor was arrested. I assumed it was a plea for Raver to get him a lawyer. So that verified one of those three numbers did belong to a hit man. I ran a search on the other two numbers. One belonged to a man named Jessup Wallis." She pointed to the screen. "And that is Jessup Wallis. The man who turned him in is a man named Jordy Gooch. Gooch does not belong to the church, but is a local in Paulette. I'll have to do some research to make sure he's no relation, but I think I just got number two."

"Location-wise, do you know where Wallis is?" Charlie asked.

"Now that I know which number is his, I enter it into my locator."

"If he's in Dallas, then that means you're still in danger," Charlie said.

"He's not in Dallas. Neither of them are," Wyrick said.

"How can you be so sure?" Charlie asked.

"If they've been notified about the video, they'll both be worried about who knew what they were doing, and who might turn them in. They'll be looking for a place to hide, and to deny, deny, deny the accusations."

"Are you going to stay here in the office for a while?" he asked.

"No. Rachel Dean takes precedence over this. I'm just sending an email to Jordy Gooch, telling him verification is in progress. I'll be back in the kitchen in a sec. Don't eat my PBGJ."

"As if," Charlie said. He looked long and hard at the photo again and then left.

Wyrick paused, pulled up one of her apps, entered Jessup Wallis's cell number, then waited for a cell tower to pick up on it. It took a few minutes, but when it did she relaxed and logged out.

Once she got back to the kitchen to finish breakfast, they talked about the pending search, but neither mentioned Rachel's name. The days since she'd gone missing were passing, and neither they nor the police had a clue as to what had happened to her. Charlie had promised Millie he'd find Rachel, but he didn't want to find her dead.

As Wyrick carried their cups and plates to the sink, Charlie reached for his phone.

"I'm giving the manager a heads-up that we're coming back this morning, so he'll be there to give us a key."

"Good idea," Wyrick said and loaded the dirty dishes into the dishwasher. "I'm going to get my laptop. I'll be right back."

She hurried away as Charlie made the call, and then waited for it to be answered.

CHAPTER TEN

Wayne was in the office calling a plumber when the door opened. One of the residents walked in, and Wayne held up a hand then pointed to a chair while he finished his call. As soon as he hung up, he turned and smiled.

"Sorry about that, Sonny. What's up?"

"I have an Amazon delivery that's supposed to arrive today. If you'll text me when it arrives, I'll come pick it up."

"I'll keep an eye out for it," Wayne said and then looked a little closer at him. "You don't look so good. Have you been sick?"

"No…nothing like that. But I fell the other day and haven't been sleeping well. I'm getting better, but you know when your back goes out, it hurts like hell no matter how you stand or sit, right?"

Wayne frowned. "I'm so—" Then his cell phone rang. When he saw who was calling, he grabbed it. "Hang on a second. I need to answer this."

Sonny nodded, then picked up a magazine as Wayne answered.

"Detter House. Wayne Dyer speaking."

"Wayne, it's Charlie Dodge."

"Yes, hello, Charlie. What can I do for you?" he said.

"Wyrick and I need access to the apartment again. Can we pick up the key at your office?"

"Sure. Are you coming this morning?" Wayne asked.

"Yes. We'll be there within the hour."

"See you then," Wayne said and hung up, then glanced at Sonny. "Sorry. That was Charlie Dodge again. He and his assistant are working for Rachel Dean's family, you know…trying to help the police find her."

Sonny frowned. "It's so awful. Do they have any leads?"

"I have no idea," Wayne said.

Sonny leaned forward, resting his elbows on the arms of the chair. "His assistant is that Wyrick woman, right?"

Wayne nodded. "Yes. They were here yesterday morning, but not for long. I guess they want to take a closer look or something…who knows?"

"Is she as stunning as she looked on TV?" Sonny asked.

Wayne shrugged. "She's very tall and quite striking. A most unusual woman, would be a better way to describe her."

"I see…well, I'm going to be running some errands in a bit, so I may miss seeing her. Just my luck. Anyway…thanks for holding my delivery for me. I'll be waiting for your text."

"Of course," Wayne said and waved as Sonny left the office, then got the passkey so he'd have it ready.

Sonny left the office in a panic. He'd had no idea the famous duo was on the case. If she was as psychic as they claimed, she might see guilt all over him, maybe even without needing his presence. He couldn't let that happen. But he needed to set up an alibi, showing him leaving the property before Charlie and Wyrick ever arrived.

He made a point of waving at staff as he took the back way out of the building to the parking garage, then got in his car and drove out the front gate, making sure the security cameras would pick him up leaving the grounds.

But as soon as he was out of sight of the building, he circled the area, came back to the house through the alley behind it and parked next to the dumpster.

He came in the back gate, making a point to stay behind the old-growth crape myrtle concealing a brick garden shed that was original to the property. He slipped into the shed and went straight to the storage closet. The moment he walked in, an LED light came on.

He paused, listening, before pulling an old box of cleaning supplies aside, revealing the door in the floor and a set of steps leading down. A light came on as he descended, and when it did, he pulled the door shut above him. His heart was racing as he reached the floor below.

Knowing Rachel was behind the big metal door to his right was tempting. But he didn't have time to deal with her, and so he just kept running, down the long passageway, up another set of stairs with a landing on the first floor, and another set of stairs that went up to the second.

Motion detector lights came on as he exited on the first floor passage, and headed for his apartment, anxious about what was ahead of him. He didn't have time to prepare as he normally would have, but the consequences of ignoring this could be disastrous.

Charlie drove them to Detter House in grim-lipped silence. Wyrick knew something was bothering him, and she hated secrets.

"You know you don't have to sulk. If you wanted my PBGJ sandwich, you could have had it."

Charlie frowned as he took an exit off the beltway.

"What the hell are you talking about?"

"Well, we were fine when we sat down to breakfast, and then you weren't. Once we get to Detter House, we need to be focusing on Rachel, not something else, so what's wrong?"

Charlie sighed. "It's not you. I just can't get that face out of my head."

"Face? What—you mean Jessup Wallis?"

Charlie nodded.

She rolled her eyes. "He's just another face to me, and they're all beginning to look alike."

"He's a threat," he muttered.

"No. I'm a threat to him now. And he's running, Charlie, I promise."

"How do you know that?" he asked.

"Because, after you left the office I entered his cell phone into my locator and pinged his current location. Not only is he not in Texas, he's not in Louisiana, either. He's halfway through Arkansas and northbound."

"Really?" Charlie said.

Wyrick rolled her eyes. "Yes, really. And as soon as we get home this evening, I will let the rest of the world see his face, then you won't be the only one responsible for me. Savvy?"

He nodded. "Sorry."

"No apology needed. I'm fine. We're working a case, and that's our focus. Not me. Deal?"

"Deal," Charlie said.

A few minutes later they arrived at Detter House, pulled into guest parking and went inside, then straight into the manager's office.

Wayne was at the computer when they entered.

"Hello again. Here's the key. Just call if you need anything."

Charlie palmed the key. "Thanks. We'll drop it off when we're done."

Charlie and Wyrick rode the elevator up to the second floor

again, heading to apartment 210 in the north wing. The yellow crime scene tape was still dangling from the side of the door as he unlocked it.

"Me first," Wyrick said.

Charlie stepped aside, then followed her in.

"What's your pleasure?" he asked.

"There can't be hidden access in the inner walls because they exit into the hall. And, according to the blueprints, nothing has been altered in the exterior walls. But there's something off. I can't tell what it is, but it doesn't feel right."

"What do you mean?" Charlie asked.

Wyrick paused. "Have you ever walked across a floor that had a slight slope?"

"Maybe, but—"

She frowned. "I'm not explaining this right. I felt it when we were here last time, but that headache distracted me. Right now we're standing here facing the hall leading into the kitchen, and the muscles in the backs of my legs are pulling, like I'm having to keep myself from falling forward."

"But the floor is flat. Level. I can see that," Charlie said. "I think it's just your Spidey senses on alert. How about I start checking out the living room, and you start in the kitchen. I'll join you shortly."

She nodded, but instead of going into the kitchen, something kept pulling her toward the bedroom at the end of the hall. Her footsteps were muffled by the carpeting as she passed a half bath, and the linen cabinet a few steps down. When she walked into the bedroom she paused, trying to figure out what was off about this room. She walked into the bathroom, then back out into the room and turned and stared at the bed again when it hit her. There were no windows anywhere in the master bed or bath.

She went back to the kitchen, and the window overlooking

the back of the property with a view of the grounds, the pool and one end of the parking garage.

She stood there a moment, thinking. The interior wall of the kitchen was even with the backside of the living room wall. And there couldn't be hidden accesses in the floor because of the residential living areas below.

At that point Charlie walked into the kitchen and saw her staring out the window.

"What?" he asked.

She turned. "Do you remember how many windows were on the back of the house on the original blueprints?"

Charlie thought a moment. "I know there were windows, but I didn't count them."

"Come look in the bedroom again," Wyrick said, then led the way into the room. "Now, tell me what's missing in here?"

He stood a moment, looking past the ornate furniture, the elegance of the old crown moldings and the tray ceiling above the bed, before he saw it.

"There aren't any windows!" Charlie said.

"Right. So who builds bedrooms without windows? Allen Carson said there were no physical alterations to the exterior of the old mansion when he turned it into apartments. So what's the deal here?"

"I'll call him right now," Charlie said, but when he reached for his phone, it wasn't in his jacket pocket. "My phone. I think I left it in the living room," he said and left the room.

Wyrick moved into the walk-in closet. The back wall was shelving. The clothes hanging on the racks were color-coded, and the shoe rack below was full of shoes. Nothing out of the ordinary.

She could hear Charlie's voice as she came out of the closet. He'd obviously found his phone and was talking to Allen Carson. Maybe he'd have answers.

She was standing with her hands on her hips, waiting for Charlie to return, when she had a sudden sense of danger. Before she could turn around, there was a sharp pain in the back of her neck. She was losing consciousness too fast to call out, but she knew when it was happening that this was exactly what had happened to Rachel Dean.

Sonny was in the old servants' passage, standing on the other side of the wall in Rachel's bedroom, waiting for Dodge and Wyrick to arrive.

He'd found the passage by accident right after he moved here, because there was one in his room. Once he knew it was there, he had to know where it went. Finding out it ran the entire length of the backside of the house was surprising, and then intriguing.

It occurred to him that, if there was a hidden access in his room, then there could be more in the other apartments, as well. So the entire first week of his residence, he began searching for more secret doors.

What he discovered was that some of the doors were now blocked because of the interior restructuring. But there were three other apartments in the building with access doors that still worked. After doing a little remodeling of his own, he had peepholes into those people's lives—a plus for the Peeping Tom fetish he'd developed during his teens.

As the apartments were leased, he'd had his own little behind-the-scenes playground. A safe place where he could jack off without being seen, watching them dressing and undressing, overhearing their phone conversations. Witnessing their fights with their lovers. Witnessing every intimate aspect of the residents' lives without their knowing it.

After a time he became so embroiled in their personal lives, that by the time he took his first woman, he had convinced himself that they were lovers. And it had worked. Perfectly. Until now.

He didn't know Rachel Dean had a sister. He'd gotten sloppy in his research. And now this was happening. He was alternating between being hyped beyond anything he'd ever felt, and scared out of his mind. There were too many variables and too many loose ends to enjoy this.

The sad part was not being able to play the game with Wyrick, but he couldn't let this go on. She'd figure it out. And he'd be toast. He also knew he couldn't take both of them down. All he could do was hope the opportunity arose when she'd be in the bedroom alone. He didn't need more than ten seconds to take her down and get her out.

The problem was going to be Charlie Dodge. He was a giant of a man skilled at finding lost people. He would not take kindly to losing his partner right under his own nose.

When he finally heard their voices inside the apartment, he tensed. The expectation of seeing Jade Wyrick in the flesh was a sensual high. The first time she walked into the bedroom, he got hard. And just watching her walk, seeing the glint in her eyes, he could only imagine how she was processing what she saw. And then she walked out before he had a good chance to come at her unobserved. He was silently cursing his luck when she and Charlie came back.

Looking at Charlie Dodge from up close and personal was intimidating. He was one big son of a bitch. Sonny had always wanted to be taller. But he'd had to settle for shoe lifts and toning up the rest of his body instead.

He was silently cursing the situation in general when Charlie suddenly left the room.

Yes!

He moved down a few steps, still waiting, watching...

Oh, God, let this happen...

Wyrick was standing in the room with her back to him as he pulled the syringe from his pocket, popped the cap and made his move.

Just like all of his other girls, she never heard him coming. He had the needle in her neck before she knew what was happening, and then she was on the floor.

He could hear Charlie talking in another room, and had no time to hesitate. Ignoring his own pain, he reached down to pull her up and throw her over his shoulder, but she was taller than he was, and all arms and legs.

Son of a bitch! He couldn't lift her!

Now he was in a panic. With only one option, he slid his hands beneath her arms and began dragging her into the closet, then into the passageway. He closed the door behind them, then began dragging her unconscious body down the passage, inches at a time.

Allen Carson answered Charlie's call on the second ring.

"Hello, Mr. Dodge. This is Allen. Do you have any news?" he asked.

"Not yet. Wyrick and I are in Rachel Dean's apartment and we noticed there are no windows in her bedroom. We know you said you did not change or alter the exterior of the building in any way, but it's strange not to have windows there. Did you, by chance, close them up?"

"No. It's just the way the floors got divided. We worked with the original windows, positioning them in the rooms that would be best served with exterior and interior light. There are several apartments that wound up that way, both in the front and the back. The windows are where they are. And anyone with an apartment on the backside may or may not have a window in their bedroom. The people who lease here always know in advance, and make their choices."

"Okay…that answers our question for now. Thanks a bunch," Charlie said.

"Anytime," Allen said.

Charlie walked out of the living room into the hall.

"Hey, Wyrick!" When she didn't answer, he thought nothing of it and just jogged back down the hall. "Wyrick! Allen said nothing was changed!"

Then he entered the bedroom and it was empty.

"Wyrick, answer me, dammit!"

Total silence.

Then he saw the drag marks in the carpet leading into the walk-in closet and his heart stopped.

"Oh, hell, no," he muttered and pulled up the tracking app for her that she'd put on his phone.

The blip came up moving south on this level. But that was away from him. Something she would never do without letting him know. Now his entire focus was on finding her.

The drag marks into the closet ended at the shelving, and he began pounding on walls, then pushing and pulling on shelves, trying to find a trigger to open an access, but nothing happened. Getting desperate, Charlie yanked everything from the shelves, then started kicking and tearing at the entire cabinet until it began coming apart.

Then he grabbed shelves with both hands, pulling at the wood, cutting his fingers and palms until they were bloody and slick, making it harder to get a grip. The blip was moving farther and farther, and panic set in. He began kicking at the wall, stomping it and kicking it until there was a hole.

When he saw light inside the access, he grabbed sheetrock, pulling it away in chunks, and then the plaster and lath behind it, pulling it away until what was left of the hidden door suddenly swung inward.

Seconds later Charlie was inside the passageway, running and shouting Wyrick's name.

Sonny was struggling.

Wyrick's dead weight was more than he had bargained for.

When he began hearing the shouting, and then the pounding, he began pulling harder, digging in his heels for leverage to move her faster, because Dodge knew she was gone.

When he paused to get a better grip, he felt her muscles tense beneath the pressure of his fingers.

No, no, no. This couldn't be happening! She was regaining consciousness! He had not used enough of the knockout drug for someone her size. This was turning into a serious cluster-fuck.

When he heard wood shattering, and then the sound of running feet, and Dodge shouting her name, he turned and ran, flying through the passage, down the stairs, then through the tunnel, past the room where Rachel was and then out of the shed, moving swiftly through the thicket of crape myrtles.

Once he was back in the alley, he headed for his car. His heart was hammering as he jumped in and sped away, taking the alley for two straight blocks before making his way to the beltway, then going straight for the Galleria.

Normally, he enjoying shopping at his favorite mall, but since he'd established his exit from Detter House earlier, this time he just needed to come home with purchases to tie up the alibi.

Charlie was still running and shouting Wyrick's name when he suddenly saw her on the floor ahead of him, her silver jumpsuit glittering beneath the light, like a diamond in the dirt. She was alone, and she wasn't moving. He could hear footsteps in the distance and wanted to give chase, but she was what mattered most.

Seconds later he was on his knees beside her, holding his breath as he felt for a pulse. Only after he found the slow, steady beat did he give himself permission to breathe.

"Thank you, God," he said softly and then began trying to wake her. "Wyrick! Can you hear me? Wake up, honey. Come on, wake up."

She moaned.

"Yes, yes, open your eyes. Come on, Jade. Look at me."

She moaned again, and at that point Charlie picked up his phone and called 911.

As soon as they were dispatched, he called the manager.

"Hello, this is Wayne. What's up, Charlie?"

"Wyrick was just attacked in Rachel Dean's bedroom. I've already called 911. When they arrive, get them up to her apartment."

"Oh, my God! Attacked? By who?"

"Likely whoever took Rachel."

"Lord, oh, Lord," Wayne cried. "Yes, yes, I'll take them straight up the moment they get here."

Then Charlie disconnected and made another call, this time to Detective Floyd.

Floyd and his partner were coming out of a meeting with their lieutenant about the closed cases of the three missing women.

After pulling the old files, they had discovered a letter in each file that had been sent to the Detter House manager, lightly explaining away a sudden decision to move. Asking that their clothing be donated. Of course, the manager quickly notified the police, turned over the letter and the case was closed. But when it happened again, there was a different manager, who had no knowledge of the first incident, and when he received a letter from the second woman with an explanation that she'd eloped, and he'd turned it over to the police, that case was also closed. When the third woman went missing the manager at that time had no knowledge of the other two incidents, and had received a similar notice. And that letter was turned over, and that case was closed. And in all three cases, different detectives within the department had worked the cases.

But after viewing the letters side by side, it was determined that the handwriting on all of the letters was the same. With the added fact of the inactivity of their social security numbers, a horrible truth was beginning to emerge. There was a serial killer right beneath their noses, taking women from the same address for the past eleven years and no one had seen it happening.

The current manager of Detter House had only been here three years, and Rachel was a relatively new resident. Neither of them would have had any knowledge of other women having gone missing, and had it not been for Jade Wyrick's attention to detail, they might never have seen this for what it was.

It was a shock to their lieutenant, and to the whole Missing Persons bureau.

They were still talking about the revelations when Floyd's cell phone rang. He glanced at it, frowning.

"It's Dodge again," he said and answered as they walked. "Hey, Charlie, what's up?"

"We're at Detter House. Wyrick was attacked and dragged into a hidden passage through a door in Rachel Dean's closet. There's no sign of a struggle, which leads me to think she was drugged. I've already called 911, but you're gonna need your team from the crime lab back in here stat. He left her in the passage and ran when he heard me coming. There has to be some DNA on her."

"Is she okay?" Floyd asked.

"I think so, but she's still unconscious. I'm waiting on the ambulance," Charlie said.

"We're on the way," Floyd said and hung up.

"What's going on?" Mills asked.

"Someone attacked Wyrick and was dragging her away through a hidden passage when Charlie found her. She's unconscious and the assailant fled."

"What about Rachel Dean? Did they find her?" Mills asked.

"I don't think so. He didn't mention her. Call it in. We're going to need the crime lab team again."

CHAPTER ELEVEN

Wyrick could hear Charlie's voice. Then it felt like she was floating. She didn't know that he was lifting her up, holding her tight against his chest.

They were moving now, but she couldn't think what had happened. All she could feel was the throbbing pain in her head and neck. She tried to talk, but the only thing that came out was a moan.

Charlie reacted to the sound by holding her tighter as he kept carrying her back.

"I'm here, honey. I'm here," he said. "You're safe. Just hang on. Help's coming."

Moments later he emerged from the passage, moving through the debris-filled closet and back into the bedroom, then he carried her to the bed, gently easing her down.

His fingers were still bloody, and now so was she. He wiped them on his jeans before checking her pulse.

When she moaned again, he ran the back of his hand down the side of her face, wanting her to feel human contact and hear his voice.

"You're safe, Jade. You're safe. I've got you, and whoever took you is gone."

She moaned again and then reached toward the back of her neck.

"What is it?" Charlie asked.

"Pain," she mumbled.

"Let me see," Charlie said and rolled her onto her side.

The red puncture mark was plainly visible. The bastard knew his stuff. Injection into a vein instead of a muscle could cause a victim to go into instantaneous unconsciousness.

"The bastard drugged you," Charlie said as he eased her back down.

"Gone?" she mumbled.

"Yes, but not for long," Charlie muttered.

Wyrick was desperately trying not to pass out again, but the drug was interfering with her ability to focus. She could hear Charlie's voice, but the words were all jumbled. All she knew was that he was here and she was safe, so she gave in to the darkness washing over her.

Charlie felt her sliding away. She went limp again, and it was just as well. Pain would not visit an unconscious victim.

Within a couple more minutes he began hearing sirens, then a few minutes later the sound of footsteps running in the outer hall, then into the apartment.

"In here!" he shouted.

Seconds later EMTs were pouring into the room, throwing questions at him as fast as they were working on her.

"What happened? Where's her wound?" one of them asked, while another was taking her vitals.

"The blood is mine," he said and showed them his hands.

One EMT frowned and started to reach into his bag.

"You tore them up pretty bad. You need to—"

"Just tend to her," Charlie said. "I'm fine. She was attacked in here," Charlie said. "I think she was injected with some kind of knockout drug. There's a red puncture mark on the back of her neck. Looks like a direct hit into her carotid. But she was dragged into a hidden passage behind that wall. I found her about fifty yards down. Just know that the police are going to want what she's wearing, to check for DNA."

They made notes of the info and began assessing her condition—blood pressure, pulse rate, checking her pupils for signs of a head injury, getting her ready to transport, and all Charlie could do was stand by, helpless to do anything but watch as they transferred her from the bed to a gurney.

"Where will you be taking her?" Charlie asked.

"Baylor Medical Center on Gaston Ave," they said.

And on that note, Detectives Floyd and Mills arrived.

Floyd stopped the EMTs as they were wheeling her toward the foyer.

"How is she?" Floyd asked.

"Stable. No obvious wounds other than a puncture mark on her neck. She'll be at Baylor Med. We have to go."

The detectives stepped aside and then saw Charlie right behind her, and the blood all over his hands and clothes.

"What the hell?" Floyd asked.

"I'm okay," Charlie said, then pointed back to the bedroom. "Go look in the closet. I found a hidden door with access into a passage behind the wall."

"How the hell did you find her?" Mills asked.

"We were in the bedroom. I needed to make a call, but I didn't have my phone. I left to go looking for it. Found it in the living room and made the call. When I came back here, she was gone. I saw drag marks in the carpet that led into the closet. I have an app on my phone that tracks her location. The blip was in motion, so I kicked in the wall until the hidden door opened on its own. I went in running, calling her name. Whoever took her must've heard me and took off. I could hear him running away as I got to her, but I don't know where he went. I gotta go. If you want more info, I'll be with her."

Then he went after the EMTs, leaving the detectives behind.

Floyd and Mills headed for the bedroom and were stunned by the hole Charlie had put in the wall.

"Holy shit! He tore that thing apart with his bare hands. No wonder they were bloody," Mills said, pointing to what was left of the shelves that had been concealing the passage.

"Well, now we know how Rachel Dean disappeared. What we don't know is where the hell she was taken," Floyd said.

"I want to see that passage," Mills said.

"I do, too," Floyd said. "But we'll have to wait for the team to go over it first. We don't want to screw up the possibility of recovering DNA in there. If he's been doing this for years, there should be prints and DNA galore."

"We've got those three other missing women to account for, too," Mills said. "We need to find out what happened to them, and hopefully find Rachel before it's too late."

Rachel's room was soundproof, so she'd heard nothing of what was happening. Most of the time she was unconscious, and the few times she came to, she was now too weak to get herself up for the water she craved.

She had moved past fear, and the idea of dying alone was no longer an issue. Her mother was with her all the time now. She heard her voice, saying the same thing every time. Telling her over and over... *Hold on, baby girl, hold on.*

So that's where she was.

Holding the knife.

Holding on to the blanket beneath her chin.

Trusting her mama's words with every beat of her heart.

Holding on.

★ ★ ★

Police were all over the premises, and everyone who'd had the misfortune to be home today was an immediate suspect.

Not only were they horrified at needing an alibi for their whereabouts during the attack, but they were also in a panic over finding out that there were hidden passages in the building, and fearing they might become the next victim was the last straw. Four of them had already called the office, demanding to be let out of their leases, and Wayne had no authority to tell them anything.

During the investigation Amazon delivered Sonny's package to the office. Wayne was up to his ears with panicked residents and assisting the police before he finally remembered to send Sonny a text.

Sonny responded with a quick thumbs-up emoji, and Wayne mentally marked off that task as done and made a phone call to the owner, Allen Carson.

The call rang and rang, and Wayne was sick to his stomach, afraid it was going to voice mail. He needed guidance here, and had no authority to proceed without it. Then his worries ended when Carson answered.

"Hello."

"Mr. Carson, this is Wayne Dyer. I'm the manager at Detter House."

"Oh, yes, hello, Wayne. What can I do for you?"

"Sir. We have a situation here. There was another attack. Two investigators were here in Rachel Dean's apartment, when one of them, Jade Wyrick, was abducted right out of the bedroom. Her boss, Charlie Dodge, found a hidden door in the walk-in closet that led to a secret passage. The man got away. Wyrick was taken to the hospital, and the place is crawling with cops. Residents are being asked to provide an alibi for where they were, and after learning that the secret passage goes all through the house, a bunch of them are already demanding to be re-leased from their leases."

"Oh, my God," Allen muttered. "So there *is* a secret passage?"

"Apparently," Wayne said. "What do I do?"

"I'll be there within the hour to speak to the police and to the residents. Just hang with me, Wayne. We'll figure this out."

"Yes, sir. Thank you," Wayne said.

The call ended. He leaned back in his chair, took a deep breath and then reminded himself that there was a positive to this day. He was in the office when Wyrick was attacked, and Charlie Dodge was his alibi, because when Charlie called to tell him about the 911 call, he'd been there to take the call. Now the cops had to quit looking at him as a suspect. He might have the passkey to the apartments, but he couldn't be in two places at once.

Upstairs, the techs from the crime lab were all over the old passage, lifting prints, finding a random hair now and then. One was found caught on an old nail. Another pulled from between a wood sliver and the wall. There was even a tiny piece of fabric caught in the floor.

They followed the passageway to a little set of stairs that led into the basement, taking pictures, prints and DNA. There were no security cameras down here. Only the other stairs that led up to the main house. And up there, there were too many ways someone could have left the building. They would have to go through security footage now.

The dead end was disappointing, but the evidence had been gathered, and once again the team from the crime lab was gone.

Sonny came home in the middle of the chaos, loaded down with sacks from several different stores in the Galleria, and for good measure he was carrying a cold drink he'd gotten from a fast-food drive-through on his way home.

He parked in the garage, then headed toward Detter House with his game face on, ready to run the gauntlet of uniformed officers all over the grounds, until finally, one stopped him at the back entrance into the lobby.

"What's going on?" Sonny asked.

"There was an attempted abduction. What's your business here?"

"Oh, my God!" Sonny said and shifted his bags to get a better grip. "I live here! Am I allowed inside? I got a text on the way home that I have a delivery to pick up at the office."

"What's your name, sir?" the cop asked.

"Sonny Burch. I live in apartment 115. Ground floor."

"I'll walk you in," the cop said and then led the way inside.

They crossed the lobby and went straight up the hall to the manager's office, passing detectives and uniformed officers on the way.

Sonny didn't have to fake the uneasiness and shock of what was happening. Nothing had gone as he'd planned. The only thing he still had going for him was that no one had seen his face, and he'd never been arrested, so neither his DNA nor prints were in the system. He needed to get rid of Rachel, but the place was too hot. There was no way in hell he could take a chance on getting her off the premises tonight.

It was a fuckup of epic proportions.

When they reached the office, Sonny entered without knocking.

"I came to pick up my package, but can you believe this?" he asked.

Wayne looked up. "It's horrible. A nightmare. They carried Dodge's assistant out unconscious, and there are police everywhere."

Sonny gasped. "The policeman told me there was an attempted abduction. Are you saying it was Jade Wyrick?"

Wayne nodded.

"Is she okay?" Sonny asked.

"I don't know," Wayne said and then his phone rang again and he pointed to a box in the corner. "There's your delivery from Amazon. I've got to take this."

Sonny picked up his package, then paused at the door to speak to the cop.

"I'm going to my apartment now."

Satisfied that Sonny was someone who belonged here, the cop let him go, and Sonny wasted no time leaving the lobby.

Charlie made it to the hospital in record time and went running into the ER. The clerk saw his hands, and the blood all over him, and assumed he was coming in as a patient until he spoke.

"Jade Wyrick was just brought here by ambulance. I'm her only family. Where is she?"

The clerk was rattled by the request and kept looking at him.

"But, sir, your hands..."

Charlie's patience was gone. There were people trying to kill her. Some nut had just tried to kidnap her, and she was unconscious when she'd left his sight.

"Ma'am! My hands are not the issue here. Where is Jade Wyrick?"

The clerk blinked, then typed in the name and waited for the info to appear on her monitor.

"She's in exam room six, but—"

"Lady! She was abducted less than an hour ago, and I just tore up a wall to get to her. Don't make me tear up another one to find her again."

"Through those doors, straight down and on your left," she said. "And get someone to look at your hands."

"Yes, ma'am," Charlie said, then headed for the doors at a lope, pushed them open with his shoulder and kept moving. He just needed to see her face. Then he heard her before he saw her and sighed. She was conscious enough to argue. He'd never been so happy to hear the sarcasm in her tone.

Wyrick couldn't stay conscious, but when she was, she knew she was as vulnerable as she could possibly be, and that wasn't good. Someone had cut the clothes from her body. She felt the air on her bare skin, and she heard someone talking about her dragon.

The dragon was hers. She was the one who chose when to reveal her, and when to keep her hidden. Some people were afraid of dragons. And people who were afraid of dragons always tried to kill them. Someone was trying to kill her dragon, but she couldn't remember who.

When she finally came to enough to open her eyes and saw where she was at, and what they'd done to her, she was livid and locked gazes with the man leaning over her.

"Well, hello, Jade. I'm Doctor Julian. You're in an emergency room. Do you remember what happened?"

Julian was waiting for a response when he realized he was looking into the angriest, darkest eyes he'd ever seen, and the tone of her voice confirmed it.

"Where are my clothes?"

"I'm sorry, but we had to cut them off you to examine—"

The sarcasm in her voice was impossible to miss.

"It had a zipper."

He grinned. "Yeah, ma'am, but since there was blood all over you, haste seemed to be the obvious solution."

Wyrick's heart skipped a beat. "I have a headache, but I don't have any other pain. Where am I bleeding?"

"You're okay. It wasn't yours. Now, can you—"

It wasn't mine?

The last thing she remembered was Charlie's voice.

"Where's Charlie? I need to see Charlie! Was he hurt?" she yelled and reached for the IV, trying to pull it out of her arm, and trying to sit up.

One nurse grabbed her hand, while another was trying to keep her in bed.

"Jade! Lie down. You're going to hurt yourself! You tell me who Charlie is and I'll see if I can find out where he is," she said.

"If I came in bloody and it wasn't my blood, then somebody better tell me where the hell Charlie is or—"

"I'm here. Calm down, Wyrick. There are sick people here," Charlie said.

Wyrick took one look at him and burst into tears.

"What happened to you?" she cried.

Now everyone was looking, and they were beginning to make the connection between the two. Her Charlie was Charlie Dodge. And this wasn't some patient named Jade. This was Wyrick. Charlie Dodge's Wyrick.

Doctor Julian looked at Charlie's hands and then pointed to a stool beside Wyrick's bed.

"Why don't you sit down there beside her and we'll all calm down. She doesn't seem to remember what happened. Maybe you can enlighten us so we can treat her accordingly."

Charlie sat, then pulled the sheet up over the dragon. "Don't cry. I'm okay. It's just cuts and scratches."

Tears were running down her face as she rolled over and grabbed his hands, turning them palms up.

"What did you do?" she whispered.

"I couldn't find the door he took you through, so I made one."

"You are a crazy man, Charlie Dodge. Thank you for saving my life," she said.

"I had to. You're the only one who knows the password to the computer in my office."

She sighed. "I don't know what happened. There was a pain in my neck and then everything went black. I remember your voice and then nothing again."

Charlie glanced up at the doctor.

"That puncture wound in her neck. It's from a needle. She was drugged. We're working a missing person's case, and I think the person we're after was afraid we were getting too close. He wanted to eliminate his biggest threat, which would have been her."

Doctor Julian eyed Charlie and smiled. "I would have assumed his biggest threat would have been you."

Charlie glanced back at Wyrick. "I'm just big and decently intelligent. She's the genius of the whole operation."

"Did he get away?" Wyrick asked.

Charlie nodded. "We'll find him again, but you're what matters now."

"I have a headache. I'm not hurt. I'm not bleeding, but you are. Don't anyone ask me questions," she said and then closed her eyes.

Charlie started to let her go, but she wouldn't turn loose his hands.

"You need to let go of him," Doctor Julian said. "We need to—"

"Stop talking," Wyrick mumbled. She was already with Charlie, feeling the pain in his hands, seeing the flesh cut from within, feeling the warmth of the blood and then zeroing in on the tiny nerves that he'd shredded to get to her.

Charlie could feel his hands getting warmer and the pain lessening. He knew she could do this, but he'd never thought she'd be doing it to him.

It was one of the nurses who first noticed he wasn't bleeding anymore, and tapped the doctor's arm and pointed. After that the room went silent. One doctor, two nurses and an orderly stood in silent awe, witnessing what could only be described as a miracle.

Charlie felt her magic and the power of her flowing through him, and knew when this was over he would never be the same. Ever since the day they'd first met, she'd been hell to live with, but at this moment Charlie knew there would not be a life without her. Whatever had been happening between them had been built on years of trust and sorrow shared.

So he watched her face, mapping the beauty beneath the public mask she always wore. Seeing a tiny blue vein in her neck that he'd never noticed before, and watching a tear seep out from beneath one eyelid and roll silently down her cheek onto the sheet. He'd never seen it coming, but he had fallen in love.

All of a sudden she turned him loose. Her eyes opened, and she was looking straight at him.

Charlie didn't look away. Couldn't look away.

"Do you hurt now?" she asked.

It took everything Charlie had to break his gaze, then finally look down. Not only had the bleeding stopped, but the cuts were already closing, too.

He shook his head, but there were tears in his eyes when he looked back up at her.

It was then that Wyrick realized what she'd done. And in front of witnesses. Her eyes widened as she looked at everyone in the room.

"Please don't tell."

Charlie heard the panic in her voice and added a plea of his own.

"I know you've all seen the video. You know a religious cult was after her. You know there were hit men sent to kill her. And this is why. Because she knows stuff...and can do stuff...

like this. But it doesn't make her anything but special. Don't make her life any more complicated than it already is. Please."

Doctor Julian lifted his chin.

"I couldn't explain what I just saw if I had to, and no one would believe us anyway." Then he looked at the others. "Do I have to say it?" he asked.

Both nurses and the orderly all shook their heads. "No, Doctor," they said.

Wyrick didn't know if she could trust them, but right now it didn't matter. Her focus was on Charlie.

"We need to go back now," she said.

"Back where?" he asked.

"To Detter House."

Charlie frowned. "Oh, hell no! You're going home to rest and—"

Wyrick held up her hand. "I need the IV out of my arm. So either someone take it out or I'll do it myself."

Doctor Julian nodded at one of the nurses, who quickly obeyed, while Wyrick kept arguing with Charlie.

"Rachel can't wait. If she's still alive, he's going to panic. His little game is ruined, and she is the only person who could identify him."

"The police will get prints and DNA," Charlie argued.

"Time, Charlie. That all takes time, and I know in my gut Rachel Dean doesn't have any left. I'm not one hundred percent, but I can focus, and I can sleep when this is over."

"Hellfire," Charlie muttered.

"No, that's where we're sending him," Wyrick said. "And I need something to wear. They cut up my clothes... Oh...and where's my phone?"

One of the nurses pointed to a sack sitting on a chair. "Those are your belongings, including the clothes we cut off you, but we were told the police would need them for DNA. Your phone is there."

"Show me," Wyrick said.

The nurse dug through the sack and then held up a phone.

"Please give it to Charlie," Wyrick said. "He has pockets right now, and I do not."

Charlie took the phone and made a point to put it in an inside pocket of the jacket he was wearing.

"Safe and sound," he said.

Wyrick nodded. "You need to wash the blood off your hands."

"Yes, ma'am," Charlie said and moved to the sink.

Doctor Julian pointed at the orderly. "Bring me two hospital gowns, the longer they are, the better for her," he said.

The orderly bolted out of the room, glad to have something to do.

Charlie was drying his hands when he saw a sliver of wood in the heel of his hand and showed her.

"You left a splinter."

Wyrick glared. "You can pick that out tonight after dinner."

He grinned, because her sarcasm meant she was back enough to keep him in his place.

Doctor Julian dispersed the nurses, then paused at Wyrick's bedside.

"I want you to know that this incident might be the most definitive moment of my career. As long as I live, I will never measure up to the healer you instinctively are, and I honor you," he said, then walked out.

Wyrick swallowed past a lump in her throat and closed her eyes.

Charlie sat back down on the stool beside her and laid a hand on her arm, just so she'd know he was there.

A short while later the orderly came back with two gowns and a wheelchair. Wyrick used one to cover her front, and the other to cover her butt. Then he wheeled her out through the ambulance entrance, seated her in Charlie's Jeep and then they were gone.

Charlie glanced at her once as they were leaving the parking lot. She had the seat reclined, her eyes closed and he guessed she was doing whatever it was she did to pull herself back together. He hated to disturb her, but he also knew she didn't like surprises.

"I assume you don't want to go back to Detter House with your butt hanging out, so I'm swinging by home first."

"My butt is not hanging anywhere. Can we please get a Pepsi on the way, and may I please have my phone?"

"Yes, ma'am," Charlie said and dug it out of his pocket and laid it in her hands, then started looking for a fast-food drive-through.

By the time they got back to the old mansion, Wyrick had downed a Pepsi and an order of fries, and was feeling more like herself.

"I won't be long," she said as they entered the house.

"Are you going to have a fit if I walk you to your room?" Charlie asked.

She sighed. "Must I keep reminding you that I do not have fits? I'm not dizzy, but I understand your concern. So yes, you may accompany me to the door."

Charlie wisely kept his mouth shut, but kept a close eye on her stride and demeanor. One stumble. One dizzy moment, and he was putting her ass to bed whether she liked it or not.

When they got to her room she paused, and then reached out and laid a hand on his arm.

"Once again you have saved my life. I have no words other than thank you. I won't be long. And you might want to call Detectives Floyd and Mills. I don't think we should go back without them."

"I don't need thanks. I just need you to keep breathing. I'll call them while you're changing," he said and went inside his room to keep from putting his arms around her.

Wyrick heard an emotion in his voice that she didn't recognize, and attributed it to her healing his hands. She had no idea how deeply that had affected him.

CHAPTER TWELVE

Charlie sat down on the side of his bed, stared down at the palms of his hands again and then shook his head and picked up the phone. But his first call wasn't to the police. He pulled up the contact number, then made the call. It rang twice and then a woman answered.

"This is Millie. Please tell me you have good news," she said.

"I have news. We still don't know where Rachel is, but we did find out how she was abducted," Charlie said.

Millie groaned and started crying. "I knew it in my heart, but hearing it hurts. What can you tell me? How did you find out?"

"Because it just happened to Wyrick less than three hours ago. We were in Rachel's apartment, in her bedroom. I walked out of the room, and when I came back Wyrick was gone. I saw drag marks in the carpet leading into the walk-in closet. After a few panicked minutes, I found a hidden access door behind shelving that led into a passage that runs the entire length of the building. Whoever took Wyrick heard me coming, dropped her in the passage and ran. And we now know that he drugs his victims. Stabs them in the neck with a syringe full of knockout drugs."

"Oh, my God! Wait? Victims? There were more than Rachel and Wyrick?"

"Three more, but that's a whole other story. We don't know details. I just wanted you to know we're making progress and I'll keep you updated. Now that we know this much, Wyrick is insistent we go back now, and I'm smart enough not to doubt her instincts."

"Is she okay to do that so soon?" Millie asked.

Charlie sighed. "Well, as she said…she'll rest when this is over. I'll be in touch."

Then he hung up and made yet another call to Detective Floyd.

Floyd was still on the scene when he got the call, and was hesitant to answer for fear it would be bad news.

"Hello? This is Floyd. I'm almost afraid to ask, but how's Wyrick?"

"She's good. I had to bring her home to change clothes because they cut up her others, which, by the way, got bagged for the cops to pick up for DNA, but she's insistent on coming back today and wants you guys along."

"Are you serious? Is she up for that?" Floyd asked.

"It's Wyrick, so yes."

"We're still on site. As soon as you get here, give us a call. We'll meet you at the office."

"Will do," Charlie said. "And thanks."

He dropped the phone back into his pocket, stared at the splinter still in the heel of his hand, the swiftly healing cuts, and stood.

He didn't hurt, but he felt like he was going to jump out of his skin. He didn't know whether it was because of what she'd done to him, or the fading adrenaline of thinking he'd lost her. Either way, this had been one hell of a day, and it wasn't over yet.

Wyrick had come home with no clothes, and his were covered in blood, so he went to change. And, since they were about to go crawling in the guts of that old mansion again, he was wearing different clothes—the kind you wore to hunt for killers and lost women.

As for Wyrick, the moment she closed the door between her and Charlie, she laid her phone on the bed, then went into her closet to pick out more clothes, but this time nothing fancy. Only she couldn't think about putting them on until she'd showered. Too many strangers had touched her today, and in ways she couldn't remember.

By the time she emerged from the bathroom, she felt more like herself. Putting on old jeans, soft from a thousand washings, and a long-sleeve T-shirt felt safe. She added a jacket, knowing it was going to be cold behind those walls. She was hesitant to show her real face in public right now, but there was no time for full makeup. The urgency for speed was still with her. So she dug through her makeup drawer, swiped her eyelids with black shadow and then dabbed a cotton swab through red face paint, and beginning at the corner of one eye, put four red tear drops down the side of her face—one for each of the women who'd gone missing—and in a rare move, left her lips bare.

Satisfied that she was hidden enough, she chose running shoes instead of her usual boots, then put her phone in the hip pocket and walked out.

Charlie was leaning against the wall near his door, reading something on his phone. He looked up.

"We need to stop by the kitchen on the way out and get some candy. God only knows when we'll get home tonight."

"You're just saying that so you won't have to cook dinner," she said. "But the candy is a good idea."

He grinned. Wyrick was back.

They walked down the stairs, then down a long hall to get to the kitchen.

"Want another Pepsi?" Charlie asked as he opened the refrigerator.

She nodded. "Do you want a Snickers bar or a Hershey?" she asked as she dug through the candy drawer.

"Snickers," he said and handed her a cold bottle of Pepsi.

She handed one to him, then got a Hershey with almonds for herself as they headed out the door.

"Want to take my car?" she asked.

"No."

She frowned. "Why not? I'll let you drive."

"Because I cannot fold myself up small enough to even sit in it, let alone drive the damn thing."

She shrugged. "It's faster."

"Not happening," Charlie said and loaded her into the passenger side of his Jeep and shut the door.

Wyrick buckled up, loosened the lid on her Pepsi and then unwrapped her candy bar as Charlie took off.

"You called Detective Floyd, right?" she asked.

"Yes, and I called Millie Chriss to give her an update."

"Oh… I should have thought of that," Wyrick said.

"I'm not completely useless," Charlie said.

Wyrick popped a piece of candy into her mouth to keep from smiling. It felt so damn good to still be alive that she stayed mute. Charlie had moved mountains…and part of a wall today to find her. He deserved to have the last word.

Sonny was staying put in his apartment. He had his television on and some stew reheating on the stove, trying to settle back into his normal routine.

He wasn't about to screw up his carefully planned alibi of being gone when all this happened, because it had cleared him tonight. Cops were still all over the place, and the last thing he wanted was to be noticed again.

But his choice to stay under the radar also made him unaware Charlie and Wyrick came back in full force, walking as if nothing had ever happened. Not only were Floyd and Mills waiting for them at the office, but they had two more uniformed officers going with them, as well.

Floyd couldn't believe it when he saw them approach.

Wyrick had gone out unconscious and on a stretcher, and was walking back in a couple of hours later as if nothing had ever happened.

"Ma'am. It's good to see you like this. You must be part Energizer Bunny."

"Something like that," she said.

Mills glanced down at Charlie's hands, expecting to see them in stitches, or at least in bandages, and then what he saw left him in shock.

"Charlie! Your hands! What the hell?" he asked.

Charlie shrugged. "They weren't as bad as they looked. Doc washed them off and cleaned them up. I've always been a fast healer. Are you guys ready to do this?"

"More than ready," Floyd said.

"Wyrick's the one with the gut feeling here," Charlie said. "So she's calling the shots. The rest of us are here for backup. We don't need a repeat of this morning."

"Got it," Floyd said. "Ma'am. Lead the way."

Wyrick took off for the elevator with Charlie at her side, weaving her way through the lobby and the continuing chaos of the investigation.

It wasn't until they got back into the bedroom of Rachel's apartment that Charlie moved in front of her. "I go first."

She didn't argue. But when they stepped into the closet and she saw what Charlie had done to get to her, she froze.

At that point Charlie warned her.

"Watch where you're walking. There's a lot of debris."

But she was still standing, staring in disbelief.

Charlie turned, saw the look on her face and sighed. She wasn't going to let this pass. And he was right.

"Charlie?"

"Yeah?"

"Did you do this?" she asked.

"I couldn't find the fucking door," he said.

She looked up.

"I can't believe you just said *fucking*."

She heard the men behind her chuckling, but she couldn't see past the look on his face.

"Now you see the danger of getting between me and something I want," he said.

Breath caught in the back of her throat. What did he mean by that? And why did he say it just now, with a closet full of witnesses, when they were on a search?

"Whatever," she mumbled, then picked up a blue paisley scarf from the floor of the closet and wrapped it around her hand. "Okay. If you're going first, get moving," she said.

Charlie frowned, then looked back at the crew behind them.

"Don't let her fall," he said.

"We've got this, Charlie," Mills said and moved up a little closer behind Wyrick.

Satisfied, Charlie turned and went through the doorway, triggering the lights within the passage, and then Wyrick was inside with the police behind her.

"So there was a passage here, after all," she said. "Where was I when you found me?" she asked.

Charlie pointed. "About sixty yards or so south. So I'm going to start walking. You're the one with the Spidey-sense radar, so if you want us to stop just say so. Otherwise, I'll keep moving."

She nodded, but she still hadn't moved.

"What are you feeling?" he asked.

"Him. He's everywhere here."

"Can you see his face?" Charlie asked.

"No. But none of them have seen his face here. They were unconscious here."

The lack of emotion in her voice made Detective Floyd shudder. She was picking up on the helplessness of the victims, and it gave him the creeps.

"Are you ready?" Charlie asked.

Wyrick took a deep breath and then exhaled slowly, letting go of everything except the trail of his energy, and it was dark, so dark that she was afraid of what they'd find.

"Yes. Let's go."

And so they started walking, moving slowly along the passage, letting Wyrick set the pace. As she walked she began telling them what she was seeing.

"There are other rooms like Rachel's. Three more, but I don't know where they are."

They kept moving. As they moved past the place where Sonny had dropped her she stopped and looked behind her, near where two of the officers were standing.

"Charlie, back there…is that where you found me?"

"Yes. How did you know?"

She shrugged. "I'm not sure. Maybe because back there felt heavier, and now the energy is different. Like he went on alone?" She glanced at Floyd. "Does that make sense?"

Floyd just shook his head. "Something has to be understandable to make sense, and so far I don't understand one iota of what makes you work…but I am in awe, if that counts for something?"

Wyrick nodded, then waved Charlie on.

Another twenty feet down she paused again, then turned to face the inner wall. "I think there's another door here."

Charlie stopped. "How can you tell?"

"He's standing at this wall and jacking off."

Floyd and Mills moved her aside, and within a couple of minutes found a trigger that released a door into a whole other apartment, and as they did, found a peephole in the door concealed within a decorative plaque.

"Jesus. We should have figured this," Floyd said. "A Peeping Tom can go from being a voyeur to actual physical attacks."

Wyrick put her hand on the wall, then looked at Charlie.

"He thinks they love him."

They backed out, closed the door and kept moving.

Wyrick kept rubbing the scarf she'd picked up, trying to see Rachel here, but all she felt was an energy different from the assailant.

They were almost at the end of the passage when Wyrick stopped.

"There's another door here. Same vibe. Same visions of what he was doing."

This time the detectives knew what to look for, and quickly found the trigger.

There was a couple inside the apartment, and when they heard talking inside their bedroom, they came running in disbelief.

Detective Floyd immediately flashed his badge.

"Sorry for the scare. Wyrick is helping us find the hidden doors giving access into apartments. We're making note of them for the owner."

The woman turned to her husband and started weeping.

"This is horrible, just horrible, Johnny. We have to get out of this place. I'll never feel safe here again!"

And then Wyrick came out of the passage and into the room, and when they saw her, a hush came over the both of them, and then the woman moved toward her a few steps.

"We saw them carry you out on a stretcher just hours ago. You were unconscious."

"And now I'm not," Wyrick said. "When a secret is revealed,

it is no longer a secret, or a danger. Rest assured, all of this will soon be going away, along with the man who's been causing all the trouble, and everyone will be safe here again."

Charlie yelled at them from the passage.

"Hey! Come look at this!"

They disappeared, pulling the door shut behind them.

Wyrick ran to where Charlie was kneeling. He had a flashlight aimed toward the wall and his pocketknife out, digging at something caught in a crack.

"What is it?" she asked.

"Something shiny. Looks like it might be…" All of a sudden it popped out, and Charlie picked it up. "It's an earring."

He dropped it in Wyrick's hand.

Wyrick was eyeing the pearl in the platinum setting when she had a vision of a man in this passage, walking away from where she was standing, with the body of a slender blonde woman, dangling lifelessly over his shoulder.

"What's happening?" Mills asked.

"She can see who this belonged to," Charlie said. "Just wait."

Wyrick felt a sense of sadness. This was lingering energy from something that happened a long time ago. When she turned and handed the earring to Detective Floyd, she was crying and didn't even know it.

"First victim. Her name was Linda. She's not alive in the world. That's all I know."

Floyd stared at the earring, then at the tears on her face before bagging the earring as evidence.

Charlie stood, then pulled a handkerchief out of his pocket and handed it to her.

"What?" she asked.

"You're crying."

Wyrick sighed, wiped her face and handed it back.

"We're almost at the end of the passage," Charlie said.

"It doesn't end," Wyrick said. "I'm still feeling that pull to fall down. Like I did in Rachel's apartment. I think, now, that I'm feeling stairs. Hidden doors. Hidden staircases. We need to go down. Find a door, Charlie. Find a door."

"Maybe it's another way down into the basement," Floyd said. "There's one set of stairs on the main floor that leads down."

At Wyrick's urging, Charlie moved the last few feet to the end of the passage, and began shining his flashlight all along the crevices on the wall to their left, where all the other access doors had been found.

"No. The other side, Charlie."

He pivoted and began shining the light and feeling for a similar trigger again, and within moments found it. The door swung inward onto a landing, and then a set of stairs going down into darkness.

"Is there a tunnel?" Wyrick asked.

"I can't tell," Charlie said. "There's no light. I'm going down. Don't come off the landing until I say so," he said.

Wyrick was clutching the scarf with both hands now. The urgency of getting down there was almost sickening.

"Hurry, Charlie. Find a light."

He saw the way she was holding the scarf, and remembered all the other times when she'd keyed in on someone's location like this, and didn't hesitate.

He aimed his flashlight down the steps and started down into the dark. But before he was halfway down, lights came on, revealing yet another secret to Detter House.

"It's a tunnel," he said and stopped and turned. "Safe to proceed."

Wyrick reeled on the first step down. Charlie was already running up to catch her when Mills caught her from behind.

"Are you feeling sick?" Charlie asked.

She shook her head. "No, no, but I do have that same feeling I had in Rachel's apartment, like I have to brace myself to keep from falling forward."

"You already knew the steps were here," Charlie said. "You just had to find them. So…here's what's going to happen. You're going to get on the step behind me, hang on to my shoulders and we're going down together."

And so they did, until they were all on the ground floor and staring down a long tunnel.

All of a sudden Wyrick pushed past Charlie and started walking, her stride long and hurried.

He didn't bother to question why.

She was a dozen yards ahead of him when she suddenly slid to a stop and turned and shouted.

"Hurry! Hurry!"

By the time the men arrived, Wyrick had her phone out and was rapidly searching for something online.

"Oh, my God! Look at the size of this metal door," Floyd said, then swung his flashlight. There was no doorknob. Just a handle, and then he saw the security panel on the right. There was no key to this thing. They needed a code to open it.

"We're going to have to get someone in here with a cutting torch," Mills said.

"No. Wait," Wyrick said. "I can get it open."

Charlie peered over her shoulder, watching her fingers flying on her phone, then pulling up the specs to a security panel just like this.

"This won't tell you what the code is," Floyd said.

Wyrick just ignored him.

"Charlie, can you get the face off the security panel?"

"Does it matter if it's still in one piece?" he asked.

"You don't have to smash everything. It should pop right off," she said and kept typing and searching, and then she stopped, muttering to herself as she scanned the specs. "Pull off the front," she said.

Charlie pried it off with his knife, revealing a conduit of tiny colored wires. "Now what?" he asked.

"Officers, you did not see me do this," Wyrick said, then pulled up an app on her phone that Charlie had never seen. "Stand back. It might spark a little," she said.

All of a sudden a light came shooting out of the camera lens on her phone and straight into the panel. There was a loud pop and a flash of fire. When the smoke cleared, there was nothing left but smoldering wires.

"Holy shit! What was that?" Floyd asked.

"Um…a kind of laser," Wyrick said, then closed the app and put her phone back in her pocket.

Charlie pushed the door.

It swung inward to a total absence of light, so he swung his flashlight to the right of the door.

"There's an old mattress in here," he said and stepped inside and swung the flashlight into the corner, and what he saw made his skin crawl.

"Oh, my God. You did it, Wyrick, you found her. Hold this," he said and gave her the flashlight.

She moved in behind him, focusing the beam on the tiny body curled up beneath a blanket, while the police moved in behind her.

"Is it Rachel?" Floyd asked.

"Yes," Charlie said.

"Is she alive?" Floyd asked.

Charlie was on his knees beside her, feeling for a pulse.

"Barely. She's burning up with a fever."

"Call it in!" Floyd said.

"There's no signal down here," Mills said and turned to one of the officers with them.

"Go back up and—"

"No," Wyrick said. "There's a set of stairs just beyond this room. They'll take you up and out onto the grounds."

"Then go, go," Floyd said. "We need another ambulance and the crime lab back down here."

He didn't have to say it twice.

Both officers took off running, and within seconds they were up the stairs, out of the garden shed and running back toward the house.

When Charlie pulled back the blanket, and saw the knife hanging loosely in her hands, he stopped. "Hey, guys. You're gonna want to bag this for evidence."

Wyrick flashed the light on the knife, and then saw the wound beneath Rachel's chin.

"Charlie…her neck…her arms…there are cuts all over her."

"Did she do this to herself?" Charlie asked.

"No. He cut her. Somehow, she got it away from him."

"The light's broken," Mills said, shining his flashlight up to the ceiling. Then he swung it down toward the floor. "There's broken glass all over."

"She's only wearing one shoe," Charlie said as he picked her up in his arms, then tried to shift her to an easier position without causing her more pain.

"Let's go," Wyrick said.

"We'll stay here on scene," Floyd said.

Wyrick swung the flashlight toward the floor, then up at the ceiling to the broken bulb.

"She used her shoe. She threw it at the light until she broke it."

"But why would she want to be here in the dark?" Floyd said.

Wyrick's eyes narrowed. The horror of the room was beyond explanation, but she could see Rachel throwing the shoe…over and over and over.

"Because when the kidnapper came back, she would have the advantage. She was lying right by the door. With a knife. It was probably her only chance to get out."

"Only he didn't come back," Charlie said. "I wonder why?"

"Because we came," Wyrick said and led the way out, running toward the stairs and shining the light for Charlie as he carried Rachel up, then out onto the grounds.

At that point Charlie's horror at her condition grew. Seeing her in this light revealed every physical injury her kidnapper had inflicted, along with the infections that had developed, and those were just the ones he could see.

"I don't know if you can hear me, Rachel Dean, but you're safe now. Your sister, Millie, sent us to find you, and the next time you open your eyes, she'll be there."

And then he took off in long, hurried strides, with her held close to his chest and Wyrick at his side.

CHAPTER THIRTEEN

Allen Carson was on site when Charlie and Wyrick came into the lobby. The officers on scene saw them coming, and Charlie Dodge carrying the missing woman in his arms.

Within seconds they began forming a phalanx around them, moving them through the lobby and out to meet the arriving ambulance.

As they moved past the office, the shock of seeing the woman in Charlie's arms was something Allen would never forget.

"Is she alive?" he called out as they moved past him toward the exit.

"Barely," Charlie said and kept going.

Allen pulled out his phone and made a call.

"This is the Ritz-Carlton. How may I direct your call?"

"This is Allen Carson. I need to speak to the manager, please."

"One moment," the operator said and then his call went through.

By the time Allen hung up, he'd reserved rooms for every resident of the Detter House, with the understanding that they would be there on his dime until the renovations were complete. Then he walked into the office.

"Wayne, I need you to send a list of the present residents' names to the Ritz-Carlton Hotel here in the city. Send it to the attention of this man. He's the manager, and the one I've already spoken to."

Wayne took down the information. "Okay, got it, but…what's going on?" he asked.

"I'm furnishing another place for them as a temporary residence," Allen said.

"Wow! At the Ritz-Carlton?"

Allen nodded. "Now, I need you to start calling the residents and let them know that, for the time being, their new residence will be at the Ritz. Tell them to pack a bag and just show up. The hotel knows they're coming, and the cost is on me until the situation here is resolved. And that includes you," he added.

"But who will—"

"I'll deal with it," Allen said. "I can't believe that this happened on my property, but I won't have one more person put in danger here until this is remedied."

"This is very generous of you," Wayne said. "I'll start letting them know."

Within the hour the panic that had been building within the complex was fading. Knowing that the owner was sincere in his need to tear down the hidden passage, and remove and remodel the walls with the hidden access doors, was extinguishing the demands to be released from their leases.

Everyone was relieved…except Sonny.

He was in a panic. His apartment felt like a holding cell. He was trapped, and just waiting to be found out and charged. They'd found the tunnel. They'd found Rachel. Unresponsive but alive. They'd seen his playroom—and were lifting all manner of prints and DNA. The next step would be demanding DNA from everyone in residence here. For all he knew that was already a plan of action they had yet to implement.

As for going to the Ritz-Carlton, it was just trading one holding cell for another, but he wanted to set up another alibi, so that his absence from the Ritz was not an immediate flag that he was on the run. He didn't have time to waste, and began throwing clothes into suitcases, packed up his laptop, all the chargers and the technology he used, and then called back to the office.

Wayne answered. "Detter House."

"Wayne, this is Sonny. I just wanted to let you know that I'll be staying with family here in the city while the remodeling is being done. They're close to my work, and it'll be much more comfortable than the hotel. Of course, you have my cell number so I'll be available for contact, should the need occur."

"Sure thing," Wayne said. "I wish I had family in the city. I'd do the same. Take care."

"You, too," Sonny said and then he was gone, heading east out of Dallas.

Charlie and Wyrick stood on the sidewalk, watching the EMTs loading Rachel up into the ambulance. He knew Rachel's chances of survival were iffy. But she was still alive and on her way to the hospital, and that was what they'd set out to do.

And he could tell by the look on Wyrick's face that she was exhausted. He had to get her home before she crashed.

"Get in the Jeep," he said and aimed the remote to unlock it.

"But what about—?"

"They know where to find us. They can call. Walk or I'll carry you," he said.

She turned, stumbled and seconds later she was in his arms.

"Oh, for the love of God," she hissed.

"I'm not doing this for God," Charlie said and carried her across the drive to guest parking and put her down beside his car.

Everything washed over her as she slid into the seat of Charlie's Jeep. The exhaustion of all the energy she'd used, and the remnants of the drug still in her system, had done her in.

Charlie got into the driver's seat, looked at her and then leaned across the console and buckled her in.

"You did good…damn good," he said. "Close your eyes. We'll be home before you know it."

"Call Millie," Wyrick whispered.

"Yes, ma'am. I'm putting the call on speakerphone and calling her right now."

Then he started the engine and pulled out of the parking lot before making the connection.

Millie had been pacing the floor of her hotel room ever since Charlie Dodge's call. She'd sent Ray a text, only to get a message back from him within minutes that he was catching a flight to Dallas, and he would be there before midnight.

At that point she sat down and cried. The stress of dealing with this on her own had nearly broken her. She hadn't been able to sleep more than an hour or two at a stretch. She couldn't bring herself to face people, and had taken to ordering room service, and then wasting most of the food they delivered because she couldn't eat for thinking of Rachel.

She'd paced the floor for hours until her feet and legs were aching, and now she was just standing at the window, looking down at the street below. All those people were coming and going about their lives, and Millie felt like hers had come to a complete stop.

When her phone rang again, she raced to answer it.

"Hello?"

"This is Charlie. We found Rachel. She's in bad shape and unconscious, but she's alive. They're taking her to Baylor Scott and White Hospital."

Millie dropped into the nearest chair, trembling from the shock and the relief.

"Oh, my God, oh, my God! Where did you find her? Did they catch the man who did it?"

"In a hidden room off a tunnel beneath the building, and no, ma'am, they still don't know who's responsible. The rest of this case will fall back to the police department. Our job was to find Rachel."

"Yes, yes, and I'm so grateful. There aren't enough words to—"

Wyrick interrupted.

"This is Wyrick. There are things I can do to help the police find him, and I give you my word I'll stay with the case until it's over."

"Thank you," Millie said. "You are both angels on earth. I can't thank you enough."

"You're welcome, ma'am. Drive safe. Dallas traffic is pretty bad," Charlie said.

"I'm not letting a little traffic stop me from getting to Rachel," Millie said. "I got this."

Then she was gone.

Charlie glanced at Wyrick. Her eyes were closed.

"So we're not done here?" he asked.

"We can't quit yet," Wyrick said, thinking of that vision she'd had in the passage after Charlie handed her the earring—of the small blonde woman slung over the killer's back. "Someone has to find the other women who went missing."

Charlie sighed. "Okay."

Detective Floyd pulled up his contact info for Rachel Dean's sister and made a quick call. Even though the family had hired Charlie Dodge, the Dallas PD was still on the case. Rachel had gone missing on their watch, and it was his duty to notify the next of kin, regardless.

He called Millie Chriss and waited for her to answer.

Millie was in traffic when her phone rang again, but she'd already switched to Bluetooth so she tapped it to answer.

"Hello, this is Millie."

"Millie, this is Detective Floyd with Missing Persons. I wanted to let you know that, with the help and cooperation of Charlie Dodge and his assistant, Wyrick, we have found your sister, Rachel."

"Yes, yes, Charlie just called me. I'm on my way to the hospital now. I am so appreciative of the way you coordinated and cooperated with me, wanting to hire private help, as well. Thank you. Thank all of you. Rachel means everything to us."

"Yes, ma'am. I know she's unconscious right now, but if she begins to wake up, please let us know. We need to talk to her. We still don't have an identity on the man who took her."

"Yes, sir, I will. I want him caught as much as you do. When her condition changes, I will let you know."

"Yes, ma'am. Thank you," Floyd said and then hung up.

He paused then, looking around the lobby at all the chaos. Residents were coming and going, carrying luggage to their cars, and there was nothing he could do about it.

He was unhappy that Carson had moved all of his suspects without notice, even though he could not have expected them all to stay put after what had happened. And then Allen Carson walked up and Floyd frowned at him.

"The least you could have done was run this mass exodus by me first," Floyd said.

Allen's disapproval at being reprimanded showed, both by the look on his face and the tone of his voice.

"Surely, you did not expect they would stay here. I've been inundated with people wanting to break their leases. Some of them were already packing up to leave anyway. I have to tear down that passage and tunnel, remove those access doors and rebuild the walls. You should thank me that I've kept them all in one place for you."

"Okay, I'll admit that foresight was wise, and it will help," Floyd said.

Allen shrugged. "We just need to both pray that Rachel Dean wakes up and names the bastard. Oh…just so you know. This will be your only notice. Get all of the pictures and evidence you need from this property, and whatever else you want to take to make your case, because in two days we're tearing into this place like a Texas tornado. I'm sick that this passage was never revealed to me when I bought it. And I can't believe it wasn't discovered during remodeling. If it had been, none of these women would have been fair game for a madman. Do we understand each other?" Allen said.

Floyd nodded. "Understood."

Allen was satisfied he had a plan, but he wasn't going to be satisfied until he found out why that passageway had ever existed.

He knew two people who might be able to help him. One was a historian, familiar with the city of Dallas, and the other was the last living relative of the original family. He'd never spoken to the old man, because he'd never had a reason to, but he was going to do so now.

Wyrick was asleep when Charlie drove through the gates of the old mansion, taking care to close them behind him before driving around back to park.

"We're home," he said as he pulled up at the doorway to the basement apartment where she used to live.

Wyrick opened her eyes then sat up, but Charlie was already out and opening her door to help her out.

She looked up at him from inside the Jeep and then pointed a finger at him.

"I'm walking in. I do not need to be carried."

Charlie said nothing.

She rolled her eyes and got out. Now all she had to do was stay upright, or he would ignore what she'd just said. She just knew it.

As they started up the steps of the old veranda, she held on to the railing, and Charlie held on to her. She was too shaky to care. This felt like chemo. Like she was hollow. The only thing missing was the nausea and pain.

By the time they got inside, Charlie was out of patience and picked her up anyway.

"Nobody's looking now, so don't gripe. You and I both know you're not gonna make it up the stairs, and you're not gonna make it to the elevator, either."

She laid her head on his shoulder and closed her eyes.

Charlie's heart hurt for her. All the way up. All the way down the hall to her room. Even after he laid her down on her bed and pulled off her shoes.

And when she rolled over onto her side and curled up in a ball, it was too reminiscent of how he'd found Rachel. Tears welled as he pulled a blanket over her shoulders.

"I will be back to check on you," he said, then walked out of the room, closing the door behind him.

Barrett Taylor had a visitor. He knew it was his lawyer, but he didn't know why he was here, unless it was to tell him they'd been given a trial date. Still, it was a break from the routine of jail so he didn't mind.

Marsh Fielding was sitting at the table in the visitation room when the guard brought Barrett into the room, cuffed and shackled.

Barrett took a seat on the other side of the table, and waited as the guard cuffed him to the table.

The guard glanced at Fielding. "I'll be right outside the door. Ring the bell when you're ready to leave."

Marsh nodded, and then as soon as the guard stepped out of the room, Barrett leaned forward.

Marsh leaned back and folded his hands in his lap.

"What's going on?" Barrett asked.

"Jeremiah Raver is dead. Killed by one of his money-laundering associates. The FBI and the ATF are in the process of taking down the whole ring."

A cold chill went all the way up Barrett's spine. His preacher man was even dirtier than he could have imagined.

"What does this mean for me?" he asked.

"Legally, it changes nothing of your charges. Technically, it will make you look even worse in the eyes of a jury, being a known associate, even though you might have had no knowledge of the illegal activities…other than agreeing to go kill an innocent woman."

Barrett's eyes narrowed.

"You're my attorney. You're supposed to help me wangle the legal system."

Marsh Fielding shrugged. "And that's the other thing. The man who hired me to be your attorney is deceased. He had yet to remit a retainer. Do you still want to go to trial, or do you want to change your plea?"

Barrett was stupid about some things, but not the legal system. He'd screwed himself and he knew it.

"What's my best bet?" he asked.

"Plead guilty and have a bench trial…let the judge rule in your sentence, rather than a jury."

Barrett sighed. "Will you do that for me before you quit?"

"Yes. I'll stay with you through the sentencing. It's my own fault for doing this without the retainer."

"Thanks," Barrett said.

Marsh shrugged. "It's what I do." He hesitated, and then stared Barrett straight in the eyes. "May I offer a word of suggestion?"

"I'm listening," Barrett said.

"You're going to be inside for quite a stretch. It would behoove you to think of something else to do with what's left of your life besides cause other people trouble. That's all. I'll let you know when we have to appear before the judge. In the meantime…the byword is low-key."

And then he was gone.

Barrett was taken back to his cell and left to ponder the lawyer's advice.

Farrell Kitt was down at the pigpen feeding hogs, and his wife, Judy, was in the house making supper.

Their kids were outside playing in the yard, and Farrell could hear their playful squeals and laughter. He couldn't quit thinking about how close he'd come to losing all of this, and how gullible he had been, believing Jeremiah Raver's claim that he'd had a vision from God, ordering him to send Jade Wyrick back to the hell from whence she'd come.

There was a part of him that still believed the woman should have never been born, but he hadn't counted on her calling their bluff and calling them out. He couldn't bring shame upon his family. Thank God no one knew.

He headed back to the house with a bounce in his step, looking forward to a good meal. Judy was still angry with him, but he knew in time she'd get over it.

He was walking toward the house when a car drove up into his yard. Moments later Judy came out of the house with their two-year-old on her hip. The kids who were playing all stopped and stared.

The visitor was Junior's teacher, Mildred Pete.

Farrell started walking faster, hoping Junior, his eldest, hadn't gotten into trouble at school today. Junior had his moments, and was sometimes a little hard to handle.

Judy was already at the car talking to the teacher when Farrell walked up.

"Evening, Miss Pete."

She gave him a strange look.

"Is something wrong?" he asked.

"That's what I came to ask you," she said. "Your son was doing some bragging at school today. He said something to the effect that his daddy was worth a quarter and a bazillion dollars, cause he'd done a job for the Lord. And when his daddy got paid, he was going to buy candy for everyone."

"Oh, my God," Judy said. The look she gave Farrell was somewhere between "look what you've done" and pure horror.

Farrell went numb. He could still see the teacher's lips moving, but he couldn't hear what she was saying. After all of the conniving and lying to his brother, their own child had outed him. But how? They'd been so careful.

"Well, what do you have to say for yourself?" Mildred cried.

Farrell just kept shaking his head when all of a sudden, Junior was among them.

"Teacher, did you come to eat supper with us?" Junior asked.

Mildred shook her head. "No, but thank you. I'm on my way home to my own supper."

"Daddy don't mind," Junior said. "He's got lots of money, don't you, Daddy?" Then he looked up at Farrell and smiled, waiting for confirmation.

Farrell's thoughts were in free fall. He just kept shaking his head.

"No, son. I don't have lots of money. You go get your brother and sister and get them in the house. Tell them to wash up. Supper's almost ready."

Junior glanced at his teacher, then frowned.

"But, Daddy, I heard you and Mama talking about a quarter and a bazillion dollars that was on you."

Judy grabbed her son by the arm and headed toward the house, dragging him as they went, leaving Mildred and Farrell alone.

"I knew it! I knew it the minute he said it! You're the other one, aren't you?" Mildred cried. "You and Jessup Wallis went and lost your good sense listening to that Jeremiah Raver. He's never amounted to a hill of beans, and never did anything but preach hellfire and damnation to all his church members about their mortal sins. And all the while, he was partaking in criminal activities, and look where that got him! He's dead, and you've shamed yourself and your family."

Farrell just kept shaking his head. "No, no, that—"

Mildred jabbed her finger in his chest. "You were willing to kill a woman for how she looked, and now you're trying to call an innocent child a liar? You're willing to throw your son under the bus to save yourself? You are one poor excuse for a father, Farrell Kitt. Now… I've had my say. But just know that every kid in school probably went home today and told their parents what Junior said. So prepare yourself. Your dirty secret is out, and if you so much as lay a hand on your boy's innocent little head for telling a truth, I'll report you to CPS myself. It would serve the both of you right if they came and took all your kids. You don't deserve to be parents."

"Judy didn't know anything," Farrell said, and the moment it came out of his mouth, he realized he'd just confirmed her suspicions.

"I knew it!" Mildred said.

She whipped out her cell phone, snapped a picture of his face, then ran to her car and locked herself inside.

Farrell was in shock.

Why would Mildred take his—oh no!

She was going to turn him in for the money!

Now the whole world would know his face. They wouldn't understand how he'd believed he was doing the right thing. They would only see a man willing to kill. He turned and ran for the house as Mildred drove away.

Judy was in their bedroom with their youngest in her lap, sobbing.

He sat down beside her, but when he went to put his arm around her, she pushed him away.

"I'm sorry, honey. I'm so sorry. Mildred threatened something about telling Child Protective Services. We need to leave. I can't lose you and my babies."

Judy shook her head. "I'm not going anywhere. I didn't go to that church. You did. You're the one who needs to leave. This is my home. Daddy left it to me. You did this to us, not me."

"But, Judy! You can't mean this!" Farrell cried.

As she stood, their toddler was all big-eyed and teary at the shouting, sucking his thumb at a frantic pace and still riding her hip as she held him close.

"I do mean it! Now, you get your clothes and get out of here."

"You can't manage this place by yourself!" Farrell shouted.

"I'll figure it out. But I won't be shamed by your actions, and I won't have my children shamed, either," she cried.

"They're my children, too!" Farrell yelled.

Judy took a step back. "You weren't thinking about me or our babies when you left out of here to go take a woman's life. Get out! Get out! I can't take any more of this."

Farrell was in shock. He packed without thought, throwing clothes in a bag, and then his razor and Bible in on top of it.

He paused in the doorway and looked over his shoulder. He'd

never seen hate on Judy's face before, but he was seeing it now, and he knew it was over.

"I need to go tell the kids goodbye," Farrell said.

She shook her head and waved him away.

"You will do no such thing. I'll tell them what they need to hear, and when they're older, they'll all know the truth. Just get in the car and drive. I don't want to know where you are, or where you go."

"Are you gonna divorce me?" Farrell asked.

"In a heartbeat, and I'll be changing our names," Judy said.

He stormed out of the house, threw his bag in the car and headed out of the drive.

He glanced up once in the rearview mirror. His youngest daughter was standing on the porch, waving goodbye. He looked away and just kept driving.

CHAPTER FOURTEEN

After Charlie put Wyrick to bed, he went to his bedroom and sent a text to Millie, asking her to keep them updated on Rachel's progress, then stripped and got in the shower. The need to remove the filth in which they'd found Rachel Dean was overwhelming. He washed and scrubbed at his skin until it was tingling before he finally got out.

Tragically, Rachel wouldn't be able to wash away the memories of what had happened to her with soap and water. They had to find this man. He needed not to be walking free ever again.

By the time Charlie got down to the kitchen to make dinner, he was heartsick and tired to the bone. He didn't know what Rachel Dean had endured, but it was remarkable how hard she'd fought back. Such a smart little thing—somehow getting a knife away from him, then thinking to put out the light to give herself a fighting chance.

He put potatoes in to bake, then started the grill. He'd promised Wyrick steak, and she was getting steak, even if it was after midnight before they ate.

The grill was still heating and the steaks were still marinating when he went back upstairs to check on her. He expected her to still be asleep, but the bed was empty and he could hear the shower running, so he hurried back downstairs, put the steaks on the grill and then sent her a text.

Your steak is grilling.

Within a few minutes she showed up in the kitchen in thick socks, leggings and a sweatshirt that hung halfway to her knees. Her face was bare, and the shadows under her eyes weren't makeup this time; they were for real.

He glanced up, then pointed to a container of French onion dip and a bag of wavy potato chips.

"Hors d'oeuvres."

"Such elegance. You really shouldn't have," she said, then plopped down at the table, swiped a chip through the dip and popped it into her mouth. "Mmm. Good."

He relaxed. If she felt good enough to sling a little sarcasm, then she was getting back in her groove.

"I baked potatoes and I'm grilling rib eyes. Want a salad with yours?"

"I want some of Merlin's tomatoes," she said and pulled off her socks and grabbed a bowl.

"Wait and I'll go with you," Charlie said.

"I'm fine. It's not dark yet, and you can watch me from the veranda."

"Are you feeling better?" he asked.

She nodded, swiped another chip through the dip then popped it into her mouth and took off out the door barefoot.

Charlie grabbed a platter and some tongs and followed.

She was already on the grounds and striding toward the greenhouse when he reached the grill. He gave the surroundings a quick scan, and then opened the lid to check on the steaks. They needed a couple more minutes before they'd be ready to turn, so he watched for her instead.

He watched as the light came on inside the greenhouse, and then saw her silhouette as she moved toward the back to pick the tomatoes. It made him smile, thinking of how much she enjoyed them. She liked them a lot, but not as much as chocolate.

He went back to check the steaks again, and this time they were ready. He turned them, and when he looked up she was coming back toward the house with the bowl cradled against her chest, eating from it as she walked.

"Did you save me any?" he asked as she bounded up the steps.

"Maybe four?"

He grinned. "Brat."

"How many more minutes before the steaks are done?" she asked.

"Maybe four."

She grinned. "I'm holding you to that. I'm starving."

Charlie looked down at her feet. "It's already getting chilly out here. I'll be in with the steaks in a few. Go put on your socks."

Once he mentioned it, Wyrick suddenly felt the cold. She hurried back inside, washed the tomatoes, then left them to drain and did as she'd been told. The warmth of the thick wool socks against her skin was instant comfort.

At that point Charlie came in, and the scent of the meat made her mouth water.

"Just sit," Charlie said. "Today you have earned the right to be waited on."

Once they had the food on their plates, they ate in silence for the first few bites, until they had enough in them to sate the hunger pangs, and then Wyrick paused.

"Uh... Charlie?"

He swallowed a bite and looked up. "Yeah?"

"Do we have an update on Rachel?" Wyrick asked.

"No, but I did text Millie and asked her to keep us in the loop."

"Good," Wyrick said and took a bite of baked potato and chewed. She was silent for a few more moments. "Could we stay home tomorrow?"

"Absolutely. I intended to anyway because I had every expectation that you would need a whole day home to rest up."

"Thanks. I want to sleep until I wake up. No alarms. No pressure. Just here...where it's quiet and safe."

He watched her as she ate then, thinking of all that she was, and all that she owned, and all that she knew, and all she'd asked for was somewhere quiet and safe. If only he had the power to give that to her every day for the rest of his life.

They had already taken Rachel to surgery by the time Millie got to the ER, and was directed to the surgical floor.

She raced to an elevator and then waited with a half-dozen others for a car to arrive. But the shock was still with her, and she couldn't quit shaking.

As soon as the elevator car arrived, she filed in, pushed the button to take her to the surgical floor and then grabbed hold of the rail behind her back to keep from falling when the car started upward.

A woman standing beside her grabbed her by the arm.

"Honey? Are you okay?" she asked.

Millie couldn't answer without crying, so she nodded instead.

When the door opened on her floor, all but two of the riders exited with her, dispersing in different directions, while Millie headed to the nurses' station.

A nurse glanced up as she stopped.

"Yes, ma'am...how can I help you?"

"I'm Millie Chriss, Rachel Dean's sister. Rachel was just taken into surgery. I was told there was a waiting room on this floor."

The nurse nodded and made a note of the info.

"Down the hall and to your left," the nurse said.

"Thank you," Millie said, but all the way there she kept flashing on images from their childhood.

Remembering when Rachel was six and had climbed too high in a tree and was afraid to come down. Millie didn't know what to do because their parents were gone, and she was supposed to be watching Rachel, but when Rachel saw her sister's panic, she faced her fears and came down on her own.

Remembering Rachel at fifteen, being stood up on a first date, and instead of feeling defeated, went to school the next day, laughing about it. She wound up making a fool of the boy, instead of looking like one herself.

Remembering the day they'd gotten the news about their parents' deaths, and how they'd faced the grief together. Despite her small stature, Rachel had always been a fighter. Millie suspected she was still fighting, or she wouldn't have survived.

As soon as she reached the waiting room, she found a seat near a window, then sent Ray another text, telling him where she was and that Rachel was in surgery.

Now that she knew he was on the way, she couldn't wait to see his face, to feel his arms around her again. She needed to hear someone say it was all going to be okay because, until Charlie Dodge's last call, she'd come close to losing faith in a good outcome.

It was after 8 p.m. The place had emptied out, and all of the others who'd been in the waiting room were gone.

Millie was alone, and the more time passed, the more worried she had become. When she finally heard footsteps and looked up, a young man in scrubs had walked into the room and was coming toward her.

"Rachel Dean's family?" he asked.

Millie jumped to her feet. "Yes. How is she?"

"Please, have a seat," he said, then sat down beside her. "I'm Doctor Howard, Rachel's surgeon. She came through surgery, but she's not out of the woods."

Millie started crying again, but they were tears of relief.

"Thank God she's still alive," she said. "Please, tell me everything and don't hold back. I need the truth."

He nodded. "I don't want to give you false hope. She's in pretty bad shape. She was fighting infections when they brought her in, so her fever is still high, but we're working on that. She had broken ribs and a nearly ruptured spleen. We removed the spleen and reset the ribs. It was a miracle it hadn't already ruptured. She would have bled out before she was found. She was raped. Multiple times, and we repaired some tearing. There were fragments of broken glass in her hands, her knees and the bottom of one foot. It took a while to clean that up. She has a fracture in one eye socket, but her eye seems okay and the fracture was hairline. We're going to have to watch for pneumonia as she heals."

"Did she ever regain consciousness?" Millie asked.

"No, she did not," he said.

"If the law doesn't find this man, I will find him and kill him myself," Millie said.

Doctor Howard understood her rage. "I'm so sorry, but take heart. Your sister is a fighter, or she wouldn't still be here."

"Yes, that's what I keep thinking," Millie said. "I'm afraid to ask, but what are her chances?"

"You asked for the truth, so just know that the next twenty-four to thirty-six hours are crucial. After that, we'll reassess."

Millie nodded. "Thank you. Thank you for saving her life."

"The people who found her saved her life. We just did our best to put her back together again. I'll be checking in on her regularly, and she will go from recovery to the ICU. As I'm sure you know, visitation is limited there."

Millie nodded. "Thank you again, Doctor Howard."

"Of course," he said and then left her on her own.

Millie stood, then staggered. She'd been sitting there for hours without anything but coffee in her stomach. She had another long wait ahead of her and needed food. It was too late for the hospital cafeteria, so she headed to the vending machines in the corner of the room. She got a pimento-cheese sandwich, a cold drink and some chips, then sat down and ate for the sustenance it provided.

Afterward, she washed up, then went back to the nurses' station to get directions to the ICU. Once again, she headed for the elevator. But this time knowing Rachel was still alive was all the hope she needed. After she reached the ICU waiting room, she settled into a small sofa to send Ray a message. Then sent another one to Charlie Dodge.

Charlie was kicked back in bed, watching TV, when his phone signaled a text. Seeing it was from Millie, he hit Mute and grabbed the phone. As soon as he read the text, he thought about Wyrick, then forwarded the text to her. She'd either get it tonight, or when she woke up.

But Wyrick was awake, too, and read the message with mixed emotions.

Rachel was still alive. Barely. She read the details of her surgery in disbelief. The torture she had endured was obscene. They had to find the man responsible and make sure he never hurt anyone again.

She read the message again and then sent a text back to Charlie.

We have to help find the monster. I may never rest again if we don't.

She slipped the phone onto the charger and lay back down, but she couldn't sleep, and the longer she lay there, the more she began to fidget. Finally, she threw back the covers, put her wool socks back on and headed downstairs to the office.

Finding Rachel on the property, after being missing for all those days, told her that the man they were looking for was also a resident. He'd stashed her nearby, making it easy for him to visit and get back to his apartment without anyone knowing he was ever gone.

So she started with a list of people who were in residence at Detter House when the first woman went missing, and then compared it to the list in residence when the second woman went missing…and so on until there were only two names left from the original residents who still lived there today. A man named J.J. Burch, who was in his fourteenth year of residence, and another man named Lou Nunez, who'd been there a little over twelve years. Burch owned a leasing company, and Lou Nunez was a stockbroker.

She sat there staring at the names without getting any vibes on which one it might be. It was frustrating to know that he'd had his hands all over her, and yet, she had no sense of it happening. It had to be the drug. Charlie could share this with Detective Floyd. They may already be on it, but if they weren't, this drastically narrowed the field of possible guilty parties.

It was just after two when she left the office and started down the long hall to the kitchen, only to find Charlie sitting at the table, staring into a bowl of melting ice cream.

Wyrick slid into a seat across the table and pointed to his bowl. "You gonna eat that?"

He shoved it toward her.

"What's wrong?" she asked as she took her first bite.

"I knew you were up. I was just killing time until you went back to bed," he said.

She paused in the act of taking a second bite and stared.

"You got up because I was up?"

"Eat your ice cream," he muttered.

"Well, I don't have any ice cream. I'm eating *yours*," she said and poked another bite into her mouth, then talked around it as it began melting on her tongue.

"What kind of ice cream is this?" she asked.

"Vanilla."

She swallowed the ice cream and then waved the spoon in his face.

"Okay...let me rephrase this. What else did you put on your vanilla ice cream to make it taste like this?"

"Peanut butter. Some squished-up corn flakes. And a spoonful of grape jelly."

She nodded. "The cornflakes. That's what I couldn't identify." She took another bite.

"Do you like it?" he asked.

"It's growing on me," Wyrick said.

Charlie looked up at her then, thinking to himself... *Just like you're growing on me...a crazy combination of things I didn't know I liked.*

"Want a Pepsi?" he asked.

She nodded.

He got up, got a beer for him and a Pepsi for her and came back to the table. The ice cream was gone, and Wyrick had a look on her face that he knew all too well.

"What do you know that I don't?" he asked as he handed her the drink.

"Well...since we found Rachel on the property, it's logical to assume all of the other women were likely kept there, too, until they died. So I started to wonder if there were any residents still at Detter House who'd been there from the time the first woman went missing."

"And?" Charlie asked.

"There are two. One has been there fourteen years. One has been there twelve years. And the first woman went missing eleven years ago. I'm sure the police are already on the same page, but after that thought was in my head, I had to find out."

Charlie nodded. "Good for you. That sure shortened their list of possible suspects."

"Unless, of course, someone we're not even aware of has been coming in and out through the tunnel and taking them elsewhere," Wyrick said.

"Then why stash Rachel Dean on the premises?" Charlie asked. "Nobody even knew she'd gone missing for more than twelve hours. I think your first guess is the right one."

"So do I," Wyrick said and took a drink of her pop. "It would certainly make things easier if Rachel Dean would just wake up and give us a name."

"Agreed. How's your bounty hunting going?" Charlie asked.

She shrugged. "I haven't gotten back into that yet. I'll check in tomorrow and see where I am."

"Are you ready to go to bed now?" Charlie asked.

"Yes, but you didn't have to stay up," Wyrick said. "You're not my babysitter."

"No, ma'am, I am not your babysitter. At times I am your boss. Other times I am your bodyguard. But at all times I am your friend."

Wyrick paused, too stunned to respond, and then took another drink before she could get herself together enough to ask, "So out of curiosity, what got you up tonight?"

"Hunger. And you just ate my snack," Charlie drawled.

Wyrick knew that wasn't the truth, but she let it slide.

"I'm going back to bed now," she said and picked up her Pepsi.

"This time remember not to run with that," he said, pointing to her bottle of pop.

Wyrick swished herself out of the kitchen with her chin in the air. He thought he heard her laughing as she went up the stairs, but he wasn't sure.

And by the time he got everything cleaned up and turned out the lights, she was out of sight. He paused in the hall outside her room, watching the light shining beneath her door, and didn't move until he saw it go out.

Then he went back into his room, crawled back into bed and closed his eyes. It was becoming more and more difficult to keep his hands to himself on the rare times he saw her falter. She mattered. And he didn't want to lose her, but trouble followed her everywhere.

He was still waiting for the other shoe to drop when he finally fell asleep.

Ray Chriss's plane landed at DFW in Dallas, just after midnight. It took forty-five minutes to retrieve his luggage and get a ride to the hospital, then another fifteen minutes to find the only entrance to the building at this time of night. By the time he found Millie, asleep on a sofa in the ICU waiting room, it was after 1 a.m.

He set his bag at the end of the sofa and then laid a hand on her head, feeling the soft brown curls wrapping around his fingers.

"Millie…honey?"

Millie came awake within seconds and sat up. "Oh, Ray… sweetheart! You must be exhausted, but I am so glad you're here."

He sat down beside her and put his arms around her.

"I should have been here sooner. You shouldn't have had to wait this out alone. Is there any news?"

"Not really," Millie said. "I finally got to see her at midnight." Then she put a hand over her mouth to keep from screaming, and took several slow, deep breaths. "Oh, Ray…she's so hurt. She's so, so hurt."

Ray pulled her close, rocking her where they sat as Millie dissolved into tears.

"But she's alive, baby. She's alive. And this time yesterday we didn't know that, right? This is the miracle we asked for. Just to find her alive, and they did."

"You're right," Millie said and then laid her head on his shoulder. "Thank you for coming into my life so many years ago, and for loving me…and sticking with me after Rachel came to live with us, too. You're always the calm in my storms."

Ray smiled. "Well, Rachel was in college when she came to us, so it's not like we had any diaper duty or sneaking out of the house at midnight business to deal with."

Millie laughed a little, and it felt so good to turn loose of some fear.

"Rachel was never that kid anyway. She's always known what she wanted, and has never let other people deter her from going after it."

"Yes," Ray said. "And that's why she's still alive. Because she fought to stay that way. I'm holding on to the fact that she's going to fight her way back to us now. And when she's well enough, we'll take her home again and we'll love her back. She won't be the same. Just accept that now. But she'll be stronger."

Millie glanced at the time. "I slept through the 1 a.m. visitation. But we can go in at two."

"Can I go in, too?" Ray asked.

Millie nodded.

"Two family members at a time, and we have to be very quiet. There are some very sick people in ICU."

Ray nodded. "I just want to look at her and let her know we're here. You never know how much they can hear."

"You're right," Millie said. "I was so horrified when I first saw her, that it was all I could do to say her name. I'm so glad you're here. If you're hungry, the food in the vending machines isn't awful. We have to wait until six thirty before the cafeteria opens."

"I'm fine for now," Ray said. "I missed you. I just want to hold you."

And so they settled in to wait, keeping an eye on the clock until they could see Rachel again.

Rachel knew nothing. She didn't know she'd been rescued, or had surgery, or that Millie and Ray were so near. The blessed peace of clean and soft were lost on her. The fluids and food she was getting intravenously were what she'd needed days ago. Fever warred with the antibiotics being pumped into her, and right now it was still winning.

She was safe, and didn't know.

She had prayed to be rescued or to die.

She needed to wake up so she'd know her prayers had been answered. Maybe that would be the turning point, knowing she didn't have to fight her way out of that hell now to survive.

She didn't know there were nurses with her. She didn't know when Ray and Millie came in, or when her surgeon came in to check on her again before morning.

She heard nothing.

Saw nothing.

Knew nothing.

She just was.

Waiting to be Rachel again.

Mildred Pete was a nervous wreck. She'd spent the night moving from room to room with the lights out, scared half out of her mind that Farrell Kitt would come looking to silence her.

She still couldn't believe she'd had the nerve to challenge

him, but her heart hurt for Junior Kitt. He was a sweet little boy, who was now going to grow up with a big strike against him for being his father's son.

She also felt bad for Judy Kitt. It was obvious she'd known nothing about what her husband had done until it was too late. Everyone in Paulette had known that Judy Kitt took herself and her kids to the Baptist Church in town, while Farrell had become wrapped up in Jeremiah Raver's cult. That was what they'd called it, and time had proven them all right in their beliefs.

Mildred was torn about turning Farrell in. But she also knew that if she didn't, someone else would. She was almost sixty. She'd been planning to retire at the end of this school year. Having that money for a nest egg in her later years would be a blessing.

But she didn't want people in Paulette to know she was the one who turned him in. And the only way to keep that a secret was to have that money deposited in a bank in another city.

So by the time the sun came up, she was in the kitchen having breakfast. As soon as she started a load of clothes to washing, she took off to Baton Rouge, to open an account in one of the banks. She had been saving Christmas money in a sock in her underwear drawer. Nearly five hundred dollars.

It was Saturday. That meant no school, but it also meant the banks would close at noon. It would take almost an hour to get there, but by the time she reached Baton Rouge, the bank lobby would be open. And when she left, she'd have a new checking account—one where the bounty money could be sent.

She had the email all ready to send to that woman. All she had to do was send the routing number of her bank with it, then sit back and wait for whatever came next.

It was after 8 a.m. when Wyrick woke up. She rolled over to check the time and then stretched, reveling in the leisure of a slow morning, before getting up to shower and dress.

She sent a text to Millie Chriss, telling her that they were staying on the case until the man who took Rachel was behind bars, and then went down to find something to eat.

She started her cup of coffee to brewing, and poked around in the refrigerator and then the pantry.

What she wanted was pancakes and bacon, but she didn't know how to make pancakes, and frying bacon was dangerous. Food should not hurt. So she opted for a bowl of cereal. She decided to put some fruit on it, and was eyeing the bowl of cherry tomatoes, then decided that was more adventure than she was ready for, and picked a container of blackberries instead.

She was eating a blackberry and pouring cereal in her bowl when Charlie walked in. She waved her spoon and kept chewing.

Charlie grinned. "Good morning to you, too."

He made himself coffee and toast, then got butter and jelly from the fridge and joined her at the table.

"Called Detective Floyd yet?" Wyrick asked and then poked another spoonful of cereal into her mouth.

Charlie shook his head. "I wanted to wait until we were both in on the call, in case he asked for details."

She nodded, and while they were eating Wyrick got a text. It was from Millie. She read it aloud.

"Millie says Rachel is stable. Her fever is down a couple of degrees. The doctor is happy with her progress, and Millie's husband arrived last night."

"Good news," Charlie said.

Wyrick nodded, finished her cereal and carried the bowl to the sink, then sat back down at the table and started reading the morning news on her phone.

She would have rather watched Charlie eat, because everything he did was sexy, right down to licking butter off his thumb.

As soon as he carried his dishes to the sink, he refilled his coffee and came back to the table.

"Are you ready to talk to the cops?"

"Yes," she said and laid down her phone.

Charlie made the call, then put it on speaker and waited for the detective to answer. It rang a couple of times and Wyrick frowned.

"It's Saturday. Maybe he's off?"

"Not with a kidnapper on the loose," Charlie said. But just when he thought it was going to go to voice mail, Floyd answered.

"Hey, Charlie. Sorry. I was dropping my son off at his grandma's for the day. What's up?"

"Wyrick uncovered more information last night. She thought you might already know it, but just in case you didn't, she wanted to pass it on. I have the call on speaker and she's right here, so I'm going to let her explain."

"With Rachel Dean still unconscious, any help in this case is appreciated," Floyd said. "Good morning, Wyrick. I'm listening."

"Okay…here's where I went with research last night, and you are officially welcome to shoot it all down. Only I would advise you not to, but that's just me."

They heard Floyd chuckle. "Ma'am, after witnessing you in action the past few days, I'm not shooting down anything you have to say."

Wyrick continued, "Since Rachel Dean was found on site, I went with the premise that the kidnapper likely lives on site, too. Her presence there made it easy for him to come and go at his leisure. So by a process of elimination of the names of people who've lived at Detter House since the first woman went missing, there are only two men who've lived there long enough to have had access to all four women. A man named J.J. Burch, who's been there fourteen years, and a man named Lou Nunez, who's been there twelve years."

"Wow. No. We hadn't begun to dip back that far. How on earth did you get access to records that old—?"

"Don't ask," Charlie said.

There was a moment of silence, and then Floyd chuckled again.

"Okay. Message received, and, lady, you sure don't mess around."

"There's no time," Wyrick said. "You will need to interview both of them and fast, or the guilty party will likely disappear."

"They're all already gone," Floyd said. "Allen Carson moved them to the Ritz-Carlton on his dime yesterday, because most of them were trying to break their leases. He gave us two days to get finished with our investigation and evidence gathering, and then he's going to begin demolition of the passage and the tunnel, and remodeling the rooms with the hidden doors. I understand his point. It's all about damage control."

Wyrick frowned. "This isn't good. I'm not going to tell you how to do your job, but having heard this, I would bet money the man you're looking for is already gone, and I don't want him to be gone because we need to find the other three women he took. I know they're not alive. I'm not living in that fantasy. But they're lost, and lost is a hell of a place to be. You have family. You have people who know and love you. But there are a lot of people in this world who don't. And I can say, with a level of expertise, that it is a terrible thing to be so alone in the world that, if you went missing, there wouldn't be one person to sound the alarm."

Floyd was silent a moment, then they could hear him clearing his throat.

"Yes, ma'am. I'm calling my partner. We'll head out to the Ritz this morning."

Charlie added one final comment. "Keep us in the loop, because Wyrick is not going to let this go. And if you can't find him, then that means we'll be looking for the bastard on our own."

"Understood," Floyd said. "I'll check in with you later today. Thanks for the heads-up, Wyrick."

"One more thing," Wyrick added. "If one of those two men is already in the wind, get a search warrant for his apartment and let me have access. If he's left anything behind that will help us, I will find it."

Floyd hesitated. "I don't know if—"

Charlie frowned. "Look, Floyd. We're not trying to step on anyone's toes. We don't want credit for any of it. No one has to even know we're there, and whatever we find is yours to follow up on."

"Yeah, okay. Whatever it takes, I'll make it right with the lieutenant. I'll call you later."

CHAPTER FIFTEEN

Sonny Burch was home, standing on the back porch of the old farmhouse he'd grown up in, watching the sun come up in a blaze of oranges and pinks, wondering how many more sunrises he would see.

This wasn't how he had expected life to turn out, but he never had been good at planning ahead. He'd been more of a "live in the moment" kind of guy, and now he was paying the price.

He'd given himself a once-over in the mirror last night as he'd undressed for bed, and was not happy about how he looked. His chest looked like he'd been mauled, and his dick was three shades of purple and hanging a little too limp for comfort.

He'd called his leasing company, put his manager in charge and told him that he was going to be gone for a while. They knew what to do. He wasn't worried about the future of his business. But he was worried about himself.

The sun was up now. The light show was over.

He turned toward the field at the back of the house, remembering the horses that used to run there and the cattle that had grazed in the back pasture, and sighed.

Time changes everything.

Nothing lasts forever—except memories.

Then he looked toward the bench beneath a trio of trees that were just inside the yard fence, and stepped off the porch. It was time to pay a visit to the girls. Each held a special place in his heart, even though, in the end, the relationships had not worked out.

It was close to 10 a.m. when Floyd and Mills arrived at the Ritz-Carlton. They went straight to the registration desk and flashed their badges.

"I'm Detective Floyd, and this is my partner, Detective Mills. We need the room numbers of a couple of your guests who just came in from Detter House."

"Yes, sir," the clerk said. "What are their names?"

"J.J. Burch and Lou Nunez," Floyd said.

The clerk immediately turned and typed in their names.

"Mr. Nunez is registered in room 466. But we don't have a J.J. Burch."

Floyd glanced at Mills and frowned. "Do you have Wayne Dyer's phone number?"

"No," Mills said.

"What room is Wayne Dyer in?" Floyd asked.

The clerk typed in the name.

"Mr. Dyer is in room 402." Then he pointed to a bank of phones near the desk. "You can call the rooms from any of those phones."

"Thanks," Floyd said and headed for the phone bank, then called Wayne first.

Wayne was in bed, kicked back watching TV, when his room phone rang. He muted his show, then leaned over and answered.

"Hello."

"Mr. Dyer, this is Detective Floyd."

"Oh, yes, sir. How can I help you?" Wayne asked.

"We wanted to speak to one of the residents you moved here, but he doesn't appear to have registered. His name is J.J. Burch. Do you happen to have a different location for him?"

"Who? I don't know a... Oh, wait! You're talking about Sonny. He doesn't go by J.J. No, he's not registered here. He called the office when he was leaving to let me know he was going to stay with family in the city. He said it would be more comfortable, and closer to his work."

"Ah...okay. By any chance would you have Sonny's cell phone number?" Floyd asked.

"I think I brought a list of the residents' names and contact info with me. Just a moment, please. Let me go check."

He laid down the phone and ran to get his briefcase, then shuffled through some papers before he found it. He slid back onto the side of the bed. "Yes, I do. Got a pen and paper?" he asked.

"Yes, go ahead," Floyd said and took down the number.

"There's a separate number for his office. I'll give you that one, too," Wayne said.

Floyd wrote it down. "Thanks, Mr. Dyer. Oh...since you have the list in front of you, do you have a contact number for Lou Nunez, too...just in case he's not on the premises?"

"Of course," Wayne said and gave him Nunez's number. "He's a stockbroker, but I don't know if they work on Saturdays. If you don't mind, I have a question for you. Do you have an update on Rachel Dean? We've all been praying for her."

"All I know is that she came through surgery. She's in the ICU and still unconscious."

Wayne sighed. "Lord bless her heart. This whole thing is just so horrifying and ugly. You have to catch the man who did this to her. He's a monster."

"We're doing our best," Floyd said. "Thanks for the help."

As soon as he disconnected, he called Lou Nunez's room, but he didn't answer.

"This was a bust," Mills said as they left the hotel and walked back to their car. "And who's Sonny?"

"J.J. goes by Sonny," Floyd said and got in, then pulled out his notebook with the numbers Wayne had given them and called Nunez first, then put it on speaker so Mills could hear, too.

Lou Nunez was at the office with a client when his cell phone rang. He glanced at caller ID and then frowned.

"I'm sorry, but I need to take this. If you'll excuse me for a few minutes, I shouldn't be long."

The client nodded and Lou got up and went into the outer office to answer.

"Hello, this is Nunez."

"Mr. Nunez, this is Detective Floyd, Dallas PD. Do you have a few moments to answer some questions?"

"Well, sure, I guess. Does this have anything to do with Rachel being kidnapped? Because if it does, I'll do anything I can to help. We all really like her. She is a little workaholic, but a delight to be around. What do you need to know?"

Floyd had to admit the man was forthcoming, but he could also be a damn good liar.

"How many years have you been a resident of Detter House?" Floyd asked.

"Oh, goodness. Maybe eleven, no, this year is twelve years. I don't have any relatives in the state, but the amenities at Detter House are perfect for fostering a social atmosphere, which keeps me from feeling lonely."

"Are you married?" Floyd asked.

"Not now. I moved to Detter House after my divorce. What does—?"

"Are you aware of any other women going missing since you've been living there?"

"Lord, no. Look at all the turmoil Rachel's absence caused! We would have all known, you know?"

"Where were you yesterday morning?" Floyd asked.

"I was at work. You can check with my employer. I didn't find out about that Wyrick woman being abducted or that Rachel Dean had been found until I got the phone call from Wayne Dyer that we were going to be moved to the Ritz."

"Okay, I think that's it for now. Thank you."

"Sure," Lou said. "Would it be out of line to ask about Rachel's welfare?"

"No. She's had surgery and is in the ICU. I don't believe she's regained consciousness," Floyd said.

"God. This is just so tragic. I keep praying she'll pull through," Lou said. "Thanks for letting me know."

"Of course," Floyd said and ended the call.

"He didn't come across as guarded or evasive," Mills said.

Floyd nodded. "Okay, let's see what Sonny Burch has to say for himself." He made the call, waited for it to start ringing and within seconds it went to voice mail.

"Yes, Mr. Burch. This is Detective Floyd of the Dallas PD. Please call me at this number at your earliest convenience." And then he hung up.

"Voice mail?" Mills asked.

Floyd nodded. "He has it turned off because it went directly to voice mail. I'm calling his office," he said and made that call next.

Within seconds a perky little voice was on the line.

"Mid-Texas Leasing, Chelsea speaking."

"Good morning, Chelsea. This is Detective Floyd of the Dallas PD. I need to speak to Sonny Burch."

"Oh, I'm sorry. Sonny's not here. Would you like to speak to Darryl? He's the manager."

"Yes, please," Floyd said and waited to be transferred. A few moments later a man answered.

"This is Darryl."

"Darryl, this is Detective Floyd with Dallas PD. I'm trying to get in touch with your boss."

"Oh, he's not here. He called in yesterday and told me he was going to be gone for a while. I have his cell number."

"Was this a planned trip?" Floyd asked.

"No, sir. A bit unexpected, but that's Sonny. Do you want his number?"

"Sure," Floyd said, curious to know if it was the same number they'd already been given, and it was.

"Is there anything else I can do for you?" Darryl asked.

"If he calls in, have him call this number," Floyd said. "Ask for Detective Floyd."

"Yes, sir, I sure will," and the call ended.

Floyd looked at his partner.

Mills shrugged. "I think someone's on the run."

"I think you might be right," Floyd said. "We need to get back to the station and get a search warrant for J.J. Burch's apartment, then let Wyrick loose in there. She offered, and I'm not going to turn that woman down."

This was their stay-at-home day, and Charlie was giving Wyrick all the space she needed, but after a few hours of quiet, he wanted to know what she was up to, and headed to the office where Wyrick was working. After all the years they'd spent working together, he was still amazed at how fast her fingers moved across a keyboard, and how fast her thoughts were churning to be able to do that.

"You're staring," she said without looking at him.

"No, I'm not. I just came to see if you were getting hungry."

"Not particularly," she said and kept typing, and Charlie was still there.

He shoved his hands in his pockets.

"I'm hungry," he said.

"I'm not cooking," she said and pulled up a new screen to implement another search.

He laughed.

"Are you cooking?" Wyrick asked.

"No. I'm doing DoorDash. I'll pick it up at the gate. They won't be on the property, okay?"

"I might be getting hungry. What are you ordering?" Wyrick asked.

"I think Chinese," Charlie said.

She paused and looked up.

"Ooh, good call. I'll have spring rolls, sesame chicken stir-fry and dumplings. I love pork dumplings."

"You got it," Charlie said. "I'll let you know when it's on the table."

"Don't forget condiments. I will need orange sauce and hot mustard," Wyrick said.

"Anything else?" Charlie asked.

"Fried rice. What are you having?" she asked.

He arched an eyebrow. "You mean all of that is yours?"

She glared. "You know I like leftovers, and I know you're going to order Mongolian beef something and a gallon of shrimp fried rice. Meanwhile, I have my last hit man identified. I'll tell you about it over lunch."

As she turned back to the computer, there was a moment when the graceful curve of the back of her head and her long, bare neck struck him as so beautiful. And then he thought, how odd that this woman knew everything about him, and he still didn't understand a fraction of who she was.

He walked out of the office as Wyrick was rereading the email she'd received from Mildred Pete, a fourth grade teacher in Paulette, Louisiana. According to Mildred, Farrell Kitt's own son gave him up without knowing it, by an innocent comment on the playground, and when Mildred confronted Farrell, he finally admitted it.

Wyrick nodded in satisfaction. It was the verification she needed to finger Kitt as the last hit man. His phone number was also the last number she'd pulled from the preacher's phone records. Just to make sure Kitt wasn't still bent on coming after her anyway, she pulled up her tracker app, entered his phone number and waited, watching for it to ping off a cell tower somewhere. It took several minutes before she got a hit, and when she realized the phone was pinging northbound off a tower on an interstate in Ohio, she breathed a quiet sigh of relief.

It was a sad commentary for the world in which she lived, that it took an inordinate amount of skill and money to keep herself safe, but it was worth it to keep evil on the run.

She ran a second check on Jessup Wallis's location, and realized he was moving through the Dakotas. Wherever they went, the farther away from her, the better.

Convinced she had the right men, she sent the information to Special Agent Hank Raines, just so they'd have it in their records, and then made a call to one of her banks.

After verifying her identity with the bank president via a video call, social security number and the routing number of the account she intended to use, she explained the reason for her call.

"I intend to make two large money transfers into two different bank accounts, and don't want them flagged as possible hacks," she said.

"Of course, Miss Wyrick. By any chance, are these transfers in regard to the bounties you posted last week?" he asked.

"Yes, they are. Both accounts have been verified, so I expect absolute security from your bank. In no way are the names of either of the recipients ever to be revealed."

"No, ma'am. You can rest assured their privacy will be respected on this end."

"Thank you," Wyrick said.

"Of course, and thank you for your business," he said. "I'll connect you with bookkeeping right now. Please hold."

Within fifteen minutes the bounties had been paid.

Wyrick exited that screen and pulled up the last press release she had to send, posting the pictures of the other two men from the Church of The Righteous who'd been sent to kill her.

She'd written up a short commentary to go with the faces, and had no second thoughts about what she was doing. They'd intended to end her life. All she was doing was ending their life of crime. They should be happy they were still free and breathing.

And so she hit Send, and once again the info went out to the same media outlets, and that was that. She shut down her computer, then went to wash up before going to find Charlie.

The sooner people realized she couldn't be bullied, and wouldn't run scared, the better off she would be.

She was coming down the main hall and passing the foyer when she saw movement outside and went to look out the front windows.

It was Charlie, heading toward the front gates at a lope. She paused to watch because it was Charlie, and then noticed a delivery car was parked just outside the gates.

Lunch was served. She headed for the kitchen and was making herself a glass of iced tea when he returned.

"So talk to me about your bounty hunting," Charlie said as he began pulling little cardboard boxes out of the sack.

Wyrick snagged a set of chopsticks, then sat down and opened boxes until she found her dumplings and popped one into her mouth and rolled her eyes.

Charlie grinned. "Good?"

She waved her chopstick for yes, chewed, swallowed, took a drink of tea, then started talking.

"The bounties have been paid. The last dude *was* Farrell Kitt, the third man on Jeremiah Raver's phone list. And you won't believe who gave him up. It was his nine-year-old son, and he didn't even know the significance of what he said."

"Damn. That's a hard one," Charlie said.

Wyrick nodded. "His teacher overheard a comment, put two and two together and confronted the man. He finally admitted it to her. She snapped a picture of him and ran. I admire her guts."

"Do you know where both men are now?" Charlie asked.

"Jessup Wallis is in the Dakotas, and Farrell Kitt is heading north through Ohio."

"May they forever stay in Canada," Charlie muttered, then finally found his Mongolian beef stir-fry and got up to get a fork. He didn't have good luck with chopsticks and rice noodles.

They talked as they ate, going over and over the details they knew about the case as it stood, and were almost through when Charlie got a call from Detective Floyd.

Charlie answered. "You're on speaker. Go for it."

"This is the promised update. Nunez has an airtight alibi for yesterday. He was at work when Wyrick was abducted, and still there when we found Rachel. He knew nothing about any of it until he got a text from the manager telling him they would be moving them to the Ritz. So he came home and packed, like everyone else."

"What about Sonny Burch?" Wyrick asked.

"He never registered at the Ritz. He told Dyer that he was staying in the city with family. Then he called his business, put the manager in charge and said he would be gone for a while. And his phone is off. When we call, it goes straight to voice mail."

"He's running, isn't he?" Charlie said.

"Or hiding. At any rate, we're waiting on a search warrant for his apartment. If we get it, can you meet us there today?" Floyd asked.

"Yes," Wyrick said. "But I have a question. Did you locate any of Burch's family?"

At this point Mills entered the conversation.

"To our knowledge, he has no family in the state. His parents and grandparents are deceased. He has two cousins mentioned in an obituary…but one lives in California and the other in Montana."

"I'll see if I can find out anything more," Wyrick said.

"When you get the search warrant, just text me," Charlie said.

"We're on our way to the judge's office now. It shouldn't be long," Floyd said. "See you soon."

He hung up.

Charlie put the phone back in his pocket and finished off the last of his shrimp fried rice.

"I have a spring roll left," Wyrick said. "You can have it if you want."

"Are you sure?" Charlie asked.

"Yes, I'm sure there's one left, but I won't repeat the offer. Eat it, or forever hold your fork," she said and pushed the box toward him.

He grinned. "Smart-ass…and thank you."

She rolled her eyes. "You're the only man I know who gives smiles with insults, and you're welcome."

Charlie pointed to a little packet of hot mustard near her glass.

"Would you also part with that packet of hot mustard?"

"Knock yourself out," she said. "But I'm keeping my leftover fried rice."

"Understood," Charlie said.

"Thank you for lunch," Wyrick said. "I'm going to change into some traveling clothes so I'll be ready when the call comes."

"You could go in the leggings and sweatshirt," Charlie said.

"As if. Nobody sees me like this but you," she said, then dumped her empty cartons into the trash and strode out of the room like the goddess she appeared to be.

Charlie was still digesting the comment as he finished off the spring roll, and cleaned up what was left of their mess, unaware Wyrick was already in search mode, determined not to let a killer get away.

She dressed quickly in black leather pants and a red V-neck shirt. The only button on the shirt was midway across her stomach, leaving more than enough of her dragon for the world to see.

As soon as she was ready, she hurried back to her office. Her first move was to get the names of J.J. Burch's parents and grandparents, and then she began searching deeds and land records to see if there were any properties still owned in their names in the state of Texas.

CHAPTER SIXTEEN

It didn't take long before Wyrick found records of the deeds, and then she began tracing deaths, and heirs, and more deaths, until she determined that the property in Dallas, once owned by his maternal grandparents, was no longer in the family.

However, the property once belonging to Burch's paternal grandparents was located in a rural area east of Dallas, and was now owned by a grandson named Joseph Jonathan Burch, who had the same social security number as the Sonny Burch who'd gone missing. She had the right place. Now all she needed was to see if Sonny was there.

She rolled her chair to a different computer, pulled up an icon on the screen and then activated her satellite search. She keyed in the GPS location of the farm, and as an aerial view came up, she started zooming in.

Burch owned a leasing company. If the house was habitable, maybe he'd leased it. Or maybe he'd just leased the land. She needed to see if there was anyone in residence, and kept zooming in until she saw outbuildings, fences and an old, two-story farmhouse.

The house looked empty. The grass in the yard was long enough that it was lying over, like hay ready to cut, and she couldn't tell if there was power on anywhere.

She moved the camera to the outbuildings, and as she did, noticed the rear end of a newer-model car parked just inside the barn. She moved in closer, and closer, until she saw the make of the car, and then zoomed in to get the tag.

She turned back to her other computer, hacked into the DMV and checked the registration, then grinned.

"To quote Charlie...hot damn."

It was registered to Burch. She began saving images of everything she'd seen to send to Detective Floyd, and when she was finished, she was pulling back on the satellite view when she saw a door open on the front porch, and then a man came out.

The skin on the back of her neck suddenly crawled. It was Burch. She recognized him from his picture on file at the DMV and immediately saved the image. And then she went back to the active screen and zoomed in on his face.

He looked so ordinary. Midforties, a nose that might have been broken once or twice, a chin people would have referred to as weak, pale eyes and blondish/graying hair.

It was horrifying to know that this man had tried to kidnap her. He'd had his hands all over her, and she could have passed him on the street and never known who he was.

This was the man who kidnapped Rachel and the other women. And if it hadn't been for Charlie, she would have been the fifth. A bitter taste was suddenly in the back of her throat, as if she might vomit. She leaned closer to the screen until they were digitally face-to-face.

"I'm taking you down, you sorry bastard, and I'm doing it for free."

Then she heard Charlie coming up the hall at a fast pace and guessed he'd heard from Floyd.

She dragged all of the photos into the desktop folder she'd made for the deeds and land records and sent in the whole thing as an attachment to Floyd's email just as Charlie came into the office.

"We have to go," Charlie said.

"Call Floyd," she said.

"But we'll see him at—"

"Please. Just call him now."

Charlie pulled up the number and called.

Floyd answered promptly. "Did you get my text?"

"Yes, just now, but Wyrick needs to tell you something. She's on speaker."

"Hey, lady. What magic have you conjured up now?"

"Sonny Burch inherited his paternal grandparents' farm east of Dallas. It's north off Highway 80…between the towns of Elmo and Edgewood. He's there…now."

"How in the world do you know that?" Floyd asked.

"Check your email. I just sent you satellite photos of a car parked inside a barn on the property, and the GPS location. I also got the make, model and license plate number of the car. It belongs to Burch. And I have satellite photos of him coming outside and standing on the porch."

"Okay… I'm not even asking you how you have access to a satellite you can manipulate to suit yourself. We'll contact the Dallas County Sheriff's office, and ask them to pick him up for questioning. But we're already on the way to Detter House. Are you coming?"

"Wouldn't miss it," Charlie said.

"Then we'll see you there. And once more, thank you, Wyrick. If you ever want a job with—"

"Everybody always asks, but she's mine, so no poaching," Charlie said.

Floyd was still laughing when Charlie ended the call.

Then Wyrick stood up, and Charlie's gaze went from her face to the dragon's eyes staring at him, and then back to her face again. He pointed at the visible dragon beneath her shirt.

"He glared at me. Tell it I'm on your side," Charlie said.

"Don't be so touchy. She already knows that, and I'm ready when you are."

Charlie felt as if the ground had just gone out from beneath his feet. *Ready when I am? Am I ready for you?*

"Uh…ready to…?"

"To leave," Wyrick said. "Do you want me to drive?"

Charlie hit the earth with an emotional thump.

"We've already had this conversation," he said. "Let's hustle."

Minutes later they were in his Jeep and leaving the property. Wyrick set the security alarm as the gate swung shut behind them, and then they were gone.

While Charlie and Wyrick were on their way to meet the detectives, Floyd had already sent a request to the Dallas County Sheriff to pick J.J. Burch up for questioning in the abduction of Rachel Dean, and the attempted abduction of Jade Wyrick. He readily agreed and sent two officers to the farm.

Sonny was spending his last hours as a free man and didn't know it. Part of him knew the possibility was inevitable, but he had yet to accept it.

He'd spent the night on a dusty bare mattress and missed the irony of how dirty bare mattresses were playing out in his life. Then he spent the morning outside, visiting with the girls before the weather had driven him back indoors.

The wind was picking up and when he went out to check the sky, it was clouding up in the north. He'd heard weather reports earlier of a storm moving south through Oklahoma, and guessed Texas might get some of that down the road.

He'd brought some food from his apartment, but it wasn't

going to last forever. And he was going to have to make a decision as to where to go from here. He could have just kept driving, but he'd had a need to say goodbye. Now that he was here, he was second-guessing his decision.

The house was nearly bare, and there was a layer of dust all over everything. In addition to the one and only bed, which he'd slept in last night, there was an old table and two chairs still in the kitchen. But that was it. Normally, the dirt would have mattered, but not this time. Cleanliness was the least of his troubles.

The scabs on the front of his chest were beginning to itch, but he didn't dare scratch. And his belly was complaining of a lack of food, so he dug through the sack, opened a can of tuna and a sleeve of saltines and sat down to eat.

Back in the day, the lights would have been on, and good things to eat would have been cooking on the stove. His mother and grandmother would have been laughing and talking, and his dad and grandpa would have been outside doing chores. But that was before the fantasies began.

He didn't remember when he first started thinking about hurting women. But as he moved through his teen years, the thoughts became all-consuming. As he got older, prostitutes suffered the indignities of his fantasies, until he caught an STD, and after that the rage to hurt them more kicked in.

But this time there would be no more hookers. He went for the nice girls. The good girls. And got rejected.

Sonny had never dealt well with rejection, so one thing led to another, and now he was here, on the run, eating tuna on crackers in the shadows of his past.

He was scooping out the last bit of tuna on a cracker when he thought he heard vehicles approaching. He swallowed the final bite and got up to look out. When he realized the vehicles were from the Dallas County Sheriff's Department, his heart began to hammer.

He watched the two officers get out, their hands resting lightly on their weapons as they headed to the front door. He gave the inside of the old house one last look, then went back into the kitchen and cleaned up his trash, tossing it into the sack with his other food.

He heard the knock and closed his eyes, trying to pull the silence of the old house around him like a hug, but the cops ruined the moment when one of them shouted.

"J.J. Burch! This is the Dallas County Sheriff's Department."

At that moment Sonny gave up the fight. He was too big of a coward to kill himself. He didn't know what prison was like, but he was guessing he was about to find out. If it had not been for Charlie Dodge and that Wyrick woman, his game could have gone on forever.

The officers knocked again.

He glanced out the kitchen windows one last time and then walked through the house and opened the front door.

One officer asked, "Are you J.J. Burch?"

He nodded. "What's all the ruckus about?"

"You're wanted for questioning by the Dallas PD."

"What on earth for?" Sonny asked.

"Regarding the assault and kidnapping of Rachel Dean, and for the attempted kidnapping of Jade Wyrick. Put your hands behind your back."

And so he did. Without argument. Without demanding a lawyer, or to see a warrant for his arrest. Rachel Dean had taken away his power, and Wyrick had defeated him.

The cuffs were hard and a little tight on his wrists. After he was cuffed, they began to pat him down for weapons.

He cried out when they roughed up his chest and cried out again when they patted him down below the waist, checking the inside of his legs for concealed weapons.

"Be careful," he yelled. "I'm hurt."

One of the officers pulled up his shirt and saw the scratches. "A friend's cat," he said.

"Your friend has fingernails," the officer said.

"Would you please pull the front door shut?" Sonny said. "I don't want the property damaged."

One officer turned the lock inside the door then pulled it shut, while the other one put Sonny in the back of the car and then drove away.

Detective Floyd still had a passkey to the apartments, and since they hadn't been able to find Burch to serve the search warrant, they notified Allen Carson of the search.

Allen was shocked about the request.

"Is Sonny Burch the man who abducted Rachel?" he asked.

"He's a suspect in the case," Floyd said.

"Lord. Do I have to be there?" Allen asked.

"No, sir. We're just covering our bases by letting you know we're on the property and about to search his residence," Floyd said.

"Then search away," Allen said. "I will be so glad to see the guilty person behind bars, and my renters safely back in their homes and unafraid. I also want to give you a little backstory about the property. I spoke to a woman from the historical society, and then the last living relative from the original owners, asking them about that passage. The historical society didn't have much to go on, but the relative told me something that made things fit. Back in the old days, after the original owners had passed, one heir actually turned it into a gentlemen's club for a time, with a secret access into the property without being seen, which might explain the tunnel. As for the secret doors in the building itself, at the time they weren't secret, and the women inside were high-class prostitutes, waiting to service whoever came through that door. Then he died, some relatives from Boston inherited without knowing the details of the place, and through the years that knowledge was likely lost from one owner to the next."

"Wow," Floyd said. "Interesting, and explains the whole mess. Well, happy renovating."

"Oh, have no doubt," Allen said. "That's about to be gone."

"Okay, thanks for the info," Floyd said and disconnected.

He and Mills were waiting in the hall in front of the office when Charlie and Wyrick arrived.

Floyd first saw them walking across the drive toward the entrance. Looking at Charlie Dodge made Floyd wish he worked out, but it was Wyrick who held his focus. No hair, no boobs, and she was, without doubt, the sexiest woman he'd ever seen. And from his partner's comment, it was apparent that he agreed.

"Damn," Mills whispered. "Charlie Dodge is one lucky son of a bitch."

"I don't think they have that kind of relationship," Floyd said. "His wife recently died after a long bout with Alzheimer's, and Wyrick has worked for him for years. They're partners for sure, in the best sense of the word."

And then Charlie and Wyrick entered the building, and both cops clammed up.

"We have a little info for you," Floyd said. "Allen Carson found out why the passage and tunnel were likely there in the first place," and then related the story as Carson had told them.

Charlie was dumbfounded. "Good Lord. So the original reason was just a way for rich guys to see hookers without their wives finding out."

"Secrets and lies are never really buried," Wyrick said.

"Yes, ma'am. Are you ready to do this?" Floyd asked.

Charlie nodded. "Lead the way."

The detectives turned and moved through the lobby, then

down a long hall on the south end of the ground floor to apartment 115.

"This is it," Floyd said, unlocked the door and walked in, turning on lights as they went.

Wyrick moved through the rooms, looking at the layout and the fixtures and the bookshelves surrounding the gas fireplace in the living room on their left.

"This apartment is a reverse layout of the one Rachel Dean was in," Charlie said, then glanced at Wyrick. "Everything okay?"

She nodded. "Just getting a feel for the place."

"So what do you think?" Charlie asked.

She shrugged. "Even though the lights are on, it feels dark. I'm going to walk through all of the rooms first and then backtrack to begin a search and go from there."

"You and Charlie do your thing and give us a shout if you find something," Floyd said.

"I'm going this way," Wyrick said.

"Then so am I," Charlie added. "I already left you on your own once in this damn place, and I nearly lost you. That's not happening again."

Wyrick wasn't going to argue with that, and began walking through the rooms but nothing popped. So she backtracked and began in Sonny's bedroom, picking up small items, trying to get a feel for him, or lock in on a vision. Except for a slight nausea just being in the energy, she got nothing, but she knew it was because the girls had never been here.

"We're not going to find souvenirs or trophies of his conquests," Wyrick said. "He's too careful...and patient."

"That's for darn sure," Mills said as he searched through the drawers of a dresser. "I've never worked a case where a killer waited so long between kills. And if you hadn't caught on to those other women being missing, we would never have known Rachel was one of four."

"He's right," Floyd said as he walked out of the bathroom. "But once we pulled those case files, little things began to add up."

"How so?" Charlie asked.

"Oh. Right! We never did share what we learned as to why the cases on the other missing women were closed."

Then Floyd began to explain about the carefully crafted letters that led each manager at Detter House to assume the missing woman had simply moved on to greener pastures.

"But when we compared the letters from each file, the writing on all three letters was the same," Mills added.

Floyd nodded. "Right! And *then*, as we began backtracking, we also found out there was a different manager in charge at each time, so that when another woman went missing, there was no one to raise concerns about this happening before—no continuity to be tracked. And there were so many years between abductions, that the officers in Missing Persons never caught the location as being a hot spot for missing women…until Wyrick saw it," Floyd said.

"Serial killers are often particular about attention to details. We need to look for some of Sonny's handwriting," Charlie said. "If it's the same as what's in the other files, that will be one more fact to add to your case against him."

"He doesn't have a study," Wyrick said. "But there's a small desk in the living room. We can look there. And if we don't find anything here, we can always go to his office."

They left the detectives in the bedroom and headed back to the front of the apartment.

"I'm going to check the kitchen first for handwriting…to see if he wrote a grocery list rather than putting it on his phone," Charlie said, but there were no signs of lists.

Afterward, they went to the living room. Charlie headed straight to the desk, but Wyrick kept looking at the shelves of books. The titles told her nothing. They were a random assortment of fiction and nonfiction self-help books, and some on realty and flipping houses. There were no classics. No literature. And none of the books were in any kind of organization. They were just poked in the shelves without thought, almost as if they were there to fill up shelves…*and hide something in plain sight.*

The thought had come out of nowhere, and it startled her.

"Hey, Charlie…"

He paused, then looked up.

"Yeah?"

"We need to go through these books."

"Really?"

She nodded and went to the bottom shelf on one side of the fireplace, started with the book at the end, pulled it out, leafed through it, then held it by the covers and shook it upside down.

Charlie followed her lead and started on the shelves on the other side of the fireplace. They were still going through books, and then tossing them on the floor, when Floyd and Mills walked in.

"What's going on?" Floyd asked.

Wyrick shrugged. "Just following a gut feeling."

"We'll help," they said, and soon all four of them were pulling books from the shelves and shaking them out before tossing them aside.

When they got to the top shelves, nobody could reach them but Charlie. So he began pulling down books and handing them to the trio below to search. He had just grabbed a handful and as he was pulling them down, a book that had been hidden behind them fell flat onto the shelf.

"Uh-oh," Charlie said and handed Floyd the books.

"What?" Wyrick asked.

"There was a book behind those. It just fell."

"What is it?" Wyrick asked.

Charlie felt along the shelf until it was beneath his fingers, then pulled it out and frowned.

"Weird. *The Velveteen Rabbit* is a kid's book."

"Is it? I've never heard of that," Wyrick said and held out her hand. "May I?"

Charlie hid his shock as he handed it to her. Wyrick had never heard of *The Velveteen Rabbit*? And then he watched as she opened the cover and touched the inscription inside with a kind of reverence.

"There's something written on the flyleaf. It says, *To Sonny, with love, Granny.*"

"Ah, just a keepsake," Floyd said and kept searching.

But Wyrick wasn't so sure. She turned the book upside down and shook it.

"A page fell out," Charlie said.

She reached down and picked it up. "It's not a page. It's folded paper," she said and even as she was unfolding it, she knew it had something to do with the missing women.

"It's a map," Charlie said. "But it's not a road map. This was torn from a plat map. Those lines are section lines, and the other lines and notations are the way the sections of land have been surveyed and sold off. See, half section, quarter section and some even smaller. This is how rural land is mapped."

Wyrick was still holding the paper, staring at it. What she'd first thought were just stains or mold spots in one area, she now saw as ink spots. She took the map over to the desk and spread it out, then laid her hand over the marks and closed her eyes. Almost immediately, she saw a woman's face, and then a second, and then a third. And they were crying. She yanked her hand back as if she'd been burned and handed it to Floyd.

"I don't know which county his grandparents' farm is in, but these dots are where he buried the three missing women."

Floyd looked at the paper.

"How can you be sure?"

Wyrick nodded. "I saw their faces."

He shook his head. "Ma'am, I don't know how you do this, but you two are helping us take a real bad man out of circulation. If it had not been for your help, he could have done this forever. Those women can't thank you, but we can. You put yourself in danger to help us, and don't think it will go unnoticed."

"No...please. Don't tell anyone we helped you," Charlie said. "It just makes it harder on her."

"Oh...right. I understand," Floyd said and was refolding the paper when his phone signaled a text. He read it and grinned. "Some boys from the Dallas County Sheriff's office just picked up Sonny Burch. They said he offered no resistance."

"He's a coward," Wyrick said. "He's not afraid to hurt women, but he's afraid of getting hurt. He'll talk. And he'll brag. And you'll find the bodies. Thank you for letting me help."

Charlie put a hand on her shoulder.

"You ready to go home?"

"Almost. I want to stop by the hospital to check on Rachel Dean. And then I want a Pepsi and a Hershey bar."

Charlie laughed. "Okay, now you two know the real secret to her genius. Pop and candy. And if you don't mind, we'll see ourselves out."

The detectives' laughter followed them up the hall. But even after they were leaving the building, Wyrick imagined she could still hear it...but it wasn't the men's voices she was hearing now. It was the women. They were joyful to no longer be lost.

It took almost an hour to get to the hospital because of a wreck on the beltway. Traffic was moving at a crawl, and when they finally came to an exit, Charlie took it, traveling the city streets to get where they needed to go.

Wyrick was quiet, but Charlie thought nothing of it. She never talked without purpose, but as they were parking to go inside, she finally spoke up.

"Visiting hours in the ICU are on the hour, and only two at a time are allowed. If Millie is there, and Rachel still hasn't regained consciousness, I'm going to ask if I can go in with her."

Charlie parked, then looked at her. He knew what she was thinking. If Rachel wasn't doing well, Wyrick was going to fix her, just like she'd fixed his hand.

"She's going to be hooked up to a dozen machines. Don't fry them."

Wyrick shrugged. "She needs to have something to live for. I want her to know she's safe. After that she'll finish healing herself."

"If you weren't so damn scary, I'd tell you what an angel you are," Charlie said.

"Oh, shut up," Wyrick muttered. "I am not scary."

"Why don't you want me saying nice things about you?"

She looked at him, her dark eyes locked into his gaze.

"You don't have to say anything nice to me," she replied and then opened the door.

Charlie got out and followed her into the hospital. He didn't know whether he'd just been put in his place for getting too personal, or if he'd crossed a line he hadn't known was there. When they got in the elevator to go up to the ICU, he stood in one corner of the car, and she stood in the other.

"I'm sorry," he said.

"You have nothing to apologize for," Wyrick said. "I'm not scary, but I am sometimes a bitch. It's a coping mechanism. Not a criticism of you. You are my anchor, Charlie. Don't go rocking my boat."

And then the door opened and she strode off, leaving him to follow, because she didn't want to see his face. She didn't want to see shock, or rejection, or even worse, that he might be laughing at her. She'd revealed something personal to him, and *that* was scary.

But Charlie got it. She didn't know what to do with emotion. He'd scared her, so it was time to back off.

"There's the waiting room," he said, pointing to a room off to their left, and then they walked in.

There were several groups of people scattered around the room, some talking quietly, others reading their phones and a few reading books.

The people looked up when they entered, then looked again at Wyrick's yellow-eyed dragon, breathing fire across her bare chest. They knew who she was, and she *was* scary all over again.

But it was Millie who jumped to her feet when she saw them.

"Oh! I had no idea I'd see you two again! Thank you! Thank you for coming," she said and hugged Charlie, then Wyrick. "This is my husband, Ray. Ray, this is Charlie Dodge and his partner, Wyrick."

Ray was on his feet in seconds, shaking their hands. "It's an honor to meet you both. Will you sit with us?" he asked.

"Sure," Charlie said. "We came to check on Rachel. Has there been any change in her condition?"

"Some," Millie said. "The antibiotics are working, because her fever is slowly going down, and her doctor is pleased that she's healing from the surgery."

"Has she shown any signs of regaining consciousness?" Wyrick asked.

Millie's eyes welled. "No, but I still have hope."

Wyrick reached across the space between them and took Millie's hands.

"Would you allow me to accompany you at the next visitation?"

Millie looked a little puzzled. "Why, yes, of course, but—"

Wyrick lowered her voice. "I might be able to help."

Millie's fingers tightened on Wyrick's grasp.

"You mean…?"

"I will only hold her, like I'm holding you."

Millie looked down at Wyrick's hands, pale skin and the long, graceful fingers, then looked up at the clock.

"You'll have to wait about fifteen more minutes before we're allowed to go in."

"We'll wait as long as it takes," Charlie said and then saw the vending machines.

"Hey, Wyrick, there's your Pepsi. Want one?"

"Yes, please," Wyrick said and leaned back in her seat.

"Can I get either of you anything?" Charlie asked as he stood.

"I'll go with you," Ray said.

Wyrick watched in awe of how two men, total strangers to each other, could just bond over anything and walk away, talking. Or maybe everyone was like that, and she was the oddball. Life had taught her the hard way not to let down her guard. Not even for Charlie. Even though he saw more of her truth than anyone else, she held back that which mattered most, for fear of losing him.

By the time they came back, Ray and Charlie were talking about Oklahoma/Texas football rivalries and fishing. Charlie handed her the Pepsi and then pulled a Hershey out of his pocket and laid it in her lap.

"Thank you," she said and unwrapped the candy first and took a bite.

Ray had chips and a drink for Millie so they sat quietly, having their snack, while Ray and Charlie kept talking.

Wyrick kept watch on the clock, mentally preparing for the

task ahead. The minutes crept by as she finished her food, then slipped into the bathroom to wash up.

When she came out again, new people had arrived—one a couple with a crying baby. She paused without thinking that people were watching her again. She was wondering what it would be like to be a mother. She barely remembered her own, and since chemo and cancer, would never be able to be one.

The baby was screaming, and the mother looked frazzled. Wyrick had to move past them to get to her seat. It wouldn't take a second to just stroke his head. Touching babies' heads was permitted, she thought.

The mother looked up, her eyes widening in surprise as she recognized Wyrick on sight. Then Wyrick paused and laid her hand on the back of the baby's head.

"He's so beautiful," Wyrick said and felt the softness of the baby's curls beneath her palm.

"He's cranky. Nothing seems to make him—" And then she realized he wasn't crying anymore. She looked down as he settled his little cheek against her shoulder and began sucking his thumb. "Well, my goodness! I guess—"

Wyrick reluctantly let go of the curls and walked back to her seat.

This was the second time Charlie had seen her affinity with children. It wasn't anything he would ever have expected from her, and he knew better than to comment, but it touched him in a way he could not explain.

Millie was still fascinated with Wyrick, and seeing the baby go peacefully to sleep with hardly more than a touch from Wyrick's hand was amazing. It made her wonder what magic she might render to Rachel. Could she wake her as easily as she'd put the baby to sleep?

She'd soon find out.

CHAPTER SEVENTEEN

It was 4 p.m. when people began getting up and leaving the waiting room.

"Is it time?" Wyrick asked.

Millie nodded. "Follow me," she said.

Wyrick stood then walked out of the room, towering over Millie's height by almost a foot.

They entered the ward in silence, moving past the other patients. There was a nurse at Rachel's bedside as they approached.

"Is there any change?" Millie whispered.

"She's stable. That's a good sign," the nurse said softly, then glanced up at Wyrick. She recognized the woman behind the mask of makeup, then eyed the fierce tattoo before walking away.

Wyrick moved to Rachel's bedside, quickly identifying all of the machines they had hooked to her body, then gently laid a hand on Rachel's shoulder.

"Do you talk to her?" Wyrick asked.

Millie nodded.

"Then let her know you're here. Tell her she's in a hospital, and that she's safe. Keep telling her she's safe. Tell her the man who hurt her is behind bars."

Millie gasped. "They caught him?"

Wyrick nodded, then she put one hand on Rachel's forehead, the other on her arm and closed her eyes.

She could hear Millie's soft voice, but the words were fading as she moved into Rachel's body…seeing the physical damage already in the stages of healing, and feeling the drain of the energy it was taking from her. It was the fever that was sapping her strength.

She sent all of the energy she had into Rachel, knowing when the wounds healed, the fever would abate. She put her hand over the bandage on her neck and then moved it over her heart, sending energy pulsing throughout her body, watching it seal off wounds and healing the frayed ends of tiny nerves.

And then she put a hand on Rachel's forehead and moved deeper, slipping into Rachel's psyche, feeling the horror trapped within her, and the pain and the terror of what she had experienced.

It was just as Wyrick had thought.

Rachel didn't know she was safe.

Wyrick remembered she'd sent Charlie a text with her thoughts. What if she could get her thoughts beneath the dark in which Rachel was hiding? What if Rachel heard them?

There was only one way to find out.

Rachel… Rachel Dean. Come out of the shadows. You've been rescued. You are safe. There's no one left to hurt you. He's the one locked up now. You're free, but he'll never see freedom again. Come out, come out into the light. Don't let him win. Millie's here. She's waiting to take you home. Listen for her voice. She's here. She saved you. It's safe to come home.

She stood for a few seconds, waiting to see if she felt any kind of response, and then slowly turned loose and stepped away.

Millie was on the other side of Rachel's bed, whispering near her ear, patting her arm, saying things only a sister would know to say.

Wyrick was waiting. The visitation time was almost up. She didn't want to leave without knowing if it had made a difference.

Unaware of Wyrick's expectations, Millie paused to wipe tears from her eyes, and as she did, Wyrick saw Rachel's chest rise as if she'd taken a deep breath, and when she exhaled the cannula in her nose shifted slightly.

It was at that moment that Millie looked back down and then gasped.

"Her eyelids are fluttering. Oh, my God, oh, my God!" She took off to get a nurse. They were back within seconds, and Millie pointed to Rachel's eyes, seeing movement beneath the lids.

"Look," Millie said. "I think she is trying to wake up."

The nurse immediately began checking Rachel's vitals and then called the RN.

Millie was beside herself. It was hard to keep her voice down, but she just kept talking to Rachel, wanting to hear her voice.

"Honey, it's me, Millie. You're in a hospital. You're safe. You're safe. You're going to be okay."

Rachel's lips parted.

Millie leaned over.

At first she just felt her sister's breath on her cheek, and then she thought she heard a word within an exhale.

"Yes, this is Millie. You're safe, sugar. You're safe. I'm right here."

The word was faint, hardly more than a whisper.

"Saa…"

"She said *safe*," Millie cried.

The nurses had to agree it was a cognizant response to what Millie had been saying.

"I'm sorry, ladies, but visiting time is over."

Before they could challenge her, Wyrick spoke.

"Rachel…who hurt you?"

The RN turned and glared at Wyrick, but she wasn't looking at the nurse. She was touching Rachel's leg.

"Who hurt you, Rachel?"

"Time's up," the RN said.

"Sonnn."

Millie gasped. "She said a name. She said Son. What does
that mean?"

Wyrick felt Rachel's triumph as if it had been her own.

"She didn't say Son. She's trying to say *Sonny*. Sonny Burch
is the name of the man they've taken into custody," Wyrick said
and walked past nurses and patients, and out of the ICU.

The waiting room was emptying fast. Ray was standing,
holding Millie's purse, ready to take her down to the cafeteria
to get some food.

Charlie was standing by the window, watching the gathering
clouds. It was going to storm.

Then all of a sudden, Wyrick was at his elbow.

"She's regaining consciousness," Wyrick said. "She knows
she's safe, and she named him."

Charlie grabbed her by both shoulders, gave them a squeeze
and then immediately let her go.

"Have you done all you need to do here?"

"Yes. She'll get better now."

He pointed to the clouds. "Then we need to head home."

Millie came running into the waiting room and threw her
arms around Ray's neck.

"She's waking up. She's trying to talk. I can't explain what
Wyrick did, but I witnessed it." Then she realized they were
leaving. "Wait. Please, both of you! I have to say this. You didn't
know us, and yet your generosity saved us. Giving of your skill
and time without pay, nearly getting yourself killed, finding my

sweet sister and now this. Wyrick, whatever you did in there helped her turn a corner. How? How can you do that?"

Wyrick shrugged. "I don't know. It's just part of who I am. Please let us know how she progresses. I hope you take her home to heal. It's going to be a long time before she feels safe again."

"It's okay. She's alive. We'll deal with the rest as it comes," Millie said.

Charlie put his hand on the middle of Wyrick's back.

It was her signal to move, and so she did—in long strides, all the way to the elevator. Once they were down, they hurried through the main lobby and out into the parking lot. The wind was already rising, and the clouds were rumbling and rolling overhead as they made a run for the Jeep. The first drops were just hitting the windshield as they got inside.

Wyrick was buckling up when she glanced at Charlie.

"Rachel said two words."

Charlie's eyes widened. "What did she say?"

"I asked Millie to keep telling Rachel that she was safe, because she didn't know she's been rescued, and right after Millie said it, Rachel got out enough of the word *safe* to be understood. And then right before we left, I asked, 'Who hurt you?' The nurse didn't like it because she'd already told us it was time to leave, but I ignored her."

"Of course you did," Charlie said.

Wyrick shrugged. "Anyway, right after I asked, Rachel got out the word *Son*. That's when I told Millie she'd just named her kidnapper... Sonny Burch."

Charlie grinned. "That's what Floyd and Mills have been waiting to hear. I'm driving. You call and let them know."

"Okay," Wyrick said and made the call.

Floyd was back at the precinct, writing up the report on finding the piece of map when his cell phone rang. He saw it was Wyrick and quickly answered.

"Good afternoon, lady. What have you stirred up for us now?"

As always, when they were on the job, Wyrick had the phone on speaker and told him everything that she'd just told Charlie.

"She named him. She named her abductor in front of her sister and a nurse."

"This is wonderful!" Floyd said. "You just made a good day better. I'll check in with Millie again soon, and remind her to let us know when Rachel is well enough to give us a full statement. Thanks for the update."

"Welcome," Wyrick said and disconnected.

Charlie was already out of the parking lot and back on the city streets when a bolt of lightning shot across their line of vision, quickly followed by a loud clap of thunder.

"We should have stayed inside the hospital," Charlie said.

"We're not going to melt. Turn on the windshield wipers and drive like hell," Wyrick said.

Charlie laughed. And he was still laughing when they hit the beltway in a downpour, but he wasn't driving like hell because he didn't want to die. He was having too much fun with this woman.

And then the moment he thought that, his heart nearly stopped. Having fun! It had been so long since he'd felt like this. He and Annie used to have fun. Oh, God, they could laugh. But their fun ended a long time before she did.

Wyrick always pissed him off...or made him mad. And he'd laughed at her, and with her...but they'd never just done something reckless...just for the hell of it.

"Want to stop somewhere for dinner?" he asked.

"It's pouring," Wyrick said.

"So you're afraid to get your hair wet?" he drawled.

Her lips twitched. "That's going to cost you."

"How much?" he asked.

"Corn dogs much."

He frowned. "Corn dogs? As in wieners in fried cornmeal?"

"Yes," she said.

"Where the hell do I get corn dogs?"

Wyrick grabbed her phone and began scanning locations.

"The only ones I want are from a Sonic drive-in. We can park in one of their stalls, order from the car. Eat in the car. And I don't get my hair wet."

He grinned. "You called my bluff. Deal. Find me a Sonic."

She found one closest to where they were and entered it into his GPS system.

An hour later they were parked in a stall, sheltered from the downpour by the red metal roofing above them.

Wyrick was sitting sideways in the passenger seat, one leg folded up beneath her, with her back against the door. She was working on the last of her onion rings and was halfway through her second corn dog, sipping Pepsi as she went.

Charlie had already finished a *Super*SONIC double bacon cheeseburger and a large order of fries, and was eyeing the ice cream treats available on the menu.

"You gonna want dessert?" he asked.

She glanced at the order board. "Mostly not," she said.

He chuckled. "Mostly not? I don't think I've ever heard that phrase come out of your mouth."

"It's often in my head. I'll have to remember to voice it more often," Wyrick said and smeared a little more mustard on the end of her corn dog. "I love these," she said and took a big bite.

"Why haven't you ever mentioned wanting these before?" Charlie said.

"Well, they aren't nearly as good if you don't eat them on site, while they're still fresh and hot. I used to do it once in a while…before I moved to Merlin's. But that was before UT started trying to off me."

Charlie frowned. Couldn't even go to a damn drive-in and eat a corn dog without wondering if she'd leave there alive? Every day some offhand remark she made was just a reminder of the hell she'd gone through to stay alive.

"So…are you getting dessert?" she asked.

He gave the ice cream choices a last, longing glance and shook his head.

"Mostly not."

She grinned and then wiped her lips and stuffed the napkin in the bag with the other trash.

"Are you finished?" he asked.

"Yes. Stuffed. This was a good day. We caught a bad guy and solved an eleven-year-old mystery. I witnessed a young woman decide life was worth living after all, and ate at Sonic. My life, today, is just about perfect."

"So's mine," Charlie said. "Sack up our trash and I'll dump it on the way out."

So she did.

It was still raining when they got back to the old mansion. Wyrick refused to care about what was happening online about the pictures she'd posted, or whatever fallout was happening in their personal lives. Their own stupidity and guilt led directly back to Jeremiah Raver, and nothing she'd caused. She was so glad to be home that all she wanted to do was sleep.

"I'm going to the den to watch football," Charlie said as they came in out of the rain.

"I'm going upstairs to change, then play the rest of what's left of this day by ear," Wyrick said.

"You can always come watch football with me," Charlie said.

"I'll pass," she said and wrinkled her nose. It was her only sign of distaste.

"So you want to play quarterback?"

She frowned. "I have no idea what that means."

He grinned. "You're smarter than me. You'll figure it out," he said and walked out of the room.

Wyrick grabbed her phone and went straight to Google, typed in football and then quarterback and started reading. "The player who calls plays, throws passes, et cetera…"

And then she got it. Charlie was going to watch football. She said she wanted to pass. He said *so you want to play quarterback*, so…

A slow smile spread across her face. She didn't want to play football, but she liked playing with Charlie like this. This teasing thing between them felt safe. Charlie made everything okay.

Two days later

Rachel Dean had been slipping in and out of reality without an awareness of time. She knew she was in a hospital, and she knew she was safe. Someone told her that, but she didn't remember who. She remembered praying for someone to find her, and now she knew they had.

The times she heard Ray's and Millie's voices she would cry, the tears seeping out from beneath her closed eyelids because she knew they were there.

Sometimes she thought she was still dreaming about them coming to find her, but most of the time she was sure they were real and present. Millie patted her arm when she talked to her, a physical presence she could not deny, and Ray's voice was deep, reverberating within her body like the echo of a bell.

The fever that had racked her body was almost gone, and the pain of hurting to breathe had eased. She was more sore than broken now. It was a blessed, blessed thing to be aware of all sensations.

The cool, wet cloth on her forehead, the cleansing of her body as they changed her bandages. She knew they were there, but she just wasn't ready to open her eyes, for fear the rescue was all a dream, and her reality was still hiding in the dark, waiting for him.

And then Millie appeared again. Rachel knew the stride of her walk, the solid click of her heels on the floors. The urge to see her was becoming stronger than the fear that had kept her hidden. Then she felt her sister's hand on her arm and heard a joy in her voice she hadn't heard before.

"Hey, baby…it's me, Millie. I have such good news! They have charged a man named Sonny Burch with your kidnapping. He has so many other charges against him, too, including three counts of murder, so he will likely never be free again. He can't hurt you anymore. Not ever again!"

And then she leaned over Rachel's bed and gave her a quick hug, and when she did, Rachel reached for her, trying to put her arm around Millie's neck.

Millie felt it and gasped and pulled back.

"Honey…oh, honey!" she said, then cupped Rachel's face, waiting.

Rachel opened her eyes.

Millie smiled.

"There you are, my sweet baby. There you are. Welcome back. Welcome back."

After that, Rachel's recovery hastened.

Within another day she'd been moved from the ICU into a regular room, and after that either Ray or Millie was with her every moment, refusing to leave her alone.

Rachel talked…about everything…except what he'd done to her. She knew she had to give a statement to the police. She would do it, but then she didn't ever want to discuss it again.

Her ad agency, Addison-Tunnell, sent a huge bouquet of flowers with a message on the card she kept close to her heart.

Whenever you are ready, no matter how long, your job and your office are waiting for you.

Love from all of us…can't wait to see you again.

And then on the same day, Millie got a call from the police. They wanted to know if Rachel was well enough to give them a statement, and she said yes.

Millie helped her wash her hair and let it air-dry into a tumble of curls. Her bruises had faded to pale greens and shades of lavender, and her ribs had healed enough that she could sit up for short periods of time with hardly any pain. It was as ready as she was going to get. She was ready to meet the men who'd helped save her life and put Sonny behind bars.

Millie was standing on one side of Rachel's bed, with Ray on the other, when the detectives walked in.

"Good afternoon, Rachel. I'm Detective Floyd, and this is my partner, Detective Mills. We are so happy for your continuing recovery."

"Thank you," Rachel said. "I understand I have you two to thank for my life…and for catching Sonny Burch."

"I'd like to take credit for all that," Floyd said. "But just between us…if it hadn't been for your sister hiring Charlie Dodge and his partner, Jade Wyrick, to assist in the case, this could have had a whole other ending."

Rachel nodded. "Yes, Millie told me about all of that. I'm just so grateful to still be alive."

"Yes, ma'am," Floyd said, then he and Mills shook hands with Millie and Ray and got down to business.

"We know this isn't going to be easy," Floyd said. "My partner will be recording this, so anytime you need to stop filming to take a break, just say so."

Rachel nodded.

"I'm not going to ask you many questions. We just want to hear your story from the beginning to the last thing you remember. I also know this will be hard to do, but we need details of what he did to you to corroborate the injuries you had when you were found. Start off by stating your name and then begin your statement."

Rachel swallowed, then reached for Millie's hand.

Millie grabbed her and held on.

Rachel took a breath and then began, "My name is Rachel Dean. The day of my abduction, I had stayed late at Addison-Tunnell, the ad agency where I work, because I had a big presentation for a client the next day. I came home sometime around 8 p.m. The cleaning crew had been in my apartment that day and everything smelled good. I changed out of my work clothes, gathered up a load of laundry and started them to wash. The next thing I did was to heat up some soup for my supper. I was eating it as I read, when I began hearing voices in the back of my apartment. I went to investigate and found the television on in my bedroom. It wasn't on when I'd come home, so it puzzled me. But when I went to get the remote, it wasn't on the table by my bed where I kept it. It was across the room, beside the TV. Again, I thought it was strange, but shrugged it off. I was on my way to get the remote when I felt a sharp pain in my neck. I thought it was a bug bite…maybe a spider. I think I was raising my hand, like to feel for it, and then everything went black. I don't remember anything until I woke up in that room."

She shuddered and reached for her water.

Millie grabbed the cup and straw. "Here, honey. I've got it," she said and held it while Rachel drank.

Rachel nodded her thanks, then picked up where she'd left off.

"I woke up on the floor, on a bare and filthy mattress, but I couldn't stay awake. The drug, I guess. There was a light in the ceiling. It was always on. The room was concrete. It had an ancient toilet and sink. As the drug began to wear off, I saw more details. There were stains on the mattress, old, faded stains. They looked like blood. I had no sense of time, but each time I woke, I would get up and beat on the door, screaming for help. But no one came."

She paused. Her voice was beginning to shake, and Ray was in shock, wondering how she would ever be Rachel again, when she picked up the story.

"He came when I was asleep. I woke up and he was on top of me. I recognized him instantly and tried to push him away, and when I did, he knocked me out. The next time I woke up we were both naked and he was inside me, holding a knife to my throat. He talked ugly, and dirty, getting off on my pain. He made little cuts all over me, then told me if I moved he would cut my throat. Then he said it wouldn't matter, because he'd fucked dead women before. I don't know how many times he raped me afterward."

Millie bit her lip to keep from screaming.

"You're doing great, Rachel. Do you need to take a break?" Floyd asked.

Tears were welling. She shook her head.

"He had brought me food. I ate it after he left, because I knew I had to stay strong enough to survive. It became routine for me to beat on the door and scream for help." She felt her throat...remembering. "After a long while, the cut on my neck finally stopped bleeding, but it became sore and festered, and I was so cold. The next time he came he brought food and a blanket, but I was already getting sick. I had a slight fever, and so I pretended to be out of it. He tried to get me to talk, but I pretended I could barely keep my eyes open. He hit me. A lot...and cut me, using pain to try to wake me up. I still didn't comply. He stripped me again, but I stayed motionless, letting it happen. Then he stripped, and had the knife with him when he straddled my legs."

Rachel paused again, remembering. Then she scrubbed her hands across her face as if trying to wipe the memory away.

"He was going to use the knife on me again, and I knew it. I saw him look away for just a second, and when he did, I grabbed his erection, dug my fingernails into the flesh and twisted it hard...so hard. He dropped the knife, screaming as I dug my fingernails into his chest and raked them deep. He was screaming and bleeding and punching me, but I wouldn't let go. He was trying to get away, but he couldn't move for fear I would tear it off. One minute I thought I had him, and then he knocked me out. When I came to, he was still there, crying and moaning and trying to get up to get to the sink. I saw the knife and grabbed it just as he saw me. He could barely stand up, and he knew I was coming at him, so he managed to get his clothes and get out before I could catch him. The door slammed in my face, and I never saw him again."

"Damn," Mills whispered.

"We found you in the dark," Floyd said. "How did that happen?"

"Oh, right," Rachel said. "I did that. I wanted to catch him off guard when he came back. I dragged the mattress to a corner by the door, paced off the distance from it to the toilet and sink over and over until I knew how many steps it took to get there and back to the mattress, and then I threw my shoe at the bare bulb until it broke. The downside of that was I got so sick that I forgot about all of that broken glass. I woke up disoriented and walked in the glass...and of course I'm missing one shoe. It was somewhere in the room...in the dark. Stepping on the glass both startled and hurt me. I fell, so then I had glass in my knees and hands, as well. I picked out what I could feel and crawled back to the mattress, rolled up in the blanket and held the knife, waiting for him to come back. But he never did.

"I had dreams...hallucinations. My mother was always with me telling me to hang on. Sometimes I thought it was Millie.

I knew I was sick. I was mad at God. I kept begging Him to either let me die or send someone to find me. And so He did."

"And did you know your assailant?" Floyd asked.

Rachel nodded. "Yes, immediately. His name is Sonny Burch, a resident at Detter House."

"Did you ever have a personal relationship with him?" Floyd asked.

"No. Never. He was just someone I'd speak to in passing. I haven't had a personal relationship with anyone since moving to Dallas some years back. I was alone. And I guess, a sitting duck for someone like him. That's all I have to say."

"That's more than enough," Floyd said.

Mills stopped the video, packed up their things and they were gone.

As soon as the door closed behind them, Rachel stared down at her hands, took a deep breath and then looked up at Millie and Ray.

"Look. I know I'm broken. But he didn't break *me*. My body is healing. Eventually, so will I. I will be going to counseling. But I really, really don't ever want to talk about this with my family again. I'm not trying to bury it. But I also don't intend to keep it alive. It has already changed me. But it didn't kill me. And I have to work with what I've got. Okay?"

"Absolutely," Ray said.

"Very okay," Millie said, then patted Rachel's hand. "Can I get you anything? Maybe something cold to drink?"

Rachel sighed. "I would love a sweet tea."

"With lots of ice!" Ray said.

Rachel smiled. "You remember!"

"Of course I remember," he said. "I'm heading down to the cafeteria right now and bringing back one for all of us."

But as soon as he left the room, Millie laid her head down on Rachel's leg and wept.

Rachel tunneled her fingers in her sister's hair.

"I know, Millie. I know. It was…it was…a nightmare. But I'm alive. I fought back. I hurt him, too, and he'll have nightmares about me for as long as he lives. And that's what I'm going to hold on to. I am not a victim. I am a survivor."

CHAPTER EIGHTEEN

The storm had passed sometime during the night, but the old mansion was cold when Charlie woke up. He got up, turned up the thermostat in his room and then went to shave and shower.

It was Sunday, his take-it-slow day. But he didn't know what was on Wyrick's agenda, because if she had one, that meant he was along for the ride.

He turned up the thermostat in the hall as he headed down the stairs, and then turned up the one downstairs, as well, before heading to the kitchen.

The last thing he expected was to see Wyrick sitting at the kitchen table, wearing old sweats, red wool socks and watching something on her laptop.

"Morning," he said. "What's up?"

"You mean, besides me?"

Charlie grinned. So this was how the day was going to begin.

"Now I'm afraid to comment," he said.

She looked up at him and frowned.

"I'm watching a YouTube video on how to make pancakes. I can build rockets and make medicines. I can build cloaking devices for anything. I can hack anything on the planet without leaving a sign. I can heal people by just touching them, and play the stock market like a boss. I can create video gaming that is making me rich as sin, but I cannot freaking cook. From itch."

Charlie stifled a laugh. "From scratch. The term is *from scratch*."

"Yes, that," she muttered. "I want pancakes. And I do not want to leave this property to go get them. I don't even know if we have the stuff to make them, but if we do, I'm going to make pancakes."

"I know how."

She slammed the laptop shut and stood. "Then will you teach me? I only need to see it done to understand it."

"Absolutely," Charlie said. "Get a bowl and a whisk."

"What's a—"

He pulled the wire beater out of a container of spoons and spatulas and held it up.

"This is a whisk."

"I'll get the bowl," she said.

"Get one bigger than the one you make salad in."

"Yes," she said and pulled out a clear glass bowl and set it on the counter.

"Okay, now we need eggs, milk, flour, baking powder and salt, sugar and vegetable oil."

Wyrick looked at the counter and then toward the pantry, and then at Charlie.

"Do we have all that?"

"In labeled containers in the pantry. Come with me."

He loaded her up with the baking powder, salt and vegetable oil, while he carried the canisters of flour and sugar to the counter. "Now get the milk and two eggs from the fridge, and we're ready to mix."

Wyrick was almost dancing as she flew to the fridge and came back carrying the gallon of milk and the eggs, then set them on the counter. She watched Charlie getting measuring cups from the cabinet, and a set of measuring spoons from a drawer and put them down beside the bowl. She was as focused on what he was doing as she would've been in a lab at UT, watching one of the scientists working on an experiment.

"Get the one-cup measure," Charlie said. "The sizes are on the handle. I'll talk, and you follow my instructions."

She nodded.

"Take the lids off the flour and sugar so you don't have to do that later. And when you're making a batter, always start with all the liquids first. This glass cup is for liquid measures. These other cups are for measuring dry ingredients. So first, measure out two cups of milk and pour it in the big bowl."

So she did, and the delight on her face when the first ingredient went into the bowl was pure joy.

"Okay, crack the eggs and add them into the milk," Charlie said.

She cracked and dumped them with a degree of skill, learned from making herself scrambled eggs.

"Now we need about two tablespoons of oil in the liquid. I never measure, because I can pretty much guess, but for your first time, take that one-fourth-cup measure and fill it about half-full. I say half, because there are four tablespoons in one-fourth of a cup, so half of that would be two tablespoons."

"Why can't I use the measuring spoons?" she asked.

"You can, but then you'll need two sets of measuring spoons if you're going to measure wet and dry. If the spoons are already wet or oily from measuring a liquid, then when you try to measure out a dry ingredient, it won't come off."

"Oh! Smart thinking!" she said.

Charlie grinned, watching as she measured and added the oil.

"Okay, now take that whisk and gently whip the liquid stuff

together until it's all mixed up…making sure the eggs are well incorporated."

"Whip?"

"Like this," Charlie said and showed her once.

After that she was all about the whisk, and incorporating the liquid ingredients.

"Perfect," Charlie said.

She nodded because *perfect* was how she rolled.

"Okay," Charlie said. "Now it's time to add the dry ingredients. A fancy cook would tell you to mix the dry ingredients all together first, before you put them in the liquid, but I'm all about expediency. Measure two cups of flour and just drop them into the liquid. Don't stir."

She shoved the cup into the container, and Charlie realized he'd missed a step.

"Oh, wait…you can't pack flour when you measure it or whatever you're making will be too heavy or too tough. I just kind of stir the flour in the container with a spoon or a knife…like this…and then scoop the flour like this and level it off with the knife. I'll do this one, and you do the second cup."

Wyrick didn't miss a detail, and repeated his actions perfectly when she measured the second cup of flour.

"Now add two tablespoons of sugar. Use that one…see, it says tablespoon. Just level them off…yes, like that, and dump it in on top of the flour. Now add two teaspoons of baking powder and a teaspoon of salt."

Wyrick was so focused on what she was doing that she didn't realize she was all but leaning against Charlie in an effort to get close, and their hands and arms had bumped a half dozen times in crossing while he was showing her how to measure. She didn't know it, but Charlie did, and he liked it. This comfortable, doing-something-together shit rocked.

"Okay," Charlie said. "Now whisk it again until all of the dry ingredients are mixed in."

She grabbed hold of the bowl with one hand and the whisk with her other, and began beating the ingredients until it had become a smooth, silky batter.

"That's looks perfect," Charlie said. "You just made pancake batter."

Wyrick stopped, looked down at the bowl and then up at him and beamed.

"Now, show me how to cook them without burning. And I'll warn you, I can't even flip a fried egg without making a mess, which is why I always eat them scrambled."

Charlie wanted to hug her. Instead, he put a hand on her shoulder.

"Chill. I have faith in you."

He didn't see the flash of tears in her eyes, because he had turned to get a big griddle out of a lower cabinet, but it was all Wyrick could do to get herself together. Never in her life had anyone ever said that to her.

Charlie was talking about preheating the griddle, and about nonstick surfaces and others that had to be oiled, then he showed her spatulas versus what he called pancake turners.

She was nodding and watching, but she was also painfully aware of the deep rumble of his voice in her ear, and the musky scent of his aftershave.

"Okay," he said. "This is how you know when the griddle is hot enough." He dunked a spoon in some water, then let a couple of drops fall onto the griddle. "See how that sizzled and almost danced across the griddle? That's how you know." He picked up the one-third measuring cup, dipped up some batter and poured it onto the griddle. "Like that," he said. "Now, you do the rest and see how that one is spreading...so...leave room between each pancake for it to spread and cook. Makes turning them easier."

She nodded, repeated his actions and soon had six perfect little round pancakes cooking on the griddle.

He picked up the pancake turner, then pointed again. "Watch for the edges to start getting a little brown…and when the bubbles start coming up in the middle of the pancake, that means it's ready to turn."

Wyrick's focus was laser-sharp as she watched, and when the first ones began to appear, she pointed.

"There's one! And another, and another. There are three bubbles. Is it time to turn?"

"I'd say yes," Charlie said. "Let's see." He slid the turner beneath the pancake, then gave it a quick flip. It landed raw side down in a perfect little plop, revealing a golden-brown surface on the side they'd just cooked.

"Perfect! It looks perfect!" Wyrick said.

"Now you do the rest," Charlie said. "Just wait for the bubbles."

Within seconds the next one was ready to turn. She struggled a little and then got it turned, and after that she was a pancake-making machine, flipping each one as if she'd done it all her life.

"Now check the first one we turned to see if it's done," Charlie said and showed her how. "Looks done to me," he said and took it off the griddle.

Again, she followed his instructions with surgical precision and had the six-stack done, and all she could do was stare at it.

"I just made pancakes," she said, then looked at the rest of the batter. "You can have those. I'm going to make more," she said and turned her back on Charlie to begin adding new batter to the grill.

Charlie carried them to the table, got the butter and syrup and, as he ate, watched the joy and satisfaction on her face as she kept making and flipping pancakes until the batter was gone and she had a platter full of pancakes, which she carried to the table.

She sat, took four pancakes from the platter to make her stack, buttering and adding syrup between each one and then added a little extra to the top one.

When she took the first bite, she rolled her eyes in delight, then chewed, swallowed and sighed.

"Thank you, Charlie. For the first time in my life, I have accomplished something I didn't innately already know. You cannot imagine how this feels. The only thing I can relate it to is sex."

Charlie choked. *Jesus and Mary.*

And then he remembered. She'd had a fiancé. They must have been intimate before she got sick. Why did he think she'd never— He stopped himself. But the image of her in unbridled passion, those long legs wrapped around a man's body, put a knot in his belly that had nothing to do with all the pancakes he'd eaten.

"Happy to have been of service," he said, then stared down at his plate, afraid she'd go all psychic and know what he was thinking.

Wyrick, completely unaware she'd stirred up more than pancake batter with Charlie Dodge, took a sip of lukewarm coffee and then finished her breakfast.

"We have leftover pancakes," she said. "What do we do with those?"

"You can reheat them. They're not as good, but they're worth keeping," he said.

"Awesome," she said and got up to hunt for some plastic wrap.

"You cooked. I'll clean up," Charlie said.

"Deal," Wyrick said. "I need to check the stock market, call my broker and finish up a new game for PlayStation VR."

Charlie blinked. "I'll just be here washing dishes," he said.

"'Kay," she said and walked out, completely unaware of how unbelievably awesome she was.

"Well, she couldn't make pancakes," Charlie muttered and began cleaning off the table.

The following day was Monday, and by daylight the forensic team from the Texas Bureau of Investigation was on site at the old Burch property east of Dallas.

By 9 a.m. they'd found the first body. It took hours to photograph and dig it up and bag it.

They found the second body just after three and again, they spent hours photographing and bagging the remains.

The sun was setting when they found the third body. But they were old pros at this, and simply set up floodlights and proceeded as they had with the others, photographing all they could before dark, then carefully removing the remains of the last one with artificial lighting.

By the time they left the property, Sonny Burch's fate was sealed. He just had to go through the court system to find out where he'd be spending the rest of his life.

The following day was a Tuesday, and Barrett Taylor's day did not start off with pancakes. He had jailhouse oatmeal before being cuffed and shackled and transported to the Dallas County courthouse.

His lawyer, Marsh Fielding, was in the courtroom when the guards marched him in. He took a seat at the defendant's table with his lawyer and sighed. He'd been this way before, and every time he'd gotten out, he'd sworn he wasn't going back, but Barrett had failed himself again.

He lowered his voice and leaned toward Marsh.

"Any idea of the sentence coming down?"

Marsh shook his head.

Barrett nodded. He'd agreed to this, so it was what it was.

A few minutes later the bailiff stepped forward.

"All rise, courtroom three. Honorable Shane Dupree presiding."

They stood.

The judge, sporting a black goatee and black hair peppered with shades of gray, walked in and took a seat behind the desk.

Barrett watched all the protocol that followed with a jaded eye. He just kept thinking, ditch the ritual and get this misery over with.

And Dupree finally obliged.

Barrett Taylor was staring at the US flag behind the judge when the charges were read and the verdict was given, and then they led him away. He was going to die behind bars. It was a risk he'd taken, and he blew it.

Jessup Wallis hadn't known Wyrick had published his photo until he stopped in North Dakota for fuel, and saw himself on the TV behind the counter. He just kept his head down, paid for his snacks and the gas and didn't look back.

His goal was Canada. And when he reached the border, the relief he felt was huge, but short-lived.

The guards took one look at his passport and the rest of his ID, then refused him entry.

He was shocked. "But why?"

"Sir. You are an acknowledged hit man. You have a bounty on your head. We do not welcome known criminals into our country."

Jessup was stunned. There was nowhere to run. Nowhere to hide. She had doomed him. And then what was left of his good sense kicked in.

No. Jade Wyrick had done nothing to him. Until he came

after her. He doomed himself. He got back in his car, turned around and drove away, disturbed and just a little bit scared.

He didn't have any particular skills except hunting, fishing and construction work, and he needed to think.

So he drove back to the nearest town, got a six-pack and a motel room, and locked the door behind him.

Two beers in, he had decided to grow a beard.

Three beers in, he began googling how much it cost to change a name.

By the time the six-pack was gone, he was riding a good drunk, and had decided to bury Jessup Wallis. He always wanted to be called Will, so he was going for William, and would use Banner, his mother's maiden name, as his surname. As soon as he made that happen, then he was going to Utah. There was lots of land and very few people. It was the best he could make out of a bad situation.

Farrell Kitt was heading for Bangor, Maine.

All he'd ever known was farming and hunting gators during season. He'd never fished for a living, but he was thinking that knowing how to snag a gator with a treble hook and pull it in close enough to shoot was enough like commercial fishing to get himself hired.

He'd been driving all night on Interstate 80, and was planning to stop at the next town and get a room, when he drove into a thunderstorm. The traffic was heavy, and he found himself boxed in, following a semi on the outside lane. The truck was throwing up a crazy amount of water. His wipers were on high, and he was trying not to hydroplane, when the truck's brake lights suddenly came on.

He slammed on the brakes, and was trying to stop without getting rear-ended by the car behind him, when the brakes locked. He was doing seventy miles an hour when he slid into the back of the semi, ending his plans, and his life.

He had never expected to go home again, but the people who picked up what was left of him sent him there anyway.

It was a cruel twist of fate for Farrell, and a shock to Judy Kitt and her children, and to Farrell's family, as well. Just when they were getting ready to denounce him as their own, he boomeranged back in a box.

The irony that Judy was now a widow was a financial boon. She would collect widow's benefits through Social Security, and all of their children would get death benefits until they reached the age of eighteen—even the baby Judy had yet to birth. But she refused to stand up in a church as a grieving widow, and left the burying of him up to his family.

It was an inauspicious end for a man on the run, and better than he deserved.

Jordy Gooch bragged he was the one who'd turned in Jessup Wallis, and hardly anyone in Paulette blamed him, and knowing he'd come into money now, almost everyone wanted to be his new best friend. But he was already making plans to head for colder weather. This was his one chance to change his life, and he wasn't going to blow it.

Judy suspected Junior's teacher had turned her husband in, but she didn't hold it against her. Only Mildred showed no signs of a sudden influx of money, and kept teaching her classes and living her life just as she always had. Judy decided it had to be someone else. Farrell hadn't been able to get away with murder, but Mildred had gotten away with being the snitch.

The day after Farrell's funeral, someone set fire to the Church of The Righteous. Neighbors saw the smoke. A few even went to see what was on fire, then let it burn to the ground before they called it in. It was a bad reminder to everyone, even those who'd attended it and were trying to outlive their shame.

CHAPTER NINETEEN

Detective Floyd called Charlie to let him know that the CID had found the bodies of the three missing women. Wyrick was in on the call.

"I never found any family for the three missing women," Wyrick said. "When you go to inter them in a cemetery, pick a nice place, bury them side by side and send me the bill."

Floyd was touched. "You don't have to do that. The city has a fund for—"

"I know I don't have to," Wyrick said. "But they were tortured, murdered and buried on land belonging to their killer. I think they deserve better than charity burials."

"Yes, ma'am," Floyd said. "I'll make sure the right people know."

"Thanks for the heads-up," Charlie said.

"Of course," Floyd said. "I have one more bit of news regarding Barrett Taylor's sentencing. We didn't work the case, but you and Wyrick have done so much for us, I thought she might like to know. Taylor is forty-five years old, and he just got handed a sentence of thirty-five years, with no possibility of parole."

Wyrick gave Charlie a thumbs-up and walked out of the room.

Charlie grinned. "We appreciate that," he said. "Have yourself a good day."

Late that same day, Wyrick found out about Farrell Kitt after the media picked up on the story, posting the byline "Hit man dies by his own hand."

She read it, then deleted the story. Burch was off the streets. The missing women had been found. Now Farrell Kitt was gone, Raver was gone and Taylor was in prison, and wherever Wallis was, he'd be on the run. She no longer felt the need to trail him, because the fortress of the cult he'd been with had come down like the walls of Jericho.

A calm was settling within her.

She searched YouTube for cooking demonstrations, and was online daily looking for a new recipe to try. Learning was a passion, and she'd never had a passion before.

Charlie became the taste tester, and she grew more confident of herself as a person, and not just "the test-tube genius" she'd been before.

Charlie loved it. And he was falling deeper and deeper in love with her.

It had been so long since he'd had these feelings, but he remembered them, and the longings and the passion for more that came with them.

But this was Wyrick. And he wouldn't cross that line and risk losing her.

About two weeks after Rachel Dean's rescue, Charlie was working at his desk when he got a text. He stopped to check the message, and then got up and took it to show Wyrick.

"Look," he said and laid his phone down in front of her.

It was a brief text.

We're Tulsa bound.

There was a picture with the text, of Millie and Ray, with Rachel standing between them. They were all smiling, and Rachel was holding up a sign that read:

THANK YOU FOR SAVING MY LIFE.

"It was a good save," Wyrick said. "Tell her we say you're welcome."

"Done," Charlie said and went back to his office and sent it.

That evening when they went home, Wyrick felt the stirrings of a new level of peace. Maybe, just maybe, there would be a way to regain some personal space, and as much anonymity as a woman like her could expect to have.

But Wyrick had forgotten about the little girl named Bethie. Unaware that what had taken place between them that day at Stackhouse Burgers had been filmed, she didn't realize how tenuous her new joy had just become.

And Bethie's parents had forgotten the incident, too, until they took Bethie back to her doctor for her next round of blood tests.

Lola Franklin, Bethie's mother, knew her daughter had been eating better. She even let herself believe Bethie was getting a little color back in her complexion.

Her father, Bud, had always read to Bethie every night after they put her to bed, and often had to rub her legs to help her fall asleep, because she lived in constant pain.

But lately, she'd hadn't cried about the pain, and was falling asleep without the rubs. So they were hopeful that maybe, just maybe, the cancer in her body was going into remission, and maybe the tumor in her head was shrinking enough to alleviate some of her pain. They knew they were grasping at straws, but hope was all they had left when they took her in.

The lab drew all of the usual blood work, and took all of the usual X-rays and scans, and then they sat out in the waiting room among other families just like them, and they were easy to pick out.

There was the pale, frail teenager, barely able to walk on her own, sitting beside her mother, waiting.

A baby in arms, lying limp and crying in a thin, breathless wail, while the parents sat huddled in hollow-eyed silence, waiting for a doctor to see them again.

There was a man sitting alone, staring at a picture on the wall that he'd seen a thousand times before, waiting to see if his second round of chemo had triggered a remission.

Bethie was playing a game on her mother's phone, and Lola and Bud were carrying on a conversation about nothing that mattered, because discussing the elephant in the room was not done in front of Bethie, and had become too painful to discuss at all.

As they sat, one patient after another was called back, and still they waited.

An hour passed, and Bethie was getting tired and wanting something to eat, when a nurse stepped into the waiting room.

"Bethie Franklin."

Thank God.

Bud and Lola jumped to their feet and took Bethie's hand.

"That's us, sweetie. Just a little visit to say hello to Doctor Welch, and we'll go get some ice cream, okay?"

"Okay!" Bethie said and clutched her mother's phone as they followed the nurse into an exam room.

"Hello, Bethie. You're looking very pretty today. I love your shirt. It looks great with your cute jeans. Blue is my favorite color."

"Mine, too," Bethie said and climbed into her mother's lap to wait for the doctor to come in.

His red hair was always a little bit awry as if he ran his fingers through it too often, and his stethoscope was hanging halfway out of the pocket of his lab coat, bouncing against his leg as he walked.

He came in, shut the door and then picked Bethie up and sat her on the exam table without saying a word.

He looked into her eyes.

He listened to her heart.

He had her breathe for him, and saw for himself the pink in her cheeks, and then he turned around.

His voice was shaking, and Bud and Lola grabbed each other's hands, afraid of what he was about to say.

And then Welch held up his hands in a gesture of disbelief.

"I don't know what happened. I have no explanation for it. But there is absolutely no sign of cancer anywhere in Bethie's body, and the tumor in her head is gone. It's just...not there."

Bud and Lola jumped to their feet, crying. They hugged each other, hugged Doctor Welch, and then they picked Bethie up in their arms and began dancing around the room.

Bethie was laughing because they were laughing, but she didn't quite get the gist of all that had been said.

"What's happening, Mommy?" she asked.

They stopped, then Lola hugged her and put her down on the exam table again.

"A miracle happened, baby. You're not sick anymore. Your cancer is gone, and the tumor that made your head hurt is gone, too. You're well."

"Will my hair grow back?" Bethie asked.

"I would certainly assume so," Welch said. "There's no need for more chemo, which is what made it fall out."

Bethie touched her head, then leaned over and whispered in her doctor's ear.

"My friend Jade rubbed my head and it quit hurting."

Lola frowned. "Wait, who's Jade? What are you—?" And then she looked at her husband and gasped. "Oh, my God! I had completely forgotten!" She cupped Bethie's face. "What do you mean, she made it quit hurting? You never told us that."

Bethie shrugged. "Well, she did. She made all the hurt go away."

"I'm totally confused," Welch said. "Who is this Jade? And why—"

"Wait. I'll show you," Bud said and began searching the photo gallery on his phone for the video he'd taken that day they'd gone in for burgers. When he found it, he handed his phone to Welch. "We were in Stackburgers. Just hit Play."

Welch recognized the restaurant, and then he saw Bethie standing by a table where a man and woman were sitting. The woman was bald, like Bethie, and when she leaned over and let Bethie touch her head, his heart melted. But it wasn't until he saw the woman cup her hand on Bethie's head and close her eyes, that he realized what the Franklins were getting at.

"You aren't trying to make me believe that some woman just laid hands on Bethie and healed her? In Stackburgers? Come on, now."

"That's not just some woman," Lola said. "That's Jade Wyrick. Remember? She did a live press conference a few months back revealing everything about the people who'd created her by manipulating her DNA. She said they killed the woman that gave birth to her to get her back, and the revelations were horrific and endless. After numerous attempts to kill her, they shot down the helicopter she was piloting and Charlie Dodge found her. After she healed, she put herself on public display and destroyed her personal life just to take down those people, resulting in the closure of hundreds and hundreds of illegal laboratories, and a worldwide human trafficking ring. It blew a hole the size of the Grand Canyon in global illegal activities. It was all over the news for weeks."

Welch just kept staring at the video. "And that's her?"

"Yes," Lola said. "And she was the sweetest thing to Bethie. Our baby had just made a mess at the table, and we were cleaning it up and didn't realize Bethie had slipped away. We had a moment of panic until we saw her." Lola pointed at the couple in the video. "That's Charlie Dodge. And that's Wyrick. Everyone in the room knew it was them when they came in."

Welch looked at Bethie and then stroked his finger down the side of her cheek.

"What made you go up and talk to that woman?" he asked.

Bethie patted her head. "Because she was so pretty…and she was just like me. She let me touch her head. She said her hair can't grow back. But she said mine would, and then she touched my head and her hand was warm, and then it got hot, but the pain in my head went away."

Welch shrugged. "I have no scientific explanation for any of this. And this video is all you have. So however it happened, and whoever set it in motion, right now Bethie is as healthy as the day she was born. Go home. Live life. And if the need arises, you know what to look for, and you know where I am. God bless," he said and started to walk out of the room, and then stopped. "Hey, Bud, would you do me a favor?"

"Absolutely, Doc."

"You have my cell number. Would you send me a copy of that video? I think I'm going to need it."

Bud smiled. "Consider it done."

Doctor Welch left the office, and a few moments later his nurse came back and escorted them to the outer office.

As they were leaving the building, Bethie looked up at her mother.

"Are we still going to get ice cream?"

Bud swung her up into his arms. "Honey, we're going to eat ice cream today, and tomorrow, and every day we want some, forever. Okay?"

Bethie giggled. "Okay!"

"This is a miracle," Lola said. "That woman is a gift from God."

Wyrick was waiting in line to pick up a grocery order when she got a call from Charlie.

"Yes?"

"Are you okay?"

She frowned.

"Yes. I'm at Whole Foods, waiting to pick up our order."

"There is a situation. As soon as you get it, come home."

Her heart sank.

"It is me?"

"Yes. You're all over social media again."

"Why?"

Charlie heard despair in the question, and it broke his heart.

"It seems you healed a dying child of cancer and it was recorded by the father. Her doctor just confirmed the cancer in her body and the tumor in her brain are both gone."

Tears welled. "Bethie."

"Yes," Charlie said.

Wyrick's heart sank. "I didn't know that was being filmed, but I wouldn't change what I did."

"I know," Charlie said. "But this isn't going to be the end of it."

"It never is," Wyrick said. "I'll be home soon."

"I'm sorry," Charlie said.

"I can only imagine," Wyrick said. "This is not what you signed up for."

She disconnected and searched until she found it, then sat and watched her life going down the drain.

Charlie's heart sank. He'd never heard her sound defeated before. She was going to try to push him away in some grand gesture of self-sacrifice, and he wasn't having any of it.

He was anxious all the way up to the moment he saw her drive through the gates then head for the back of the house to carry in the groceries, and he met her coming in.

A chill blast of wind came with her, and he blamed the cold wind for her pale face and cold hands as he took the bags from her.

"I'll get the rest. Go do whatever it is you need to do."

"I'm making spaghetti," she said. "I have a new recipe."

"Yum," Charlie said, then put the bags on the counter and went back for the rest.

Wyrick's steps were dragging as she went upstairs to change. She came back down in old jeans and an even older sweatshirt from the University of Maryland.

"Nice shirt," he said.

"I bought it in an airport years ago because I was cold and it was pink."

Charlie laughed. "How does the dragon feel about your passion for pink?"

She almost smiled. The image of the red-and-black fire-breathing dragon wrapped around her body, then hiding it behind pink, was a dichotomy of images and colors.

"I never thought of it like that, but she gets me, so I suppose she's tolerant of my foibles. One has to be tolerant to put up with my life," she said and then went to the sink to wash her hands.

She helped him put up the food, keeping out what she wanted for the meal.

"Need any help?" Charlie asked.

"If I do, I'll give you a shout. I kind of need to be alone for a bit."

"Have you seen the video?"

She nodded. "I watched it while they were loading the order. I have this ability…and the child is well, and that's all that has to matter."

Charlie nodded, then left her in the kitchen with her recipe and her thoughts.

That night, as they were cleaning up after their meal, Charlie stopped in the act of putting away the leftovers to fork one last meatball from the sauce.

Wyrick glanced at him, secretly pleased when he popped it into his mouth.

"I can't believe you have room for even one more bite," she said.

"I don't have room. I just love these meatballs. You are turning into the best cook."

"I enjoy the challenge of conquering something I've never done before," Wyrick said.

Charlie waved his dish towel at her like a white flag of defeat.

"I have already yielded to your wisdom and your skill, and now I have yielded to your skill in the kitchen. The only thing I have going for me now is that I'm bigger and physically stronger than you. So next time you need a wall kicked in, I'm your guy."

He was laughing when he said it, but Wyrick couldn't laugh.

"You were everything you ever needed to be before you even met me. You could do everything I did and find just as many lost people as we've done together. All I did was help you do it faster. And I will always need you to keep me grounded, and remind me that I am human and not a freaking accident of nature. I will always need you to bust a head or kick in a wall for me when the need arises. I am gratified that my cooking pleased you, and I'm going to the office."

"Are you mad at me?" Charlie asked.

She stopped. "No. I'm mad at myself because I don't know how to even say thank you without getting my…my…what is it you say?…getting all wadded up?"

"Getting your pants in a wad?"

She nodded. "Yes. That," she said and left him standing with a dishrag in his hand.

Charlie saw the slump in her shoulders as she walked away, and knew the news of the latest video had shaken her newfound joy. He hurt for her, but he kept telling himself they would figure it out.

But Wyrick wasn't so sure.

She felt something she couldn't put a name to. It was as if the ground beneath the old mansion was crumbling at her feet. Were the walls high enough? Were the gates strong enough? Was there enough security on the grounds to keep the madness away?

Barrett Taylor was in jail, but in a way, so was she. She loved Charlie Dodge with all her heart. But he was here because of a duty he felt to keep her safe. He was always with her, and yet, she felt so alone.

She sat down at her computers and then paused, looking around at all of the technology and knowing that she had the world at her fingertips at any given time.

She also knew that everything she knew and could do, could be weaponized if it fell into the wrong hands. She understood things in the universe others had yet to even know existed, and she wasn't about to show them, or explain it, because it would never be used for good. There was always going to be someone greedy enough for money and power, who was willing to walk over bodies and souls to get it.

The simple existence she'd known before that day on the

boardwalk when her mother had taken her to ride the merry-go-round, was a painful memory she rarely revisited.

She kept thinking about that book in Sonny Burch's apartment. The one his grandmother had given him. The one he'd used to hide his secrets. *The Velveteen Rabbit*. She needed to read that one day, just to see what was special enough to keep it.

She didn't understand how someone could turn into a monster, when they started life with so much going for them.

And why had it been monsters who had created her? Why couldn't she just have been born—like a regular child with normal parents—so she could have lived a normal life? But if she'd been normal, she would likely never have known Charlie Dodge, and that wasn't something she would ever regret.

Wyrick thought of Bethie.

She'd cured Bethie's cancer, just like she'd cured her own. But she would never forget that it was getting cancer in the first place that finally set her free.

So how could she be sad? Healing that child had set her free to live again, too, so she couldn't regret one second of her decision. Whatever came from the video Lola Franklin had uploaded was on Wyrick's head and no one else's, and so it would be.

Last week she'd been an alien…and a demon…and today she was a healer sent from God. If that didn't speak for the insanity of the human race, then nothing would.

She turned to the computer she had up and running and put her hands on the keyboard. Within seconds she was looking at images of choppers. She'd been chased on the ground and shot out of the sky, and she was still standing. She would be damned before she'd let other people's madness dictate her quality of life.

She liked flying. The convenience and availability of having a chopper had been instrumental in helping solve many cases. Who knew when they'd need one again? She had the urge and she had the money. It was time to get her wings back again.

And while she was searching, Charlie was on his laptop, monitoring the surge of posts on social media about Wyrick and the video, and the longer he sat reading the posts, the more worried he became. Enough so that he went upstairs long enough to get his handgun. He'd spent too many years as a soldier to ignore what he was feeling. There was an enemy encroaching, and he did not want to be caught unprepared.

Even after Wyrick finally went up to bed, he stayed downstairs in the dark, standing watch from a window overlooking the front gates. The security system was armed, and so was he.

It was after sunrise before the chaos began. Charlie was standing at the front windows overlooking the grounds, sipping on one of the countless cups of coffee he'd had throughout the night. He was thinking about making some toast when he realized the car passing beneath the fading streetlights just now had come this way before. And when it came around the third time, his skin crawled.

He put down the coffee he'd been drinking and stepped into the shadows to keep watch. Within a few moments he saw another car, and then a trio of people on foot were suddenly standing at the gate, and then cars began lining the streets and the people emerging from them were either pushing someone in a wheelchair or carrying children in their arms.

"Oh, hell," Charlie said, and was already calling 911 when the security alarm went off. Someone was coming over a wall. At that point the number of lights and sirens that intrusion set off was startling enough to send the guy back to the other side, but they didn't leave the premises—and then Wyrick was suddenly at his side, in a panic, and still in the sweats she'd fallen asleep in.

"What's happening?" she said and then started toward the window when he grabbed her and held her back.

"I've already called 911. Just don't let them see you," he said.

She nodded and then peered between the curtains he'd pulled. He heard her groan, and then she sank to the floor with her back against the wall and covered her face with her hands.

Charlie picked her up and carried her away from the windows, then settled her on the overstuffed sofa by the fireplace. His makeshift bed was still there, quilt, pillows and all.

"It's about forty degrees outside. I think we need a fire."

So with the alarms sounding, and the sirens blaring, he began building a fire, laying kindling, and then logs, and then turned on the gas starter. Flames flared instantly.

He stood, watching until the kindling was burning and the first log was beginning to smoke, then pushed the pillow behind her back and spread the quilt up over her legs. But as he did, she took it out of his hands, pulled it up to her chin, then turned her gaze into the fire.

"The neighbors are going to hate me," she said.

Charlie touched her shoulder as he passed, then went to shut off the alarm. The silence was startling, but also rewarding, because now they could hear the sound of approaching sirens as Charlie went back to where she was lying.

"Just for argument's sake, neighbors are people who come visit you and bring you candy and cookies at Christmas. The people nearest you are strangers, just like the ones at the gate, so we don't give a fuck about what they think."

She sighed. "You said—"

"I know what I said, and I said it because I am so angry on your behalf, and because I can't go out there and raise hell with those people, because they aren't trying to hurt you. They just want you to fix what's wrong. They don't care that a couple weeks ago three men were trying to kill you. They don't care that they have scared you. They don't care that using you up to heal them would hurt you. They don't even care that it might kill you. You aren't their friend. They just want to use you up…

like a damn battery…and when the battery dies, throw you away and look for another. So get over the guilt. Right now!"

Wyrick looked at him then, towering over her in a rage on her behalf, and nodded.

"Over the guilt."

"Fine," he said. "I'm going outside now to meet the police."

"I don't want them arrested. I just want them to go away," she said.

"Yes, ma'am," he said and grabbed a jacket on the way out the front door.

She saw the handgun in the back of his jeans as he was putting on the jacket, and then looked down at the quilt he'd covered her with, and felt the pillow at her back and realized he must have spent the night here last night.

So she'd always wondered what it would be like to be with him, but lying on his bed was as close as she was going to get. So she nestled down into the pillow and closed her eyes, mentally blocking out the shouting and the sirens outside her door, while Charlie strode down the driveway to meet the police, who were already on scene.

But the people weren't leaving. They kept arguing with the police, pleading their cases, showing them their loved ones in need, trying to explain their presence as important enough to warrant the intrusion.

And then Charlie was standing at the gates with the bars between them, and when they saw him, they all pushed past the police, shouting and begging to be heard.

Charlie just stared at them without saying a word, and finally, they realized they were only talking to themselves and went quiet.

And then an officer standing nearby walked up to the gate.

"Do you want to press charges?" he asked.

The crowd began to murmur in undertones. Now it was beginning to sink in. What they'd done was arrest-worthy, and all of them were caregivers, or sick themselves, and knew they couldn't go to jail.

"If it was left up to me, I'd say yes. But she doesn't want any-one arrested," Charlie said. "She just wants them to go away."

"But she can heal, and my baby is sick!" one woman cried.

Charlie saw her in the crowd and stared her down.

"Yes, ma'am, and I'm sorry. But you don't live her life, or un-derstand. If you did, you wouldn't be here. Two weeks ago three men tried to kill her because of who she is…and this week you all don't mind using her up until she's dead anyway, just to fix what's wrong in your lives."

"But why is she the way she is, if she wasn't meant to heal?" another asked.

Charlie moved closer to the gate. "I'm not even going to re-spond to that. She didn't ask to be born like this, and she has lived hell on earth because of it. Get off this property, leave her alone and don't come back. I am her boss. I am her friend. And I am also her bodyguard, and the next time someone shows up at this gate acting the fool, I'm coming out shooting and asking questions later. Go home. Your lives are not her business, and she is none of yours."

"My baby is so sick," the woman said again.

"And you just dragged him out in forty-degree weather wrapped in nothing but a blanket? Now where's the sense in that? I'm done here." Then he looked at the officers. "If they're not gone in ten minutes, start hauling them in for disturbing the peace."

Then he turned around and started back up the driveway, and the closer he got to the house, the faster he went. Some-thing had to change, but he didn't know what, or how to make it happen and still keep her safe.

★ ★ ★

The old house was silent. There was a pall over the place, not unlike how it had felt when Merlin had died.

Wyrick had abandoned the kitchen for prowling the halls, poking in rooms on the third floor, then the second and the ground floor, revisiting the basement where she'd lived, staying longer in some places than others, but always on the move.

Charlie managed to get her to stop once long enough to eat a sandwich, and then she was gone again, her shoulders slumped, her stride slow and measured. He ached for the turmoil, but he couldn't change her life any more than she could have changed the lives of all those people at the gates.

Losing Annie had taught him that when it was time to let go, there was no power on earth that could change her fate.

So he'd stayed out of Wyrick's way, letting her prowl, knowing she would figure out on her own what she needed to do.

By noon there was private security at the gates, and he was confident enough in their presence to finally relax, and when she wanted to go out to the greenhouse, he went with her as far as the door, and then let her go inside alone.

That was her place…hers and Merlin's, and he honored her need for space and quiet. When she came out, the little bowl she'd taken in with her was still empty.

"No tomatoes today?" he asked.

She shook her head, and they went back inside.

"I'm going up to my room," she said. "I don't want food, okay?"

He nodded, and then watched her go up the stairs and stood waiting until he heard her open and close her door.

He went down the hall to the den and tried to watch TV, but he couldn't focus. He kept thinking about her, upstairs alone.

And then night fell. He checked in with the security team

outside via text. They were on the job. And then he set the security alarm and went upstairs.

He paused in the hall between their rooms, thought about knocking, then decided to just go to bed. He had the door open and had crossed the threshold when he heard her door open behind him.

He turned. She had been crying. He'd never seen her like this, and it scared him.

"I need to talk to you," she said.

"Sure. Want to come in my room?"

She nodded and crossed the hall, then as soon as he was inside she turned to face him.

"I'm leaving."

His heart stopped, but he didn't move.

"I've been talking to Merlin all day, and I've already told the house goodbye. I don't know where I'm going yet, but I can't live like this anymore. I'd rather be dead than in hiding."

He didn't ask; he just put his arms around her. Her body was stiff, rejecting his comfort, but he stood his ground and wouldn't let go.

Eventually, he felt her body give, and when he did he pulled her closer. He felt her tremble, and then she turned her face against his chest and began to cry slow, silent tears.

"Let it out. Let it go," he said softly and laid his cheek against the soft skin on the crown of her head.

His empathy was more than she could master, and his kindness pulled her under. She wrapped her arms around his waist as her quiet tears turned to sobs, and then she was crying so hard she couldn't stop.

CHAPTER TWENTY

With every choking sob that came up Wyrick's throat, Charlie tightened his grip until it felt like he was all that was holding her together. With every breath that she took, it affirmed one thing he could no longer ignore. He didn't want to let her go. She was the only important thing he had left in life, and he wasn't giving up without a fight.

He turned her loose, and then immediately cupped her cheeks, turning her tearstained face up to meet his gaze.

"I support anything you need to do. If you're leaving, then you leave, but you're not leaving me behind. I don't care if this is not what you want to hear. I don't care whether you like it or not. But you're the only person left in this world that means a damn to me. I don't need to find any more lost people, but if you want to get lost… I know how to make that happen. The only promise you have to make is to take me with you."

Still reeling from the depth of emotion in his voice, Wyrick was afraid to believe what she was seeing in his eyes, and then he began coming closer. His mouth was only inches from her lips when she saw her own reflection in his eyes.

Charlie had given her all the time to say no, or to push him away, and when she didn't, he brushed a kiss across her forehead, then wrapped his arms around her and kissed her.

Gently.

Reverently.

With a promise she could not mistake.

And then like he would die if he ever let her go.

She wrapped her arms around his neck and kissed him back. And when she did, the last of what life had broken in her slipped back into place.

Charlie swept her up in his arms, carried her to his bed, then fell in beside her, lost in the passion between them.

They were a tangle of long arms and legs, trying to undress without losing the bodily contact that had set them on fire, and then finally they were lying skin to skin, looking into each other's eyes. Charlie started to turn off the light when Wyrick stopped him.

"No more hiding," she said.

She caught a glint of fire in his eyes, and then his hands were all over her body, making peace with the dragon as he made love to her. It wasn't just the joining with a man she'd loved for years that made this matter. It was the resurrection of Jade, the woman she'd buried so long ago.

When Charlie leaned down and kissed her mouth, he didn't stop there. He took his tongue and his lips all the way down to her belly, before kissing his way back up.

"I love you, Jade Wyrick. Even if you don't love me back, trust me enough to let me stay."

She locked her hands behind his neck.

"You don't get half of nothing from me, Charlie Dodge. I have loved you forever. First, because of the way you loved Annie. And because you let me into your life and kept me there, even when I was a pain in the ass. I have loved you for so long, and accepted your friendship as enough. This moment is a gift, and you can't have it back. I want you, Charlie. I want you forever in my life."

Charlie moved between her legs and then slid into her body, and it felt like he'd always known this. When she wrapped those long legs around his waist and pulled him tighter, he began to move. She met him thrust for thrust, holding him close, pulling him deeper.

It was a dance.

It was a war.

It was the end of one thing and the beginning of another, and they would never be the same.

Wyrick had already locked herself into the rhythm of his heartbeat, and the building lust of his climax so that she could ride it out with him.

Making love to Charlie Dodge wasn't rocket science. It was, instead, the easiest, most natural thing she'd ever done, letting that first kiss, and then the shock of their first climax, launch them both into the rest of their lives.

As for Charlie, he was at peace, and out of his mind in love. He had harnessed a dragon, knowing only that he adored every wild, crazy piece of her.

And so it has been written, that once a man has conquered the wild in a creature, it is his forever.

EPILOGUE

Two years later

Summer had come to Colorado.

Even this high up on the mountain, the heavy snows of winter were finally gone.

Charlie was standing at the kitchen window of their two-story log home, watching Jade puttering about on the sunny side of the porch, picking herbs from the pots in which they were growing.

His heart was full. His life as perfect as it had ever been. If he'd known being retired would be this amazing, he wouldn't have dreaded growing old. He'd had no idea this beautiful dragon was already his life, just waiting for him to wake up and claim her.

He took delight in watching her pick the leaves from the herbs, lifting each one close to her face to savor the scents. First of rosemary and mint, and then the basil and sage.

He had a sudden urge to join her, and set his empty coffee cup down beside the book he'd given her for Christmas their first year here.

It was *The Velveteen Rabbit*, and he'd signed it.

To Jade, with love… Charlie.

When she'd said she'd never heard of the story after they'd found it in Sonny Burch's apartment, he couldn't believe it. And he'd seen the way she'd touched the words written inside Sonny Burch's copy, right before they found the map—the map that ultimately led Sonny to life in a federal prison.

Charlie also knew she had nothing left from her time with her mother, and that UT had stolen her childhood. In his heart every child should have heard this story. And as far as he was concerned, it was never too late to rectify a wrong.

She'd cried when she'd opened the gift, and then cried again when she read it. After that she read it at least once a week. He didn't know exactly what corner of her broken life it had filled, but it made him happy to know he'd been the one to fill it.

A squirrel was scolding her from a nearby tree, and she was laughing now. He couldn't resist that sound and left the cabin to join her.

Jade heard him before she saw him, and when he came up from behind her and put his arms around her, she leaned back against him and closed her eyes, savoring the size of him, and the strength of him and feeling every heartbeat of his love for her.

"Good morning, pretty girl," Charlie said. "What magic are you about today?"

She turned around and kissed his cheek.

"Whatever you and life hand me," she said.

Charlie grinned and then slid an arm across her shoulders as they stood gazing out across the forest around them.

The cabin had been a find, and with a little remodeling, it became the perfect spot for a dragon's lair. Charlie said he knew how to get lost, and he hadn't lied.

They were miles away from the nearest town at the foot of the mountain, and two thousand feet higher in altitude. The little town had a population of less than three thousand people, and without the makeup and clothes from before, Jade easily passed for just another woman who had survived breast cancer.

There was no more Wyrick. Just Jade, who was Charlie Dodge's wife. Except for the shiny black chopper in a hangar at the edge of the forest, and the little runway from it to the helipad behind the cabin, and, of course, the radio tower shooting a thousand feet up into the sky, they were just another couple who'd opted for a simpler life.

Charlie fished when he wanted to in the stream below the cabin, and kept the grounds mowed and firewood cut for the fireplace in the great room.

They had a basement below the house with little grow lights for the hothouse tomatoes—grown from the seeds of Merlin's tomatoes that she still loved to eat. She still created games and invented and filed for patents on things that would one day run a world that had yet to come into existence.

Her wealth had grown into an excessive and embarrassing amount, and so every now and then when she saw an opportunity or read about a tragedy or a disaster, a huge and anonymous donation would come to those in need.

The world had mostly forgotten about Wyrick.

Some thought she had died.

Others thought the alien world from which she'd come had just taken her home.

Only a few knew that they'd run for their lives, and out of love for the both of them, never spoke their names again.

Jade lived without a demand on her life, and without fear for it, as well.

She spent every night in Charlie's arms, loving and knowing she was loved.

Charlie Dodge had been the missing piece to her broken

life—the omega man she didn't know existed until fate put him in her path.

It was the perfect end to a tragic-filled story—living happily ever after.

★ ★ ★ ★ ★